"You're the m
Noah Buchanan **nd you**
to treat me with respect!"

"If I'm the man you married, Isobel, then you'd better do as I say. That means no taking matters into your own hands and getting somebody killed. If I'm your husband, I'm the boss. You hear?"

Simmering, Isobel stared at the towering cowboy who presumed to rule over her by his bartered title of "husband." His blue eyes fairly crackled as he met her gaze.

"You know nothing," she managed.

"I know that right now you're starting to look like a blushing bride."

"Oh, yes, my strong, brave husband," she responded, batting her eyes for effect. "I will stitch and bake—and weep for joy when I hear your footsteps on the porch."

"You do that, sweetheart." Chuckling, Noah tucked Isobel close and strolled with her toward the adobe home.

At the warmth of his arm around her shoulders and the graze of his unshaved jaw against her cheek, it occurred to Isobel that perhaps she wouldn't mind being a wife who would sew and bake and wait for her husband to come home at night. What a curious thought.

Books by Catherine Palmer

Love Inspired Historical

The Briton
The Maverick's Bride
The Outlaw's Bride

Steeple Hill Single Title

That Christmas Feeling
  "Christmas in My Heart"
Love's Haven
Leaves of Hope
A Merry Little Christmas
  "Unto Us a Child…"
The Heart's Treasure
*Thread of Deceit
*Fatal Harvest
*Stranger in the Night

*A Haven Novel

CATHERINE PALMER

The author of more than fifty novels with more than two million copies sold, Catherine Palmer is a Christy Award-winner for outstanding Christian romance fiction. Catherine's numerous awards include Best Historical Romance, Best Contemporary Romance, Best of Romance from Southwest Writers Workshop, and Most Exotic Historical Romance Novel from *RT Book Reviews*. She is also an *RT Book Reviews* Career Achievement Award winner.

Catherine grew up in Bangladesh and Kenya, and she now makes her home in Georgia. She and her husband of thirty years have two sons. A graduate of Southwest Baptist University, she also holds a master's degree from Baylor University.

CATHERINE PALMER

⁓ THE OUTLAW'S BRIDE ⁓

Steeple Hill®

Published by Steeple Hill Books™

STEEPLE HILL BOOKS

Steeple
Hill®

Recycling programs
for this product may
not exist in your area.

ISBN-13: 978-0-373-82843-2

THE OUTLAW'S BRIDE

www.SteepleHill.com

Printed in U.S.A.

Never take your own revenge, beloved, but leave room for the wrath of God, for it is written, "Vengeance is mine, I will repay," says the Lord.
—*Romans* 12:19

To Sharon Buchanan-McClure who introduced me
to the real Belle Buchanan

Chapter One

February 18, 1878

Lincoln County, New Mexico Territory

Isobel stood, her crimson boots side by side like drops of bright blood on the snow. She stared at her feet for a moment, thinking how far they had come from the sprawling pasturelands of her beloved Spanish Catalonia to this slushy trail in the New World. Weeks aboard a wave-tossed ship, days across the Texas prairie to Fort Belknap, miles along the Goodnight-Loving cattle trail toward Santa Fe…and for what?

Sighing, she pulled her lace mantilla closer around her face, lifted her chin and walked on through the scrubby, wind-whipped trees. Her emerald hem swept across fallen, brown pine needles, the ruffle on her skirt rippling along behind.

It had happened here, she thought, near this very place. A shiver of apprehension coursed through her as she looked in the twilight at the secluded forest. Five years earlier, her father—the powerful Don Alberto

Matas—had been jerked from his buckboard wagon and shot.

Isobel tightened her knotted fingers inside her muff and squeezed her eyes shut against the sting of tears. As a child, she had believed her father invincible.

Forcing away the fear that haunted her—transforming it to the more comfortable heat of anger—she gritted her teeth. Why had the lawless Americans done nothing to find her father's murderer? Not only a murderer but a thief. The killer had stolen the packet of land-grant titles and jewels that had been her inheritance—the dowry to secure her marriage to Don Guillermo Pascal of Santa Fe.

She inhaled a deep breath of crisp, pine-scented air. Five years had passed, yet the anger and betrayal still burned brightly in her heart. Despite the pain, the five years spent managing her father's vast estates in Spain had been good ones. She had overseen lands, governed workers and carved a faith that could not be shaken. And then she had traveled to America.

Though at twenty-three she knew her hopes of marriage might appear dim, she still was betrothed to Don Guillermo. She would see to it that he married her. She would recover her stolen inheritance as well. Isobel Matas was not one to cower when faced with a challenge. Glancing behind, she scanned the scrub oak and twisted-pine woods. The small party of travelers who had accompanied her from Texas to New Mexico—an itinerant preacher, a missionary doctor and his family, a schoolteacher—rested from the journey. Their horses grazed, tethered a safe distance from the trail.

The delay would put them in Lincoln Town after dark, too late for her to speak to the sheriff. She chose not to tarry and drink coffee. Instead she walked alone through the forest and thought about her father. If he hadn't come to the New Mexico Territory, he would still be alive, his golden hair shining in the sunlight, his deep laughter echoing over the rolling hills of Catalonia.

Hoofbeats thudded across the damp snow. Her eyes darted toward the trail. Highwaymen? Banditos, like the men who had murdered her father?

Alarm froze her breath. Her traveling companions were too far away to be of help, and she had left her pistol in her saddlebag. Clutching her mantilla at her throat, she melted into the shadows of a large juniper. Leaning against the rough trunk, she peered through the lace in the direction of the sound.

"Things are unhappy indeed in Lincoln Town, Noah." A young voice. English—not American.

"We're glad you're back from the trail. Mr. Chisum is wise to let you run his cattle. South Spring River Ranch profits under your management."

Isobel counted three riders, one dapper in a brown tweed coat, the others roughly dressed, their faces obscured by hats and heavy beards. Livestock behind. More men at the rear.

The man called Noah rode tall on his black horse. He wore a long coat of black leather and was massively built, with broad shoulders and lean, hardened legs. With skin the color of sunbaked adobe, his face was grim beneath the wide brim of his black felt hat. His blue eyes flashed back and forth…alert, missing nothing. This man—and not the dandy—knew a dangerous life.

"Do you suppose Mr. Chisum would take my side against Dolan?" The young Englishman's voice held a note of hope. He could not be more than thirty years old.

Noah shrugged. "Chisum stays out of a fight until it reaches his own back door."

"Don't worry, Mr. Tunstall," the third rider put in. "He'll come out of that jail fightin' mad against Dolan."

"I expect so—" the Englishman began. A raucous squawk shattered the stillness in the canyon. Isobel stiffened.

"Turkeys." Noah Buchanan rose in his stirrups and searched the gathering dusk. "How about it, boys? Let's bag one."

"Sure!" The slender man slid his rifle from his saddle scabbard. "Coming, Mr. Tunstall?"

"No, thank you." The Englishman beckoned the three riders behind the packhorses. "But go on—all of you. Perhaps Mrs. McSween will cook it for us when we get to Lincoln."

The men set off toward the nearby ridge. Noah glanced to one side, and his eyes fell on Isobel. He frowned. Reining his horse, he let his companions ride on.

"What have you there, Buchanan?" the Englishman cried out.

The American looked at Isobel an instant longer, as if to confirm the strange apparition in the woods. "Some kind of bird," he called back.

She squared her shoulders and lifted her chin. *Bird?* She knew the man might do anything. Yet there was something gentle in his manner. Perhaps it was the way he held the reins…as if he were an *artista*. She had seen the hands of a poet and she felt sure this man's hands, though large and strong, held no malice.

Glancing at her one more time, his eyes flashed with—what was it—warning? Then he flicked the reins and his horse vanished into the woods.

Isobel licked her wind-parched lips. Looking up, she saw suddenly what the others had not. Forty or fifty armed horsemen guided their mounts down onto the trail from the ridge.

"Tunstall!" A shout rang out from halfway up the slope. "That you, Tunstall?"

The Englishman reined his horse. "Who's there?"

"Jesse Evans. I'm with Rattlesnake Jim Jackson and a posse Jimmie Dolan sent to round you up. He made us deputies." The riders advanced to within twenty yards of Tunstall, and Isobel calculated they would meet directly in front of the juniper tree.

"Come ahead, Tunstall," a second man commanded. The blue light of the setting sun coated his heavy jaw and wide nose. "We ain't gonna hurt you."

"What is it you want, Jackson?" Tunstall kept riding as the men facing him lifted their rifles so the stocks rested on their knees. Isobel tensed, willing the Englishman to draw his own weapon. Could he not see these men meant to harm him?

Jackson urged his horse forward.

"Not yet," he muttered to Evans. "Wait till he gets nearer."

Isobel's mantilla buffeted her face, and she struggled to push it aside. She must warn the Englishman. But at that moment, his companions burst through the trees onto the trail.

"Take cover, Tunstall!" Buchanan shouted. "Head for the woods!"

"Now!" Jackson raised his rifle and fired. Tunstall jerked backward and dropped from his horse to the frozen ground.

Evans dismounted and ran to where Tunstall lay face down. He pulled Tunstall's revolver from its holster and shot the fallen man in the back of the head. Then he turned the gun on the horse and pulled the trigger.

Isobel swallowed in revulsion. She realized that Tunstall's friends had been too late to help him. They dispersed into the woods as the posse crowded forward, a mixture of triumph and horror written on their faces.

"With two empty chambers in Tunstall's gun," Evans crowed, "the judge'll think he fired first. Let's round up the rest of his men and give 'em the same medicine!"

Trembling, Isobel watched Evans remount and ride away. Jackson and three others remained. They stretched out the Englishman's body and wrapped it in blankets. Chuckling, Jackson pillowed Tunstall's head on a folded overcoat. Then he laid the horse's head on the Englishman's hat.

"This is abominable," Isobel muttered, icy fear melting before crackling rage. And suddenly she saw her father—lying just as Tunstall now lay—murdered, with no one to defend him.

As she stepped from behind the juniper, the wind caught her lace mantilla, tugged it from its comb and whipped it across the trail like a dancing butterfly. She caught her breath. Jackson glanced up and snatched it midair. Frowning, he spat, and stepped over Tunstall's body.

"Don't move, *señorita*." His voice dripped with contempt. "Hey, fellers. Looks like we got us a Mexican."

Isobel swallowed the last of her fear and remembered the raw wound of her father's death. A familiar anger flowed. If she must die, she would die bravely. Lifting her chin, she stepped onto the trail.

"You…" She stopped before the men. Forcing herself to think in English, she spoke. "I have seen your murder. I curse you—*asesinos*—assassins!"

"You ain't seen nothing yet, honey." Jackson whisked his rifle to his shoulder. But before he could fire, a horse thundered across the trail. Its rider leaned down and swept Isobel from the path of a bullet.

"You're dead, you little Mexican!" Jackson's voice rang out behind her. "I swear I'll kill you!"

"Keep your head down, lady." Noah rode through the trees, one arm around the woman's waist, the other controlling his horse. "They got Tunstall, didn't they?"

"The man called Rattlesnake killed him," she cried. "Give me your rifle and horse. I shall make them pay."

"Whoa, now." Noah reined his horse to a halt beneath an overhanging sandstone ledge. As he lowered his bandanna, he looked the woman up and down. Emerald gown, red ruffles, crimson boots. "Give you *what?*" he asked.

"Your horse. Your rifle. For revenge."

Around them, all had calmed—the wind, the horse, the trees, Noah's pounding heart. He studied her eyes, her nose, the high curve of her Spanish cheekbones and her lips.

"My father," she choked out. "My father was…" Covering her face with her hands, she folded inward. Her shoulders convulsed as a sob welled from her throat.

Noah set a gentle hand on her back. "Now then, little lady, don't you know revenge never did a lick of good? The Good Lord's in charge of that. One way or another, He'll see that those men pay. You put everything you saw right out of your head, hear?"

She nodded, dabbing her eyes. "They even killed his horse."

Noah shook his head, then spoke. "The woods are clear. The posse's gone to Lincoln to tell Dolan they've done his dirty work. I'll take you back to your people. I passed them on the trail. They'll keep you safe."

He turned his horse, and the rhythmic gait eased the tension in his shoulders. Darkness like velvet silk enfolded them. Noah knew he must weigh the implications of Tunstall's murder. But for now, he drank in the stillness, the quiet.

The woman had draped against him, her cheek resting on his chest. He recognized this was an improper, even dangerous, situation for a man in his position—single, bound to a mission and lonely. He had rescued her, and now, by all that was moral, he should move his arm from around her.

But she had closed her eyes. Her breath stirred the hair in his beard. Her hand…each individual finger… warmed the skin on his arm.

The horse picked its way up a hill. Noah watched the moon rise above the pines on a ridge, his heart heavy. John Tunstall had been a good man. And young, maybe in his early twenties. Now a powder keg had been lit. Though Alexander McSween was a citified lawyer, he would go after Tunstall's killers.

Noah shifted in the saddle, and his thoughts swung away, too. The woman intrigued him. Her accent was

Spanish, and she looked the part of a rich Mexican doña—green dress ruffled with red lace, red boots, jeweled comb. All this, yet her hair gleamed golden in the moonlight.

He gazed at the silken ringlet that curled down her back. If he took out her comb, the whole mass of hair would come tumbling down. Its mysterious, spicy scent would waft out into the air and—

"There is my party, vaquero," she said suddenly. "And your amigos, too. You see the fire?"

Caught by surprise, Noah shook off his wayward thoughts. He had been on the trail with Chisum's cattle many months. What else could be expected of a man who found his arms wrapped around a fine-smelling lady? He sent up a quick prayer to help him stay on task.

Tunstall's men were standing with the other travelers around the fire. There was Dick Brewer—Noah's closest friend and Tunstall's foreman—along with Billy Bonney and several others.

"Miss Matas!" A young, spectacled gentleman hurried forward as Noah guided his horse into the clearing. "We've been worried. Thank you, sir. I'm sure Miss Matas's family will reward you for saving her."

"Not necessary," Noah said. "Glad to help."

"Oh, Isobel, are you all right?" A pale woman rushed to her side. "When we heard the shots, I was terrified for you!"

Isobel's expression softened. "I'm all right, Susan. I was walking in the forest."

"Did you see what happened, ma'am?" Dick asked her. "A man was shot and killed."

Noah dismounted and lifted his hands. Isobel slipped

into his arms, but when her feet touched the ground, he set her aside. He had been distracted by the woman long enough.

As Tunstall's men gathered around, she lifted her chin. "The one called Rattlesnake shot first. Then Evans. The killers must be brought to justice."

"Yep, and you belong with your friends," Noah spoke up. "Leave justice to these fellows."

"But, Noah," Dick argued, "she's a witness. She could help us. She could testify."

"Dolan's men saw her," Noah told them. "Snake swore he'd kill her. She needs to get out of the territory fast. Where are you headed, ma'am?"

"To Lincoln Town," she replied. "To speak with the sheriff."

"Someone murdered Isobel's father here five years ago," the pale woman, Susan, explained in a soft voice. "Isobel is determined to find out who did it."

Noah shook his head. "Bad idea. If you're going to Lincoln, *señorita*, you can bet Snake will find you."

"If one of us could protect her," Dick said, "we could use her testimony."

"How about you?" Noah suggested. "Your place isn't far. She could lie low there until the trouble blows over."

Dick looked away, his gray eyes troubled. "Noah, they killed John. It's not that I wouldn't protect a woman, you know that. But I was Tunstall's foreman and his friend. I'm going after them."

"We're all going after them!" Billy Bonney stepped up. "C'mon, Buchanan, you can't expect one of us to babysit the *señorita*. You're not a Tunstall man, and Chisum's in jail. Why don't you take the job?"

Noah held up a hand. "Not me, kid. I've got papers to deliver to Chisum and my own business to see to."

"But you told us John Chisum ain't gonna sell you no land unless you can prove you're willing to settle down and knock off that reputation you carry around. Now, say you come along with this pretty *señorita*—hey, what say you marry her? Chisum would sell you the land quick if you did that. You know how sentimental he is about families."

"*Marry* her?" Noah felt the blood siphon from his face. "Billy Bonney, you're a fool. There's no way—"

"Can you be serious?" Isobel interrupted. "Never would I marry this…this dusty vaquero! I am betrothed to Don Guillermo Pascal of Santa Fe. Nor do I need a protector. I am a better marksman than most of the men in Catalonia and I ride like the wind. I shall go with you on this journey of revenge."

"You can't come with us," Billy exclaimed, eyeing Isobel as if she were possessed. "The men who killed our boss have the law on their side. And the law in Lincoln County is as crooked as this trail. You'd best get on up to Santa Fe and marry your rich muchacho."

"Not until I find my father's murderer."

"Isobel," Susan broke in, "please consider what these men are saying. The murderers have threatened to kill you, and you have no protectors. Why not take on Mr.—"

"Buchanan," Billy put in. "His name is Noah Buchanan."

Lest the conversation erupt into a shouting match, Isobel had agreed to walk a short distance from the men to discuss the situation with Susan.

"Isobel," her friend said softly. "Can you trust me?"

Nodding, Isobel acknowledged the truth. Though she had not planned to get close to the others on the journey, they had won her friendship after all.

"This is a lawless land," Susan said. "If you insist on finding your father's killer and getting your inheritance back, you must have protection. I know you ride and shoot well, but you'll never survive against fifty armed men. If you won't go to Santa Fe and get married like you should, let Mr. Buchanan watch over you."

Isobel glanced at the huddled group of men. Billy Bonney and Dick Brewer clearly were exhorting Noah to action. "Don Guillermo may not accept me now, anyway," she murmured, finally admitting aloud her fear. "Without my dowry, I cannot push for marriage. By law he should marry me, but his family is powerful."

"Then you *must* get your rightful land. And to do that, you must let Mr. Buchanan look after you."

Isobel knew it was the right decision—the only possible conclusion. She gave her friend a quick hug and hurried across the slushy snow to the men.

"Very well, Señor Buchanan," she informed him. "If you agree to protect me, I shall bear witness to the authorities about the murder."

"Sure, I'll take you on," Noah said. "If you'll marry me."

She gasped. "Marry you? *Borrachón*! What have you been drinking?"

"Not a thing." He studied her for a moment, then gave a nod. "We'll get the preacher over there to hitch us up. I'll tell folks you're the wife I brought in from the trail. That's true enough."

She stared at the blue-eyed man. "But I am already engaged."

"And the last thing I want is to get married." He glanced at Dr. Ealy, a missionary who was standing quietly in the background. "We'll get it annulled later. Extreme circumstances…marriage without parents' consent…lack of consummation…we'll think of something. Once I convince Chisum to sell me the land I've been after and you settle your business in Lincoln, you can go to Santa Fe and marry your don. Meantime, I won't lay a hand on you."

"Whoa, Buchanan!" Billy laughed. "Don't get carried away."

"Naw, kid. It'll all be on the up-and-up."

Again Isobel assessed the bearded, brawny trail boss. Did she really need his protection? Probably. Her father had been murdered despite his armed guard.

Could she delay marrying Don Guillermo? Certainly. Her fiancé had never even responded to her letter of intent to journey to America.

Retrieving the stolen land-grant titles was her primary goal. More than anything, she ached to possess those rich pastures on which to graze cattle of her own.

"Very well, Mr. Buchanan," she declared. "If you will protect me while I search for my father's killer and recover my family's stolen land, I shall marry you and prove to Mr. Chisum that you are very settled. And I shall be your witness in the law courts."

"Then I reckon we've got a deal."

Dick Brewer spoke up. "Stay at my place tonight, Noah, and head for Chisum's ranch in the morning. We've got to get Tunstall's body to Lincoln, and we can see the others safely into town."

The two conferred a moment before Dr. Ealy cleared his throat. Accustomed to unexpected weddings, funerals and the like, he had agreed to perform the ceremony and wanted to get on with it.

Isobel barely heard his words. Instead she stared down at the pointed toes of her red boots. What had she done? Minutes ago she had been planning to marry Don Guillermo of Santa Fe. Now this leather-clad cowboy who owned nothing but his horse and gun would be her husband.

The ceremony ended, and Susan presented her friend with a bundle of folded garments. "Not much of a wedding gift, Isobel. But wear them, please. Those killers will recognize you right away if you stay as you are."

As the shaken group set off down the moonlit trail in one party, Noah explained to Isobel the situation in Lincoln Town.

Jimmie Dolan had profited from his store and vast acreage by keeping the small landowners financially strapped, until the young Englishman John Tunstall had moved to the area. On the advice of his business partner, Alexander McSween, Tunstall had started his own store and ranch.

Dr. Ealy added that he, along with his wife, two young daughters and Susan Gates, had been summoned to Lincoln by McSween. "It looks as if we're already in McSween's war," he observed, "and we haven't even arrived in Lincoln."

"Just keep quiet about tonight's business," Noah instructed the group. "We'll do the same."

As Isobel watched her companions head north in the darkness, she and Noah turned their horses east. Less than an hour later, they arrived at an old cabin with a sagging front porch. With some trepidation, she followed this man who was no more than a stranger up the steps.

Without speaking, he lit two oil lamps and began to build a fire. She watched him work, appraising biceps that bunched as he placed logs on crackling kindling, brown fingers that set an iron pot he had filled with water on a hook above the blaze. Broad back. Shaggy brown hair and beard. Muddy boots. Leather chaps. Such a common man, this Noah Buchanan.

"Like to wash up?" He asked the question so abruptly that she took a step backward.

He dusted his hands on his thighs before pushing open a door and carrying her bag into a small bedroom. She followed, surveying with some dismay the narrow iron bed, the washstand with its chipped white crockery, the window fitted with paper. Noah filled a cracked bowl with heated water, then shut the door behind him.

Isobel walked to the door and listened to him whistling in the other room. Dare she trust the man? She slid her revolver from her bag and set it on a table near the tub. With another glance at the door, she changed into a nightgown. Then she removed her comb, dipped her hands into the water and finally began to relax.

Curling onto the narrow bed, she sighed deeply. But as sleep crept over her, a movement rippled behind her eyelids. Horses cantering up a trail. Men shouting. Gunshots.

Noah sat on a three-legged stool before the fire and warmed his hands. A second pot of water had begun to steam. The woman in the next room would be asleep by now. No matter how hotheaded, she must be exhausted.

He smiled and shook his head as he filled a large basin with hot water and set to shaving his whiskers off with Dick Brewer's straight razor.

Good old Dick. As Tunstall's foreman, he was bound to get into the thick of the trouble. Noah peered into a mirror hung by the iron cookstove. If Dick got hurt, he couldn't stand by, no matter what he'd promised the *señorita*.

Of course, the way she'd acted today, he'd probably have trouble keeping her out of it.

He dipped his head into a second bowl of fresh water and scrubbed his scalp. She was crazy to come after her father's killer all by herself. Of course he was just as loco to have married her. John Chisum would take some fancy convincing to swallow that one.

Trail dust was getting a little old. Noah looked forward to settling down and fixing up his own cabin. Then he could really begin to make his dreams come true.

He stared for a long time at the flames, thinking of the small packet he had brought in his saddlebag from Arizona, filled with pens and ink bottles. Soon he would start to put down the thoughts he had been having for years. Stories about trail rides, roundups, cowboys. Images and memories he didn't want to forget.

The thought of writing sent him searching Dick's cabin for paper. Maybe he would start right now—the tale of the *señorita* and the Dolan gang. He wished he had a blank notebook with him, but they were back at his cabin.

Dick never kept paper. He searched the first room and hesitated at the bedroom door, then knocked. When he got no answer, he wondered if the woman had left. He leaned closer, peered into the room, caught his breath.

She lay curled on the bed, asleep. A fan of dark lashes rested on each pale cheek. Her chin was tucked against her arm. Long, golden hair draped around her shoulders and down her side.

Noah took a hesitant step toward the bed. She wore a silky white gown but her feet were bare. He was staring at her slender ankles when she turned. A soft moan escaped her lips as she lifted her head.

Rising up on one elbow, she whispered, *"¿Mamá? ¿Dónde está?"*

She lifted her hand to her eyes.

"Who...who are you?" Her voice was husky in the night air.

"I'm Noah Buchanan," he answered. "I'm your husband."

Chapter Two

"Noah Buchanan?" With a gasp, Isobel scrambled out of bed. What on earth was the vaquero doing in her room?

"That blanket," she ordered, pointing. "Now!"

As he fetched a faded homespun coverlet from a nearby chair, she sorted through images of this so-called protector. Shaggy black beard, dusty denims, travel-worn leather.

Outlined in lamplight, his strong, clean jaw was squared with tension. His hair shone a damp blue-black.

"You look different, *señor*," she said, glancing at her pistol on the table.

"I shaved." His blue eyes sparkled as they flicked down to her ankles.

Before he could speak again, she snatched the gun and leveled it at his heart. "Take your hungry eyes away from me!" she commanded, cocking the gun for emphasis. "Stand back, Buchanan."

"Whoa, now." He held up his hands. "I didn't mean any harm. I was looking for paper."

"Paper? Why paper?"

He didn't answer.

"Why paper?" Her fingers tensed on the pistol handle.

"I wanted to write." Swifter than the strike of a rattlesnake, his hand shot out and knocked the pistol from her grip. A blast of flame and smoke erupted from the barrel. The hanging glass lamp shattered. The gun clattered across the wooden floor. As the light died, he grabbed her shoulder and stared hard into her eyes.

"Don't ever pull a gun on me again, woman," he growled. "You hear?"

"Let me go!" she cried out, the nearness of the man plunging fear like a knife into her heart.

Relaxing his shoulders, he stepped back. "I won't hurt you, Isobel. I made a vow."

She swallowed in confusion at the change in him. "I must trust you to take me to Lincoln Town. Yet I know nothing about you."

"You know me real well. John Chisum says if you want to know a man, find out what makes him mad. If you draw a gun on me again, you can say adios to the best shot west of the Pecos."

"The best shot west of the Pecos?" She laughed. "I will have to see that to believe it, *señor.*"

The moon kindled a silver flame in his eyes as he spoke. "Stick around Lincoln County and you'll see it. I can outdraw any man in the territory. But that's not what I aim to do with myself from here on."

She lifted the blanket to her chin. "And what is your aim?"

"The minute John Chisum gets out of jail, I'll introduce you as Isobel…no, Belle. Belle Buchanan, a slip of a lady I met and married on the trail."

"My name is Isobel Matas."

"You'd better be Belle Buchanan if you don't want Snake Jackson after your hide. And Belle is just the shiest, quietest little thing Lincoln Town has ever seen."

"If I'm to be Belle Buchanan, quiet and shy for your John Chisum, you had better be the fastest gun west of the Pecos—or your little wife will change swiftly into Isobel Matas, the fastest gun in Catalonia."

Noah chuckled. "I've tangled with a few women in my time, but never one as sure talking, high strung and mule stubborn as you."

"Nor as pretty," she added.

"Ornery is more like it," he said with a grin. "You put on a shy smile, and I'll keep my trigger finger ready. We'll settle the matter of my land first. Then we'll check into this question of your father."

"My father first. Then your land."

"The trouble over Tunstall's death needs to die down before we start poking around in Lincoln. We'll go see Chisum first."

"I have waited five years," she told him. "I have traveled many miles. I will wait no longer. Now, leave me to sleep, Buchanan. I must speak to the sheriff tomorrow."

"Sheriff Brady deputized that posse you saw today. He gave Snake Jackson a lawman's badge. Brady's a Dolan man. You ride into Lincoln tomorrow and you'll be eating hot lead for supper."

He headed for the open door, but he paused with his

hand on the latch. "And it's Noah...Noah to you...not Buchanan. Don't forget I'm your husband."

As he shut the door behind him, Isobel sagged against the bed frame. How could she forget? The man would be with her every moment, ordering her around, insisting on his own way. He was a bull. Rough and unrefined. Headstrong and stubborn. So powerful he frightened her.

Sinking onto the lumpy mattress, she closed her eyes. But instantly she saw him. Noah Buchanan. She felt the grip of his hand on her shoulder. He was a brute— nothing like Don Guillermo Pascal of Santa Fe.

At that thought, she left the bed again and searched through her saddlebag until her fingers closed on an oval locket. Holding the pendant up to catch the moonlight, she studied the tiny painting of her intended. His jutting chin, firm mouth, deep-set brooding eyes and shock of black hair made her proud. Here was the splendid Spaniard who could outwit the roughshod cowboy. This was the torero who could defeat the bull.

For ten years Isobel had known that Guillermo Pascal would become her husband. He owned a sprawling hacienda, a fine stable, countless cattle, land that stretched many miles across the New Mexico Territory. He was wealthy, noble, Spanish. And he was hers.

She snapped the locket clasp and slipped the golden chain back into her bag. As she crossed to the bed, she noticed the shards of glass from the shattered lamp. She ought to sweep them up.

But Isobel Matas had never touched a broom in her life. She was to be served—not to be a servant. Someone else would have to sweep the glass, someone meant for menial tasks. Shrugging, she found the fallen pistol, pushed it beneath her pillow and climbed back into bed.

The first rays of sunlight were slipping over the pine trees when Isobel waded from the shallows of slumber. She fought to catch the remnants of her dream—of that magnificent man who strode through the purple-ribboned depths, his chest broad, his shoulders strong, his eyes so blue. Blue?

Isobel frowned. Guillermo Pascal's eyes were not blue.

At a tinkling sound in the room, she eased onto one elbow. In the gray light she made out a tall figure.

Noah Buchanan.

His black hat tilted toward the back of his head. His shirtsleeves were rolled to his elbows. He wore a leather belt with a silver buckle. In his hand he held a stick. A rifle?

No...a broom.

Humming, he swept the broken glass. Unaware of her watchful eye, he raked it into a tin dustpan and stepped out of the room. She shook her head. This vaquero who could knock a loaded gun from her hand, who could guide his horse through darkness, who had walked through her dreams all night...this cattleman of the plains was sweeping!

As she rose from the bed, she caught the smell of frying bacon. He sweeps, he cooks, what else? Mystified, she peered around the door frame.

His worn brown boots thudding on the floor, the bull stalked across the room. His shoulder grazed a hanging pot, one knee knocked a rickety chair aside. But as he leaned over the fire, Noah Buchanan might have been a *cocinero* in a nobleman's kitchen. As he broke six eggs into sizzling grease in a frying pan, he hummed.

Bemused, Isobel eased the bedroom door shut and propped a chair beneath the handle. She wanted no intrusions this time. As she took a petticoat and faded skirt from the bundle Susan Gates had given her, she smiled. Noah Buchanan was rugged and earthy, but he was gentle and unpretentious, too. Perhaps they would do well together for the few days of their marriage.

A wash of guilt crept over Isobel as she slipped on Susan's petticoat. She had married Noah Buchanan under God's eyes. For as long as she could remember, she had faithfully attended church and said her prayers. She knew this marriage was a sin worthy of the harshest punishment.

As she fastened the row of buttons lining the bodice of the blue gown, she wondered what she would suffer. Would she lose her chance to wed Guillermo Pascal? Would she never learn the truth behind her father's death? Or something worse?

"Dear God," she whispered in prayer. "Forgive me, please." She knew God was harsh, vengeful, given to anger. His sacraments were not to be treated lightly. Yet she had done just that.

Struggling with the shadow such thoughts cast across the morning's bright sunlight, she slipped on a pair of boots and laced them. She would make the best of the situation, she decided. She would see to it that the contrived marriage lasted no longer than necessary. Noah Buchanan would remain the stranger he had been from the beginning. For a few days Isobel would become Belle

Buchanan—a soft-spoken, common woman, like Susan Gates, the schoolteacher.

Setting her shoulders, Isobel wound her hair into a tight chignon and buried her tortoiseshell comb deep in the saddlebag. Facing the world without her mantilla was uncomfortable. To be bareheaded in public was a disgrace.

Sighing, she thought of the trunks making their way by mule train to Lincoln Town for transfer to Santa Fe. Gowns of silk, ivory linen, satin and taffeta. Lace mantillas, velvet jackets, cloaks, stockings of every hue. She had packed ebony combs, gold pendants, pearl earrings.

But an uneven hem, sagging petticoats and a limp cotton dress were the lot of Belle Buchanan. Drawing a shawl around her shoulders, she recalled the hours she and her mother had spent choosing the perfect gowns for a dance or a visit with friends.

What would Noah think of her transformation? Cautious, she opened the bedroom door. He stood beside a rough-hewn pine table, setting out chipped white plates and spoons. Her heart softening to this strangely gentle man, she stepped out.

At a sound from the door, Noah glanced up, straightened, and let his gaze trail down the slender figure approaching. Like some Madonna of the prairie, the woman wore a gown of soft blue with a white cotton shawl around her shoulders. Sunlight from the front window framed her, backlighting her golden hair.

"Well, I'll be." He shook his head to clear the surprise and let out a low chuckle. "You sure have changed. You look regular now."

The light in her eyes dimmed as she glanced at the fire. "Susan Gates gave me the dress."

"It looks fine." He wanted to rectify his careless comment, but the words came hard. "You look pretty, ma'am. Like you belong here."

"But I do not belong here." She crossed the room and seated herself. "I belong at the Hacienda Pascal in Santa Fe. I have been trained as a *marquesa*—to oversee many servants, host officials of the government, plan fiestas and bear sons and daughters for my husband in accordance with our Spanish tradition."

"Sounds like a real humdinger of a life." He sat down opposite her. "Care for some scrambled eggs, *marquesa?*"

She bristled until he held the frying pan under her nose. "*Sí.* I suppose I should eat."

Noah set a spoonful of fluffy yellow eggs on her plate and a slab of crisp bacon beside them. He reached into an iron kettle, pulled out two steaming biscuits and tossed them onto her plate.

Bowing his head, he spoke in a low voice. "God, thanks for this new day and Dick Brewer's grub. Amen. Whew! Good thing Dick had his chickens penned up. Otherwise, we'd have been scrounging for breakfast."

At her silence, he glanced up to find her staring at him. "Was that a prayer?"

"Sure. Talking to God like always." He spread butter on a biscuit. "Tunstall did right making Dick foreman. He's got education. He can read and keep record books."

"And you? Have you an education, Buchanan?"

"Name's Noah." He took a sip of coffee. "I can read and write. Mrs. Allison taught me."

"Who is Mrs. Allison?"

"Richard and Jane Allison. He owns land around Fort Worth. English folks." He smiled, remembering. "Mrs. Allison took a liking to me. She didn't have children of her own, see. She used to invite me into the library—books from floor to ceiling. She read me all kinds of stories, mostly from the Bible. Taught me to read, too. I reckon I read nearly every book in that library."

"But where were your mother and aunties to care for you? Why did you live with Señora Allison?

"I didn't live in the big house. Mr. Allison put me in with the other hired hands when I was six or seven. I worked in the stables. What about you? Are you educated?"

"Of course," Isobel replied. "I had a tutor. Later, my father sent me to a finishing school in France. I speak six languages, and I am accomplished in painting and embroidery. Arranging homes is my pleasure."

"Arranging homes?" Noah looked up from his plate and glanced around the cabin with its tin utensils, rickety furnishings and worn rag rug. "What's to arrange?"

"Chairs, tables, pictures. My fine furniture will arrive with my trunks. You would never understand such things, Buchanan. Yet we are alike in some ways."

"How's that?"

"Books. Horses." She sat back in the chair and studied the fire. "I was away at school when news came of my father's murder. I wanted to go to America immediately and avenge his death. But my mother was devastated, and she knew nothing of my father's businesses. So I stayed with her, preparing the books, paying debts, managing the hacienda. Five years passed, and I learned that my greatest love was the land. The cattle. The horses."

"Then you're a vaquero yourself."

"Oh, no!" She laughed. "I am a lady."

"And the land in Spain? Will you go back one day?"

Her smile faded. "My mother has remarried, and my brother is grown. Now he and my stepfather fight. In Catalonia, we follow the tradition of the *hereu-pubilla.* Only a firstborn son can inherit. My brother is the *hereu,* the heir. He will win the legal battle against my mother's new husband."

"And what about you, Isobel? What about all that work you did while your little brother was growing up? You ought to get something out of it."

One eyebrow lifted. "I'm not considered worthy to own land. Nothing is left for me in Spain. I cannot marry there, because my father betrothed me to Don Guillermo of Santa Fe. I'm old now, a *soltera,* a spinster. So I came here to avenge my father's death and find the man who stole my land titles."

"It's the land, then." Noah poured himself another mug of coffee. "You want your land a lot more than you want to marry that don in Santa Fe."

"I do wish to marry Guillermo Pascal, of course. But by law the land is mine. I intend to have it."

"You won't have it long if you marry him. The Pascal family is ruthless. They'll take your property and set you to planning fiestas."

"That is not how it will be!" She pushed back from the table and stood up. "I shall manage my own land. Those grants have belonged to the *familia* Matas from the earliest days of Spanish exploration. Don't presume to predict my future, Buchanan. You are a vaquero. You know nothing. Now, saddle my horse while I prepare for the journey to Lincoln Town."

"Hold on a minute there." Noah got to his feet and caught her arm. "A cowboy is as worthy of respect as any land-grubbing don. And I didn't take an oath to be a servant to the grand *marquesa*. I'll see to your horse while you wash dishes, but we're not going to Lincoln today. We're headed for Chisum's South Spring River Ranch until the trouble dies down."

Nostrils flared, she peeled his hand from her arm. "You may go to the Chisum ranch, Buchanan, but today I speak to Sheriff Brady." Starting for the bedroom door, she paused and looked back. "And Isobel Matas does not wash dishes."

Biting back a retort he would regret, Noah banked the fire and set off for the barn. He tried to pray his way through the silence as he saddled his horse, and he had just about calmed down when he heard the woman step outside.

"You finished with those dishes?" he called.

She lifted her chin. "I am not a servant, *señor*."

He was silent a moment, his jaw rigid. Then he left the horse and strode to the porch.

"Listen, *señorita*. We have a rule out here in the West. It's called, 'I cook, you clean.' Dick let us use his cabin, and we'll leave it the way we found it. Got that?"

Her pretty lips tightened. "And in Spain we have a rule also. 'A woman of property does not wash dishes.'"

"But you don't have any property, remember? So you'd better—"

Noah stopped speaking when the haughtiness suddenly drained from her face. Her brow furrowed as she focused on the distant ridge, and her lips trembled.

At that moment he saw her as she saw herself: fallen from social class, power, wealth. Linked with a mule-headed cowboy who sassed her and ordered her around. Threatened by a cold-blooded killer. Unsure of her future, maybe even afraid.

"I...I don't know how to wash dishes." Her voice was low, soft. "It was never taught to me."

At her confession, he took off his hat and tossed it onto a stool. "Come on, Isobel. I'm an old hand at this. I'll teach you how to wash dishes."

Chapter Three

The sun painted the New Mexico sky a brilliant orange as Noah Buchanan and his bride, Belle, rode into Lincoln.

She had not expected this victory.

While up to her elbows in soapy water, Isobel had told Noah about the letter informing her family that someone in Santa Fe had begun proceedings of land transfer. Unable to learn the name of the man who possessed the Spanish land-grant titles—no doubt the same man who had killed her father and stolen them—Isobel had departed for America.

As she dried dishes at Noah's side, he suddenly relented. They would go to Lincoln instead of Chisum's ranch. But the town would be up in arms over Tunstall's murder, he warned. Rattlesnake Jackson, Jesse Evans and the rest of the posse would be there, along with Alexander McSween and Tunstall's men. It would be a powder keg waiting for a match.

"You'd better get to know New Mexico if you want to run cattle here." Noah spoke in a low voice as they entered the town. "That plant with the spiky leaves is a yucca. The cactus over there is a prickly pear."

Riding a horse borrowed from Dick Brewer, she pointed to a twisted vine. "That's a *sandía,* a watermelon."

Noah shook his head. "We call it a *mala mujer.*"

"A bad woman?"

"Looks like a watermelon vine. Promises a man relief from his hard life on the trail. But the *mala mujer* grows only cockleburs."

"And so it's a bad woman—promising much but delivering only pain?"

"Yep." He straightened in the saddle. "There's Sheriff Brady's place. His neighbor is my friend Juan Patrón. We'll stay with him."

A lump formed in Isobel's throat. She was here at last, in the town of her father's burial. And no doubt a place well known to his killer. A dozen flat-roofed adobe houses lined the road. Where it curved, she saw a few finer homes and a couple of stores.

"Listen, Isobel." Noah slowed his horse. "I brought you to Lincoln, but while we're here, you'll do as I say. Got that?"

"*Sí.* But if we disagree, you may go your way. Isobel Matas makes her own decisions."

"You're not Isobel Matas anymore, sweetheart. You're Belle Buchanan—and you'd best not forget it."

He reined in outside a small house with two front doors. "Patrón's store. He used to be a schoolteacher and a court clerk. When his father was killed in seventy-three, he took on the family business."

"Seventy-three?" She slid from her horse into Noah's arms. "My father was killed in seventy-three."

For an instant she was drawn into a dark cocoon that

smelled of worn leather and dust. Resting her cheek against Noah's flannel shirt, she relaxed in its warmth. But at the sound of his throbbing heartbeat, she caught her breath and stepped away.

"Seventy-three," she mumbled. "My father—"

"Old Patrón was murdered by a gang," Noah cut in. "The Horrell Gang went on a rampage, killing Mexicans."

"But my father was from Spain."

"Wouldn't matter. If you speak Spanish around here, you're a Mexican." He absently brushed a strand of loose hair from her cheek. "And remember, *you're* an American. You don't understand a word the Patróns are saying. Your name is Belle Buchanan. You're my wife."

She nodded, aware of his fingertips resting lightly on her shoulder. His face had grown gentle again, with that soft blue glow in his eyes, that subtle curve to his mouth. He was too close, his great shoulders a fortress against trouble, his warm hand moving down her arm.

Her eyes flicked to his. She opened her mouth to speak, but before she could form words, he bent his head and pressed his lips to hers. Gentle, tender, his mouth moved over the moist curves as if searching, seeking something long buried.

She softened. This male kiss, the first of her life, held a delight she had never imagined from the perfunctory pecks of mother and aunts. But it was over as quickly as it had begun. Noah lifted his head and focused somewhere behind her.

"*Buenas noches,* Juan," he said. "Put down your six-shooter. It's me."

"Noah?" The stout young man started across the darkened porch, walking with a limp. He was sturdy yet trim in a tailored Prince Albert coat. "*¡Bienvenidos!* You've been away too long. Come in, come in!"

"Juan, I want you to meet someone." Noah set his hand behind Isobel's waist. "My wife, Belle Buchanan."

"Your wife?" The snapping black eyes widened. "So pleased to meet you, Señora Buchanan."

"And I you," Isobel said softly.

"Noah, you are the last man on earth I would guess to take a wife. But come inside! You must meet my family."

As they started up the steps, Isobel caught Noah's hand and raised on tiptoe to his ear. "The murder! You must ask him about the murder."

He nodded and gave her hand a squeeze. She struggled to dismiss his easy intimacy. The man at her side was only pretending, after all. The kiss had been nothing more than a signal of the role each must play as man and wife.

She brushed at her dusty skirts and tucked the strand of hair into her chignon. But the burning on her lips remained as she watched Noah's shoulders disappear through a door leading from the porch.

"Please meet my wife, Beatriz!" Juan held the door for Isobel. "She is of the family Labadie, from Spain. But they have lived in New Mexico many generations. Beatriz, can you believe Noah has brought a bride?"

"Señora Buchanan, welcome." Beatriz, surrounded by children of various sizes, curtsied in greeting.

At the sight of the woman's lace mantilla and comb, it was all Isobel could do to keep from hugging her. She managed a whispered, "Thank you."

"Sit—Noah, *señora*." Juan gestured toward the fire. "How long will you stay with us? A week or more?"

Noah chuckled as he settled on a bench. Playing the dutiful wife, Isobel took her place at his side. He stretched an arm along the bench back. "We're just passing through, Juan. I need to settle up with Chisum and then—"

"But do you not know?" Juan sat forward on the edge of his chair. "Chisum is in jail! Lincoln is in a terrible state. I believe it will soon be war."

Noah's arm moved to Isobel's shoulders. "What's going on, Juan?"

"It is difficult to speak of." He lowered his voice. "John Tunstall was ambushed and killed yesterday. Shot twice. Most believe it was Jimmie Dolan's posse."

"Dolan. No surprise there."

"Tunstall's men brought his body here. The judge took affidavits from Dick Brewer and Billy Bonney and issued arrest warrants for the men in the posse. A coroner's jury is taking testimony even now."

"Who's named in the warrants?"

"Jim Jackson, the one they call Rattlesnake. Jesse Evans. Others. Maybe up to forty men."

"How's McSween taking it?"

Juan shook his head. "You know Alexander McSween. A lawyer—so mild, always thinking of law and justice. I saw the shock on his face when they told him about Tunstall. But he is busy. His house is full of guests. A doctor and his wife, their children, a schoolteacher."

Isobel bit her lip to keep from asking about Susan. Noah inquired about his boss as Beatriz set a bowl of steaming posole on a nearby table.

"Chisum won't get involved," Juan predicted,

watching his wife ladle out the spicy pork and hominy stew. "But come. I shall tell of Chisum's predicament at dinner."

Isobel followed Noah and hoped she was creating the right impression. But she might as well have been invisible for all the attention paid her.

"McSween told me the story of Chisum's jailing," Juan said after he had asked a blessing on the meal. "Just after Christmas, John Chisum, together with Alexander and Sue McSween, left for St. Louis. McSween was to settle some legal problems for a client. Chisum wanted to see a doctor. He has poor health, *no?*"

Noah nodded. "Off and on."

"When they reached Las Vegas, the sheriff and a gang of ruffians assaulted them. They knocked Chisum to the ground, and left Mrs. McSween crying in the buggy. She was taken to a hotel, but the men were thrown in jail."

"On what charges?" Noah demanded.

"McSween was accused of trying to steal money from his own clients. Chisum was charged with debt, if you can imagine that. The sheriff wanted him to reveal all his properties, you see, as debtors must."

"Dolan's behind this."

"It is bigger than Dolan, my friend. Never forget the ring in Santa Fe."

"What ring in Santa Fe?" Isobel could no longer hold her tongue at this mention of her future home.

Juan leaned across the table. "Men in high places have united in a ring of corruption, *señor*a. They take bribes, arrest innocent men, steal land titles."

"Who's in the group, Juan?" Noah caught Isobel's hand and pressed it to silence her. "Do you have names?"

"Governor Axtell, of course. But even more dangerous is the United States district attorney. Thomas Catron is a friend to Jimmie Dolan. The two are working together to take the whole territory. Your boss will be lucky ever to get out of jail."

"But McSween's here in Lincoln," Noah said. "How did he get out of jail?"

"McSween was set free to settle his business. But Chisum refused to reveal his properties."

"So he's still in jail." Noah looked at Isobel. "We may want to have you go on up to Santa Fe."

"Santa Fe?" Juan frowned. "But why?"

"Belle has relatives up there." Noah glanced at Isobel. "Juan, would you send her people a telegram? I may need to send her up there right away if things get worse."

"Of course." Juan stood. "I was planning to pay McSween a visit anyway. We'll rouse Mr. Paxton to open the telegraph office. Will you come?"

"Glad to." Noah rose and patted Isobel's shoulder. "You stay and visit with Señora Patrón, honey. I'll be right back."

"I'll go with you, *honey*," Isobel sputtered as she leapt to her feet and nearly upset her chair. Hot anger radiated from the place where Noah had patted her as if she were no more than a dog. "If you send a telegram on my behalf, I must know what it says."

Juan chuckled. "Your new wife has a strong will. You must mend your stubborn ways, Noah—or break her spirit as you break the wild horses."

Noah was silent a moment before speaking again. "Stay here, Belle. I'll take care of this."

Isobel clenched her jaw as the two men walked to the

door. The *señora* and her children eyed their guest as she stepped to an open window.

"You did the right thing, Buchanan." Juan Patrón's words carried across the night. "A woman should stay at home. If your new wife isn't happy with that now, she will be soon. You'll see."

Battling fury at Noah, Isobel shifted her attention to the bustling Patrón family. The table was spotless now, its rough pine top scrubbed clean and its mismatched chairs pushed beneath. A clamor of giggles and pleas arose from the kitchen, where Beatriz, surrounded by reaching arms and grasping hands, was doling out portions of yellow custard.

"Flan?" she asked Isobel, holding out the dish.

Isobel shook her head. "Where is Alexander McSween's house?"

"*¡No, señora—por favor!*" The woman's eyes were wide with pleading. "You must stay here! There is much trouble in Lincoln. *¡Violencia!*"

As the children swarmed their mother again, Isobel turned away. A cramped home, rough-hewn furniture, hungry children, corn to grind, clothes to mend. This was the life of a woman in Lincoln.

Thanking God that she would be leaving Noah Buchanan soon, Isobel sank into a chair. Even now he was sending a telegram to Guillermo Pascal, alerting her betrothed in case she needed a quick escape from Lincoln.

But if Guillermo came here, he would take Noah's place as her protector, as the one to help solve her father's murder. Noah would be free of her. And she of him.

Isobel closed her eyes, imagining the life she had always dreamed of having. A vast hacienda. Countless cattle. A home filled with beautiful furniture. Gracious parties attended by dignitaries.

Her eyes snapped open. There would be no visits by members of the Santa Fe Ring if she had any say. And she would have no hacienda to manage if Guillermo had his say. Noah had been right on that account. The Pascal family would swallow up her land. She would be mistress of a prison more than a house. There would be small mouths to feed, meals to plan, stitching to fill her days. How different would that life be from the difficult lot of Señora Patrón?

A gentle tugging at her skirt caught Isobel's attention. A bright-eyed little girl with shiny black braids smiled up at her. "*La casa* McSween is very close. It is just past Tunstall's store."

Isobel shook the girl's hand. "*Gracias, mi hijita.*"

The child scampered away to join her brother in a chasing game. Their mother leaned against the kitchen door, watching her children. As her son ran by, she swept him into her arms and kissed him.

Amid the laughter and fun, Isobel took her pistol from her saddlebag, drew her shawl around her shoulders and slipped outside. But a glance back at the flat-roofed house revealed a subtle transformation in what she had termed a prison. In the window, mother and child made a picture of happiness. The whitewashed adobe walls glowed almost translucent in the moonlight. The home was swept and scrubbed, the children well fed and cheerful, the mother content.

Turning away, Isobel wondered if she would find such peace with Guillermo Pascal. Passing a saloon, she saw several men leaning against a crude wooden bar and lifting mugs of beer. They were the likely compadres of a man like Noah Buchanan—common, obstinate, inconsiderate.

So why did her lips still burn from his kiss? Why did her breath catch in her throat at the memory of his hands around her waist? Worse, far worse, was the persistent image of his gentle smile. She could see that smile even as she hurried down the road, her leather boots stumbling over frozen wagon ruts. There it was as he poured steaming water into her basin, as he offered her a spoonful of scrambled eggs, when he plunged his arms into the dishwater to teach his new wife the mysteries of housekeeping.

Men were not supposed to be gentle. They were matadors, toreros—vanquishing life as if it were a bull that might rip open their hearts. Brave, strong, intelligent, bold. Fighting the sense that Noah Buchanan might be all these things as well, she hurried past the courthouse, a corral, a small shop.

As she pulled the shawl over her head, she heard the thunder of hoofbeats on the road. There! A band of men—five or six—riding at a gallop toward her. Clutching the pistol, she crossed the road toward a tumble of stones that had been cemented with mud to form a knobby tower. She crouched down into spiky, frozen grass and watched the riders approach. As they neared the tower, their leader reined his horse.

"You see that, Evans?" His breath formed a cloud of white vapor.

"See what?" Another rider edged forward. "We got an ambush?"

The first man was silent for a moment, listening. Isobel studied the low-slung jaw, the wide, flat nose, the narrow eyes searching the darkness. "I seen something run across the road just as we rounded the curve. It was her."

"Confound it, Snake, if you don't stop seein' that Mexican gal in every crick and holler, one of us is gonna have to give you what fer."

"I ain't seein' things this time, Evans." Snake drew his gun and leveled it at the tower. "She's over near the *torreón*. She had somethin' white on her head, just like that Mexican that seen us level Tunstall."

"So what if she's here? Who'd believe a no-account Mexican over us? We're deputies of the law, remember?"

Snake reached into his saddlebag and jerked out a handful of delicate fabric. Isobel caught her breath. Her mantilla! He draped it over the barrel of his gun and waved it in the air.

"Listen up, *señorita*," he called. "I got your veil—and I'm gonna get you."

"Aw, come on, Snake." Evans spat onto the road. "What is it with you and Mexicans? They ain't worth half the heed you pay 'em."

Snake flipped the mantilla into his open hand and shoved it into his bag. "Let's go, boys. Dolan's waitin'."

But when the other men spurred their horses down the road, Snake circled around and approached the tower. Isobel shrank into the shadow, her hand trembling as she gripped her gun.

"I know you're there, *chiquita*," he growled. "One of these days I'll make you wish you had never laid eyes on Jim Jackson."

His horse whinnied as he dug in his spurs. Hooves

clattered across the frozen track. With difficulty, Isobel got to her feet.

"Just try to kill me, *asesino!*" she ground out as she shook her gun at the retreating form. "Murderer!"

Her blood pulsing in her temples, she lifted her skirts and began to run, her heels pounding out her anger. The shawl slipped to her elbows, catching the frigid wind like a sail. She passed an empty lot and then came to a low-slung building. Its painted sign creaked as it swung in the crisp air.

"Tunstall Mercantile," she read aloud. "Dry goods. Bank."

Tunstall. Isobel saw again his young face, blue eyes wide with an innocence rarely found in men. The hat, the tweed coat, the brown kidskin gloves. So young, so naive. With a shiver, she set off again, knowing she must find Noah and tell him that Snake Jackson was back in town.

Grabbing up her skirts, she made for a large adobe house a few yards beyond the Tunstall store. She knocked on McSween's door. When no one answered, she turned the handle and stepped inside.

All talking at once, a crowd of men sat around a table. Isobel picked out Dick Brewer, Tunstall's foreman and Noah's friend, bent over a sheaf of papers on the table. Billy Bonney had pointed his gun to the ceiling and looked as if he might fire it at any moment. Juan Patrón was shouting at Dr. Ealy, who was arguing back.

But where was Noah? She scanned the room again until her focus came to a window. On its deep sill Noah sat watching her, his blue eyes soft.

Isobel approached, her shawl sliding unnoticed to

the floor. Her heart thundered as she came to a halt before him. Fingering a loose button at her throat, she shrugged. "I came."

He nodded. "I was waiting for you."

Chapter Four

Hand over her mouth, Isobel sagged against the wall. The men around the table turned to look, then resumed arguing. Noah took in the woman's damp hem, muddy boots, fallen shawl. Her hair had scattered across her shoulders, a golden cape.

"If you knew I would come," she murmured, "why did you tell me to stay at Patrón's house?"

"I'm supposed to protect you, remember?" he said. Though color was slowly returning to her face, she was breathing as if she had seen a ghost. Noah battled the urge to take her in his arms. "Did Snake Jackson and his boys see you?"

"Only Snake. Do the others know they're in town?"

"Not yet." He jutted his chin at the boisterous group. "They're squabbling over how to counter Dolan's latest move. Sheriff Brady appointed Dr. Appel from Fort Stanton to perform a postmortem on Tunstall's body. Appel's a Dolan man. He'll support the posse's claim that Tunstall fired first."

She frowned. "Then I must give my testimony now."

"No." He caught her hand, drawing her closer. "Don't say anything, Isobel. Stay out of it."

"Did you send a telegram to Santa Fe?"

"Yes."

"You know I won't go until I find my father's killer."

"If things blow here, you'll need a place to run. Tunstall's men are bent on revenge. Dolan's gang will do anything for him."

Noah made a place for her on the sill. He couldn't tell if the woman was terrified or exhilarated by her second brush with danger. Her hazel eyes had gone green in the firelit room. Strands of hair brushed the arch of her brows. That button she was fooling with had dropped off, and he could see the creamy curve of her throat.

Looking away quickly, he ran his thumb and forefinger around the brim of his hat. Isobel could get herself shot by Snake Jackson. The man had a reputation for killing—he and Billy the Kid over there.

Isobel was staring at her knotted fingers, and he remembered how they had felt sliding tentatively up his back when he was kissing her. That kiss was a big mistake.

Noah shut his eyes, recalling the transformation of Isobel's face from anger to hesitation to pleasure as she had rolled up her sleeves and dipped her arms into warm, soapy water. She had chattered the whole time— something about a horse she'd owned back in Spain. She'd talked on and on, unaware of the tingle that shot up his arm every time she handed him a dish and her wet fingers touched his.

The kiss had come from that, from the way she had gotten inside his mind. And now here she was beside him, her lips still beckoning. Even worse, he was beginning to care what happened to the *señorita.*

"Salir de Málaga para entrar en Malagón," she said with a sudden smile. "It's like when you say, 'Out of the frying pan and into the fire.' My father used to shake his finger and call me *la alborotadora,* the troublemaker, of my family."

"Now you tell me." Noah shook his head. "Well, Miss Troublemaker, Snake Jackson's in town, which means the constable hasn't been able to serve the warrant. He'll be at Jimmie Dolan's house cooking up a plan. If we're smart, we'll lie low the next few days and then head for Chisum's place."

"Will you ask Señor Patrón about his father's murder?"

Noah stood and took her arm. "Let's head back to the house. Patrón will go with us. I'll ask him then."

They started across the room, and Noah lifted her shawl from the floor where she had dropped it. As he drew it over her shoulders, she leaned against him. It was all he could do to keep from catching her up in his arms right then and there. A kiss…just one more…and surely his craving would be satisfied.

As they passed the throng of arguing men, he realized Patrón had gotten into the thick of the debate, his face red above his collar and his shouts adding to the chaos in the room. Noah was about to suggest they talk to him later when Isobel slipped away from him and pushed through the crowd.

At the appearance of a woman in their midst, the men around the table fell silent.

"Excuse me," she began. "My husband and I wish to return to the home of our host. Mr. Patrón?"

"Señora Buchanan," Patrón spoke up, "forgive my rudeness. Mr. McSween has been kind enough to let us gather in his home to discuss the situation."

Noah studied Alexander McSween. No older than thirty-five, the lawyer wore a drooping mustache that hung even with his chin. His tailored suit, polished boots and pocket watch set him apart from his colleagues. Noah had little doubt he was unarmed.

"A doctor has been bribed to perform the postmortem," Patrón continued. "We must find a way to avert this injustice. Dick Brewer and Billy Bonney do not agree. Dr. Ealy and I—"

"Dr. Ealy?" Isobel lifted her eyebrows as if she had never seen the man who had ridden across half the New Mexico Territory with her. "Are you a medical doctor, sir?"

Dr. Ealy gave an uncomfortable cough. "I am."

"Then two doctors must perform the postmortem," she declared. "Or Dr. Ealy might help with the embalming. It cannot be difficult to record the truth."

The men gawked in silence until Dick Brewer finally spoke up. "She's right, fellers. Doc Ealy, we'll make sure you help with the postmortem—if you don't mind. Thank you, Mrs. Buchanan."

Isobel tilted her head. "You may call me Belle."

As the sea of men parted to let Isobel through, Billy Bonney called to Noah. "Hey, Buchanan, you bringin' your pretty wife to McSween's fandango Saturday night?"

Noah's blue eyes flicked toward Isobel. "We'll see. I want to get on over to Chisum's place."

"Come on, Buchanan! I deserve at least one dance

with the lovely lady. You may be faster on the draw than me, but I guarantee I'm the best dancer in town."

"You've got the biggest mouth in Lincoln County, that's for sure." Noah shifted his attention as Juan and Isobel joined him. "Hey, Dick. Come here a minute."

The young foreman detached himself from the group. As he neared, Susan Gates emerged from the shadows of a back room. Clutching her skirts in her hands, she rushed toward Isobel.

"Susan!" Isobel caught her friend. "Susan, what's wrong?"

"You know this woman?" Patrón asked, his brow drawn into a furrow.

"I'll explain later," Noah said. "Miss Gates, meet Juan Patrón. Looks like you already know Dick."

Susan gave Juan a polite nod, but when she looked into Dick Brewer's eyes, a pink flush spread across her cheeks. Noah's friend and the schoolteacher had met only the day before, Isobel realized, but there was an obvious attraction between them.

She wondered if anyone saw such a spark between Noah and herself. Surely not. After all, Noah was just her protector. He cared nothing for her. And she had no more feeling for him than she might for a loyal stable-hand at her family's hacienda.

While he informed the men that Snake Jackson and the posse were in town, Isobel and her friend stepped aside.

"You've lost a button," Susan said. "My dress doesn't fit you well. Why don't we buy some fabric at Tunstall's store? I'll sew a new dress for you. Isobel?"

"That cowboy is looking at you, Susan." She maneuvered her friend away from Dick Brewer's line of focus. "Stay away from him. He is in the midst of the trouble."

Susan glanced over her shoulder. "Don't you think he's terribly handsome?"

Isobel shrugged. She preferred a man with a stronger frame, with broad shoulders and hands that could bring down a steer. She preferred a man whose face bore the weathering of life, who had seen good and evil—and who knew to choose the good. She preferred—

"Noah!" she gasped as he caught her around the waist.

"Let's get out of here," he growled against her ear. "This place is a powder keg."

As he led them away, Isobel turned and caught her friend's hands. "Don't let any man capture your heart, Susan," she said softly. "Never let anyone take away your dreams."

"Oh, Isobel, I…"

"I'll come tomorrow. We'll go to the shops."

Susan waved as Isobel, Noah and Patrón stepped outside. As the three started down the moonlit road, Noah spoke. "I see Dick's taken a fancy to your friend."

"Susan's red hair charms everyone," Isobel replied. "She is lovely."

"She's skinny," Noah pronounced.

"Dick was never a man to take after women," Patrón added. "Is that not so, Noah?"

"Yeah, he's like me. Prefers the company of a few good cowboys around a campfire to the meaningless chatter of women."

Isobel bristled. "What do you know about women, anyway?"

"Not enough," Patrón interjected. "I am surprised

my friend chose a wife. The rumor in Lincoln says these men—Noah, Dick, Chisum and more—were all wounded by love."

Noah grunted. "Chisum told me he proposed marriage years ago. The gal wanted to carry on being the belle of the ball a bit longer. Chisum got impatient. Told her it was now or never. She chose never."

"And he's been a bachelor ever since," Patrón concluded. "Too bad for him. But what about you, Noah? You always had a reputation as a man to leave alone. Women have given their hearts to you, but you never kept them long."

"Settling down with a wife is the farthest thing from my thoughts," Noah said. "God didn't make me the marrying kind."

"But now you're married!" Patrón exclaimed. "And you found a beautiful wife. She's smart, too. Smart enough to capture you."

Isobel held her breath in anticipation of Noah's reply, but he changed the topic. "How's your leg these days, Juan? Looks like you're walking pretty good."

Patrón patted his leg. "It is not the leg, my friend. It is my back."

"Did the Horrell Gang peg you the night they killed your father?"

"No, no. My father died in seventy-three. John Riley shot me two years later—but for the same reason. Hatred of Mexicans. Riley accused several Mexicans of stealing, and shot them dead. I demanded an investigation. When we went to arrest Riley, he shot me in the back."

"In the back?" Isobel stopped on the frozen road. "Did he face trial?"

Patrón shook his head. "Riley is allied with Jimmie Dolan. He was never even arrested."

Isobel was beginning to piece together a picture of Jimmie Dolan. The man held great power and he used it for evil.

"Did Dolan have anything to do with your father's murder?" Noah asked Juan.

"No, the Horrell Gang was just a group of worthless men." Patrón's voice held a note of bitterness. "Outlaws, renegades. In early December, the gang rode into Lincoln, shot up the town and got into a tangle with the Mexican constable. Several men were killed on both sides. A couple of weeks later, the Horrells returned for *revancha*—revenge. The Mexican community was having a Christmas dance at Squire Wilson's hall. The Horrells stormed into the room and began shooting. That night, my father was shot and killed."

Isobel walked in silence, imagining the horror of a celebration transformed into a bloodbath.

"Did you go after the Horrells?" she asked.

"Killing and more killing?" Patrón shook his head. "That is futile, *señora*. My father was dead. Another man's death could never bring him back. You understand?"

She nodded, but she didn't truly understand. Where was the *venganza*—a man's proud avenging of his father's spilled blood? By all that was right, Patrón should have gone after the killers.

"The Horrells made a pact to kill every Mexican in Lincoln County," he was saying. "For a month, they rode through the countryside slaughtering Mexicans. Finally they went to Texas, stealing mules and horses, murdering both Mexicans and gringos along the way.

Eventually, the Seven Rivers Gang ambushed and killed some of them, but the rest made it safely to Texas. They were indicted, of course, but none was ever taken into custody."

He paused. "I've heard that some of the gang—not the Horrell brothers, but others who rode with them—returned to Lincoln. But we don't talk of this. It's better left alone."

Isobel studied the tower of stones as they passed it in the moonlight. If the Horrell Gang had ridden through the countryside in 1873 killing every Mexican in sight, might they have murdered her father? His golden hair would have distinguished him from the Mexicans of the territory, but his native tongue was Spanish. Perhaps he had encountered the Horrell Gang on their journey to Texas. Perhaps they had heard him speak and gunned him down.

"These men," she said softly. "Which of them returned to Lincoln? What are their names?"

Before he could answer, Noah spoke up. "Juan, I need to tell you that my wife's father was killed near Lincoln about the same time your father was shot down. We're looking for his murderer."

"I guessed there was more to this marriage than met the eye. So you wonder if the Horrells may be involved? What else? This woman knows more than she says."

"I witnessed Tunstall's murder," Isobel admitted. "Snake Jackson has vowed to kill me."

"Noah, you must take your wife to Santa Fe," Patrón said. "To her relatives. In Lincoln County, no one is far from violence. Look at Billy Bonney. John Tunstall gave him a clean slate, taught him to read, paid him well. Now I fear the boy's past will catch up with his present."

"Billy's always hot for blood," Noah said. "The kid would rather pull the trigger than talk things over."

Patrón gave a wry chuckle. "How many men is Billy claiming to have killed now? Seventeen? Or is it twenty-one? Señora Buchanan, the men of the West will tell you many things. Do not believe one tenth of what they say, and you will have no trouble here."

Glancing at Noah, Isobel lifted her damp skirts and stepped into the warm Patrón house. If Juan was right, she should not trust her own protector. Nor could she be sure that the Tunstall-McSween faction was nobler than the Dolan gang. After all, Jimmie Dolan had the law on his side, and he was allied with the powers in Santa Fe.

Doubt slinking through her stomach, she drew her shawl tightly over her shoulders as Juan placated his agitated wife in Spanish. Isobel understood every word, of course, and had to work at maintaining a look of innocence. Once Juan had assured Beatriz she was not to blame for Isobel's disappearance, she led them down the hall to a bedroom. After unlocking the door with one of the keys at her waist, she lit a pair of candles on an ornate bureau.

Awash in a yellow glow, the guest room held a bed, a washstand, a chair. A small crucifix hung over the bed, and a cross of woven palm leaves topped the washstand. Beatriz pointed out logs and kindling, then nodded, smiled and left.

Noah knelt and began building a fire. "What was Juan telling Beatriz?"

"He said I followed you because I'm so devoted to you. And that you're in love with me."

Noah's hand halted. He glanced across at Isobel. She was looking out the window. "Juan is going to talk to you tomorrow," she continued. "To tell you the correct way to treat your wife."

Striking a match, Noah held it to the tinder. Was Juan really fooled about the marriage? Did he see something that neither he nor Isobel could admit? Sitting back on his heels, Noah spread his hands over the crackling flames. He didn't trust himself with the woman. Maybe she didn't feel anything, but he sure did.

"My parents had two bedrooms at our hacienda in Catalonia," Isobel said as she joined him by the fire. "With a door to connect them. Where will you sleep?"

Noah looked up, read the trepidation in her eyes and stood. "I said I wouldn't touch you."

"And Juan told me not to trust any man in the West."

"Do you have a choice?" At her nervous expression, he pulled a chair to the fire. "Relax, Isobel. Sit here. I want to talk about your father."

She perched on the edge of the chair. "What about him?"

Noah pushed a log with the poker, and a spray of sparks shot into the air. "Do you know which day your father was killed?"

"No. Only that it was late December. He had spent Christmas with my uncle at Fort Belknap, then he followed the Goodnight Trail north."

"Is your father buried here? In Lincoln?"

"At the cemetery. I promised my mother I would go there." Her lips trembled, and she stopped speaking.

Noah knelt again, reached out and covered her hand with his. "I'll go with you."

Isobel was cold, shivering. She clutched the ragged shawl close around her in one white-knuckled fist. How vulnerable she was, Noah realized. She was scared, too, though she would never admit it. Without her land titles, Isobel had nothing. She insisted she could shoot well enough to protect herself, but a cold-blooded murderer had threatened to gun her down.

"We'll visit the courthouse tomorrow," he told her. "They'll have the record of your father's burial. We can check the date and look for someone who remembers where the Horrell Gang was that day. But, Isobel, you'll never be able to track down the killer. You should go to Santa Fe and try to stop the transfer of the titles."

"You're asking me to forget my father's murder? Do you really think I can stop a land transfer without any documents or proof?" She shook her head. "Impossible without the titles. And without the land, I cannot marry Don Guillermo."

At the mention of her intended husband, Noah stood and slapped the wood dust from his thighs. "Who cares about ol' Don when you've got me? I mean, what more could a lady want?" He couldn't hold back a grin as her eyes went wide. "Why, there's a gal right here in Lincoln who'd be mad as a peeled rattler if she knew about this arrangement."

"What arrangement?" Isobel stood. "Your woman has no cause to feel jealous. We have a *contrato*, a contract."

Edging past Noah, she walked to the washstand, drew her shawl from her shoulders and draped it on the bed. After pouring water into the bowl, she splashed her face and rinsed her hands. Dabbing an embroidered linen towel on her cheek, she turned back toward Noah.

"For that matter," she said softly, "there are many men who would gladly trade places with you, vaquero."

Noah took a step toward her. "I don't doubt that. For a woman who's fretting over land titles and a Spanish dandy, you have a lot more assets than you know."

"What do I have? My father left me nothing but empty land in a bloodthirsty country where no man can be trusted. And Don Guillermo—"

"Don Guillermo doesn't know what he's missing." He caught her hand and pulled her close. "You've got everything you'll ever need right now. You're smart, Isobel. Gritty, too."

"Gritty? What is that?"

"Brave. You'd take on Snake Jackson and the whole Dolan gang if you had to. You know how to ride and shoot. And you're pretty. Real pretty."

She removed her hand from his and turned her shoulder. "I have gowns and jewels, but here I dress as a peasant."

"You don't need fancy gowns to be beautiful, Isobel." He lifted a hand and brushed a lock of hair from her shoulder. "You've got those eyes—green, brown, gray— what color are they?"

"My brother used to say they matched the mud in a pig's pond."

"What do brothers know?" He placed one finger under her chin and tilted her face toward the candlelight. "There's a wild cat that hangs around Chisum's bunkhouse. We call her La Diabla, and she's a devil, all right. Always in trouble, always getting into things she shouldn't. If you can catch her long enough to get a good look, you'll see the fire in her eyes—a green fire that makes them glow like emeralds. Your eyes are like that, Isobel."

For a moment she didn't speak, and Noah stood transfixed by the scent of her hair and skin. He could almost feel the velvet touch of her cheek against his fingertips. Trying to breathe, he knew if one of them didn't talk soon, he would lose himself.

"You should write a book, Buchanan," Isobel suggested, her voice husky. "Any man who sees emeralds in my mud-pond eyes has lost his senses."

"I will write a book," he told her. "And my senses never let me down."

Noah's finger now traced the line of her jaw. He knew she was unaware of how her full, damp lips entranced him. His throat tightened, and his breath went ragged with just one stroke of her skin. She was soft, silky, dangerous. Like the barnyard cat, she was elusive. He knew he shouldn't try to catch her. One look in those eyes, and all of his careful plans could go up in smoke.

"I trust my senses, also," she was saying. "And I sense you are not keeping our contract."

"I'll keep the contract, Isobel. I'm a man of my word. But your lips are telling me one thing, while your eyes are telling me something else."

"No. You're wrong."

She tried to step aside, but he caught her shoulders and drew her close. His hands slipped up and cupped her head. His fingers weaving through her silky hair, he pressed his lips against hers.

Her breath was sweet, fragrant, coming in shallow gasps as she stood rigid in his arms. Puzzled, he studied her face. Surely this gun-toting, haughty, gutsy woman had been kissed many a time. But she trembled against him, her eyes deepening to pools as she gazed into his.

"Isobel," he whispered, uncertain what to do next.

"Kiss me one more time," she murmured, her eyelids drifting shut. "Just once, and never again."

Chapter Five

Moonlight wafted through the iron fretwork on the window to drape a lacy shadow over the room. Unaware, she drifted toward him as his lips brushed hers. She slid her arms around his chest. Reveling in the rich scent of leather and soft flannel, in the rough graze of his chin against her skin, she ran her fingers down his back, which was solid, as hard as steel.

The sense that he was someone she must keep at a distance evaporated in yet another crush of heated lips.

"Isobel," Noah murmured. His blue eyes had gone inky in the flicker of the candles. "I promised not to touch you. I made a vow."

Even as he spoke, she read his plea to be released from that oath. How should she respond to the unbearable tumult he had provoked inside her? She must think of who he was—a mere acquaintance, an American, a common cattleman.

But why did his words sound like poetry in her ears and his kisses feel like music? Perhaps it was the moonlight or the crackling fire. Maybe it was the turmoil that spun through her heart. Or simply the magic of a man's touch.

"I don't know what you've done to me," she whispered.

"The same thing you've done to me. But it's not right. For either of us."

She wanted to argue, but the words didn't come. For endless minutes, they gazed at each other. Then with a deep sigh, Noah shook his head, grabbed his saddlebag and bedroll and left the room.

"Isobel." A cool hand rested on her arm. "Isobel, wake up. The morning is half gone!"

Her eyes flicked open. But instead of the man with blue eyes who had walked through her dreams, she looked into the face of her sweet friend. "Susan? Where is…what time is it?"

"After eight. Noah sent me to look in on you."

Isobel struggled to one elbow. "Where is he?"

"At Alexander McSween's house. He and Dick have been talking since dawn."

"About what?"

"I don't know. I was in the kitchen helping Mrs. McSween. Here's your breakfast." Susan set a basket of warm tortillas on a small table and glanced to the end of the bed. "Isobel, what happened last night? You look…rumpled."

Isobel touched her tender lips, remembering. "I'm all right, Susan."

"Did you and Noah…? Did he try to…?"

"No, it's nothing." She waved a hand in dismissal. "He wants me to go to Santa Fe. To Don Guillermo. Noah is…a problem. A problem for me. I'm sorry I agreed to the arrangement."

She tried to make the words ring true, but they sounded hollow and empty.

"Isobel," Susan spoke up, "if that cowboy is bothering you, we'll find a way to get you to Santa Fe. I know your don will protect you."

She herself knew nothing of the sort, Isobel admitted as she rolled a tortilla and took a bite. The more she thought about the man who had never written to her, never even sent a token of commitment to her mother, the less she trusted Guillermo Pascal.

And Noah Buchanan wanted neither a wife nor children to clutter his life. Besides, the vaquero was too common. Any connection between them was impossible.

Isobel forced a laugh as she stepped to the washstand. "Noah thinks he's a king," she told Susan. "He makes me wash dishes. He sends telegrams without my permission. He gives orders left and right."

Susan giggled. "He gives *you* orders?"

"Noah fancies himself my equal. But he has nothing."

"Nothing except a good job and a quick draw. Out West that can make a man a king. Look at Dick Brewer. He works for the Tunstall operation, but he bought land and a house, and he manages his own cattle."

"You were interested in Dick Brewer last night."

Susan's pale cheeks flushed. "I went outside for fresh air, and Dick came out, too. We talked."

"Talked?"

"Oh, Isobel, he's wonderful!" Susan hugged herself.

"He's handsome and kind and strong. I've never met anyone so perfect. I love him, Isobel."

"Love, Susan? So soon? In Spain we say, *Lo que el agua trae, el agua lleva.* It means what comes easily can also go easily. Your parents should secure a well-to-do husband—one who can give you a fine home. I stayed in Dick Brewer's cabin. It's too small for a family. His land is nothing but rocks. Keep your thoughts from love and you'll be happier."

Susan shrugged. "My Mexican friends in Texas used to say, *Más vale atole con risas que chocolate con lagrimas.*"

"Better to have gruel with laughter than chocolate with tears," Isobel translated the familiar adage. Susan was teasing her now, and she didn't like it. It was bad enough that she'd hardly had any sleep, and that all night her mind had been possessed with thoughts of Noah Buchanan, but now she could hardly focus on her plans.

"I'd rather marry a cowboy like Dick Brewer," Susan said as she helped her friend dress. "I'd rather live in Dick's old cabin and bear him seven little roly-poly Brewers than go up to Santa Fe and marry someone like your rich Don Guillermo. You don't even know him. He would protect you as his wife, but he might not care a fig about you. He can give you a big house and jewels, but can he give you his heart?"

"What do you know about a good marriage, Susan?" Isobel challenged her. "The great families of Spain have made such unions for centuries. No one sits about moaning for love. We marry well because it is our tradition. I am obligated to marry Don Guillermo."

Susan embraced her friend. "Don't be angry, Isobel.

We come from different worlds. To me, Dick Brewer seems like he stepped out of a dream."

"Dreams vanish, *pffft!*" Isobel clicked her fingers. "Like that!"

Susan walked to the window. "I always wanted to fall in love. I know it happened fast, but I do love Dick."

Fumbling with the unruly buttons of her wrinkled bodice, Isobel realized Susan looked different today. Filled with uneasiness at her memories of Noah's kisses, she hoped she didn't appear smitten, too.

"Let's go down to the mercantile," Susan chirped. "We need to sew you a gown that fits. You want to look pretty for Noah Buchanan, don't you?"

"Such nonsense you speak!" Isobel chided her friend.

Aware she was blushing, she snatched her white cotton shawl and wrapped it tightly around her shoulders as she and Susan set off. The day was sunny, and the frozen road had begun to thaw. Scraggly dogs and snuffling pigs wandered through the mud. Wisps of piñon smoke floated from beehive ovens beside the adobe houses that lined the road. The smell of baking bread hung in the morning air, mingling with the scent of bacon and strong coffee.

"Are you going to the fandango Saturday night?" Susan asked. "Folks are saying it'll help ease the tension in town. We could all use some fun."

Isobel shook her head. "I've already spent too much time in the company of rough American men."

"Last night, Dick asked me for the first three dances."

"And the wedding? When is that happy event?"

"Wedding!" Susan elbowed her friend. "Stop teasing,

Isobel. I want to teach school for at least a year. After that, who knows?"

As she walked, Isobel pictured Noah as he'd been the night before, his arms around her, his kisses burning like fire on her lips.

"Susan," she said. "Did you hear Noah Buchanan say anything to Dick about me?"

"Not this morning, no. But last night Dick told me a few things about Noah."

"Yes?"

"He said that in the past few days it seemed like something was bothering Noah. Eating at him. Dick said Noah wouldn't talk about it, but…"

"But what?" Isobel's fingers tightened on her shawl. "What, Susan?"

"Well…Dick made me promise not to tell."

Isobel stopped in the middle of the street, her sodden hem swaying against boots caked with mud. "Susan, you must tell me. Noah Buchanan is bound to me by that silly, reckless vow we made. He's going to stay with me until I've found my father's killer and recovered my land titles. You must tell me everything you know about him."

Susan heaved a sigh. "If you must know…Noah writes."

"*Writes?* Writes what?"

"Stories. He hopes to publish them in a New York magazine. But Dick says that, with you to look after, Noah figures he's going to have his hands too full to write. He sort of wishes he hadn't agreed to protect you so you'd testify."

Isobel stared down at the mud on her fine leather boots. Noah Buchanan was a *writer?* She tried to visualize his big shoulders bent over a sheaf of papers, a pen gripped in his powerful brown fingers—fingers more suited to wrestling a steer than forming letters.

Noah had mentioned the woman in Texas who had read the Bible to him and taught him to spell and count. But what tales would a vaquero have to tell? Noah had no life beyond dusty trails and herds of longhorn cattle.

How dare he resent her for keeping him from his cow stories! Well, she must put all thoughts of the man out of her head and resume searching for her father's murderer, Isobel decided. She must forget the heat of his touch and the pleasure of his lips. The best she could do for herself—and for Noah Buchanan—was to finish her business in Lincoln Town and leave.

Chapter Six

"I must go to the courthouse," Isobel announced. Turning toward the building across from the *torreón,* she heard Susan give a cry of exasperation.

"The courthouse? But Isobel, what about shopping?"

"A new dress can wait. I must find out about my father."

Whitewashed caliche walls shaded by the deep courthouse porch reminded Isobel of her home in Catalonia. She tried to focus her thoughts. She must learn where the public records were kept. Later, she would ask about church records. Striding into the large room, her head full of plans and her vision blinded by sunlight, she almost bumped into Noah Buchanan.

"Isobel." He caught her arm.

"Noah." Their eyes met and held for a heartbeat. She tried to make herself smile, but her mouth had gone dry.

He took off his hat, his hair lifting and then settling against his head. "Morning, Isobel."

"Good morning."

In that brief moment it occurred to her that she had never seen as handsome a man in all her life. He was nothing at all like the *guapo* Spanish dons who had courted her. Noah wore his broad shoulders as another man might wear a relaxed and easy-fitting coat.

Clean-shaven and smelling like fresh rainwater, Noah had on a sky-blue shirt that matched his eyes. His battered black leather jacket hung unbuttoned to the gun belt and holster at his waist. Denim trousers skimmed his thighs. His fingers touched the brim of his hat as gently as they had cupped Isobel's cheek.

"Excuse me," she breathed out. "I need to find records…my father."

"Here, Isobel. I copied out the records for you." He set a sheaf of handwritten documents in her open palm. His voice was low as he related what he had learned. "Your father died on January eighteenth, 1874."

"No, it was seventy-three," she protested.

He pointed out the written evidence. "He was buried on the nineteenth. The report is sketchy, but you'll be interested in it."

Isobel stared at the documents—proof at last of what she had traveled so far to learn. But Noah drew her attention.

"Squire Wilson," he said, indicating a middle-aged man peering at them through a pair of foggy spectacles. "I'd like you to meet my wife, Belle, and her friend Miss Gates. Ladies, Squire Green Wilson is Lincoln's justice of the peace. The town holds district court here once a year. The rest of the time, it's a meeting room and dance hall."

The heavyset man stood. "Forgive me for not being more sociable, Mrs. Buchanan, Miss Gates. I was awake most of the night taking affidavits, issuing warrants, impaneling a jury and whatnot."

"Squire Wilson found the report you needed," Noah told Isobel in a tone she found patronizing. "Wasn't that nice, honey?"

She shot him a look as the justice absently leafed through a stack of papers on his desk. "Glad I could help out. I keep these records, and nobody ever takes a second look at 'em. 'Course, now with all the trouble, you can bet the bigwigs up in Santa Fe will come snooping around."

"Thanks, Squire." Noah caught Isobel's waist and turned her toward the door. "Let's go, sweetheart."

"Certainly, honey," she replied, echoing his manner.

Noah paid her no heed as they stepped out into the brilliant sunshine and began walking in the direction of the store. "Last night," he told the women, "the jury decided Tunstall was killed by Jimmie Dolan's posse. Several of the leaders, including Evans and Snake Jackson, were named, but no one has been arrested yet."

Isobel's heart began to pound harder. "And the rest of us? Did they mention me?"

"Nobody said a word about our being there." He was silent a moment before continuing. "Cavalry troops from Fort Stanton came to town late yesterday to keep the peace. Sheriff Brady ordered the Tunstall store to provide hay for their horses. Alexander McSween accused Brady of larceny for appropriating the hay from Tunstall's estate. So, Squire Wilson issued warrants for Brady and his men. The constable arrested the sheriff this morning and the squire released him on bond of two hundred dollars."

"Everyone is arresting everyone else," Isobel remarked.

"Tempers are hot and getting hotter by the minute. McSween is using his legal know-how to bring Sheriff Brady and Jimmie Dolan to justice for Tunstall's murder."

"Did Dr. Ealy assist in the postmortem on that poor man's body?" Susan asked.

"Both doctors performed the postmortem."

"And?" Isobel's curiosity grew as she strode alongside the strapping cowboy.

"Dr. Ealy recorded the truth," Noah said. "Tunstall's body was not only shot but abused. The report confirms what you said about Evans shooting the Englishman in the head after he was already dead."

A sense of relief washed over Isobel. "I must testify immediately," she declared. "Let's go back, and I'll tell the squire everything I saw. Alexander McSween has the upper hand, and my testimony will see Dolan, Snake and the others thrown straight into jail."

"Whoa, now." Noah slowed his stride. "You march into the courthouse with that story, and you're dead if Snake has half a chance to get at you."

"Mr. Buchanan," Susan cut in. "You just tell Isobel what happened to her father. Then we'll put her into some decent clothes and send her off to Santa Fe."

Noah paused, his eyes narrowing as they pinned Isobel. "Santa Fe?" he asked. "Is that what you want?"

"I want to know about my father," she told him softly.

"It's all in the report. He was shot once—in the chest.

One of his guards was still alive when Dick Brewer found them on the trail."

"Dick Brewer!" Susan squeaked. "Dick found Isobel's father?"

Noah nodded. "He was riding to Lincoln for supplies. The guard told him a gang of twenty men had attacked their party. The man who killed your father wasn't the leader, but he was the biggest talker. After they'd shot all the travelers, the men stole everything. The guard died before Dick got him to Lincoln, poor fellow, and there wasn't enough evidence to indict anyone."

Absorbing everything, Isobel stared at the ink scribbled across the crumpled pages. Banditos had killed her father. Twenty men? But who?

"The Horrells?" she asked him. "Do you think they did it?"

"We'll ask Dick. He'll know more than anyone else."

"Let's go find him," Susan said eagerly.

Isobel shook her head. "Before we speak to Dick, I must bear witness to what I know about the murder of John Tunstall."

"Don't be a fool, Isobel." Susan's voice rose. "You should stay out of this. You'll be killed, just like your father was, and what good will that do anyone?"

Without responding, Isobel studied a store across the street. The two-story building was surrounded by soldiers sent from Fort Stanton to keep order.

"You are wise," she told her friend. "Let's purchase fabric for my new dress. Our first stop will be the store of Mr. Jimmie Dolan."

A haze of piñon smoke filtered over Lincoln as Noah escorted his wife, Belle, and the town's new

schoolteacher onto the porch of Dolan Mercantile. Four
white posts supported the porch roof, which was also
a balcony. Unlike the flat-roofed adobe *jacales* lining
Lincoln's single street, Jimmie Dolan's store had a slop-
ing, shingled roof with three chimneys. Eight windows
on the lower floor and eight above assured that Dolan
and his employees were aware of any shopper's approach
long before the front door opened.

"We need a code," Noah said to Isobel under his
breath. "You can't testify unless we're sure the killers
are the men we think they are."

"When I see the man who murdered Mr. Tunstall,"
Isobel said, "I'll say the word *yellow. Blue* will be the
man who shot second."

"Isobel." He caught her hand. "You be careful. Don't
lose your head in there."

"Of course not. Belle Buchanan never loses her head."
She initiated a chat with Susan as the group stepped
into the store. Noah lifted up a silent prayer for God to
protect them all…and to put a lock on Isobel's tongue.

"Buchanan," a gruff voice called out from a group
of men standing around an iron potbellied stove. "Don't
you know better'n to come in here?"

Noah took off his hat as the men touched the six-
shooters on their hips. "Don't get testy now, fellows,"
he told them. "My bride here is looking to make a new
dress."

"A dress?" Snake Jackson stepped to the front of the
group. "Get your saddle-sore backside outa here, Buchanan.
Jimmie Dolan don't want no Chisum men—"

"There!" Isobel moved forward and placed a hand
on Snake's arm. "Do you see that yellow fabric? Near
the ladder? Will you get it for me, sir?"

For an instant Snake's focus slid across the room and scanned the rows of brightly colored fabric bolts. Then he jerked his arm away and spat a thick, arcing stream of brown-red tobacco juice into the brass spittoon near the door.

"Get yer wife outa here, Buchanan," he snarled, "before I blast the three of you to kingdom come!"

"That'll look good on the squire's books," Noah retorted, stuffing his hat back on his head. "Belle, honey, which bolt did you want Mr. Jackson to take down for you?"

"The yellow. That bright yellow silk near the ladder."

"Ah, Mr. Buchanan. I'm afraid this is not an opportune day for shopping." A short, slender man entered from a side door. He wore a black broadcloth tailcoat and trousers, a red vest and a stiff white shirt with a black bow tie. His hair was a thick mass of unruly curls.

Noah nodded a greeting. "Hello there, Jimmie. I'd like you to know my new wife, Belle. And this is Lincoln's new schoolteacher, Miss Gates. Ladies, meet Jimmie Dolan."

"Such a lovely store you have, Mr. Dolan." Isobel dropped the barest of curtsies. "I've already found a yellow silk that will suit me just fine."

"Didn't you hear the man?" Evans growled. "We don't want a Chisum man in our territory."

"You know, dear, I also favor that blue," Isobel told Noah, her voice breathless. She turned to Evans. "Sir, would you be so good as to fetch me that blue calico?"

"Don't you hear good, lady?" Snake started toward

her, his eyes narrowing. "Jimmie Dolan ain't gonna trade with no Chisum—"

"It's all right, Snake, Evans." Dolan's speech carried an Irish lilt that might have sounded pleasant on another man. "Mrs. Buchanan, I'm afraid we've had a little trouble in Lincoln. Perhaps you'd better do your shopping another day."

Noah glanced at Susan, whose fragile face had faded from pale to white. The schoolteacher looked ready to faint. But Isobel gave Jimmie Dolan a coy smile.

"My dear Mr. Dolan," she said in a soft, buttery accent. "I am in the uncomfortable situation of having almost nothing to wear. May I see that adorable blue calico? Please?"

The Irishman glanced at the row of armed men lurking behind him. The one who was wearing a brass badge on his chest took a stump of cigar from his mouth.

"I believe Mr. Dolan just said he's not open for business," the lawman informed them.

"Sheriff Brady, what are you doing here?" Noah drawled. "If there's trouble in Lincoln, shouldn't you be down at the courthouse? It wouldn't look too good if folks knew the sheriff was hiding out at Jimmie Dolan's store."

"Hiding out?" Brady snarled.

"Sheriff. Buchanan." Dolan put up his small, ring-bedecked hand. "Men, why don't you take your seats by the fire? I'll see that Mrs. Buchanan gets her fabric."

"Why, thank you, Mr. Dolan." Isobel awarded him a radiant smile. "How kind of you."

Noah had no intention of leaving her side for a moment. Dolan made his way around the counter and hooked the bolt of blue calico down into his arms. "It's fifty cents a yard, ma'am." He tossed the fabric on the counter. "That yellow silk is five dollars a yard."

Noah sensed Snake Jackson eyeing Isobel from his position against a wooden post.

"Five dollars. My goodness!" She fingered the yellow silk and then the coarse cotton printed with tiny white sprigs on a blue field. "And the width?"

"Twenty-two inches for the calico. Eighteen for the silk."

"I'll need at least twenty yards to make a dress, won't I, Mr. Dolan?"

Noah watched her turn the dull fabric this way and that. Then, unexpectedly, she turned to face Snake Jackson. "Is there something wrong, sir?" she asked. "You have been staring at me."

Without taking his eyes from her, he straightened. "You always wear that shawl, ma'am?"

Her cheeks paled. "May I ask why you would want to know that, sir?"

"I'm looking for a woman I seen in a shawl just like that one. A woman about your size—"

"Snake," Evans called out, rising from his chair. "Get over here, and leave them people alone."

"You have a mighty odd accent, ma'am," Snake went on as Evans approached. "Like Mexican talk, maybe?"

She tried to smile. "I've never been to Mexico, sir."

"Get your snake-eyed mug back here." Evans stomped up to the counter, a half-empty bottle of whiskey dangling from one hand. "'Scuse ol' Snake, here, ma'am. He thinks he's seein' ghosties ever'where."

"I am seein' ghosties. Mexican ghosties with little lace veils."

"Let's get out of here, honey," Noah said, reaching his arm around her shoulders. "We'll take ten yards of the blue stuff, Dolan. Mark it down, and I'll send you the money when Chisum pays me."

A slow smile spread over the Irishman's face. "You'll have a long wait for John Chisum to be paying you, Mr. Buchanan. I'm afraid he's in jail."

"So I hear. They tell me some stinkin' coyote of a man is behind it."

Dolan measured the yards of fabric, his face impassive. "The coyote is a smart animal, I'm told."

"Feeds on carrion," Noah shot back.

Isobel placed a placating hand over Noah's. "Have you buttons?" she asked Dolan, tucking the fabric under her arm.

"We don't carry buttons. Most people cut the buttons off their old clothes and sew them on their new ones."

"Hooks?"

"Those we have. I assume you'll be wanting thread?"

"Blue, of course."

"Do you have a sewing machine, Mrs. Buchanan?"

"Mrs. McSween has a Wheeler and Wilson machine—" Susan blurted. "That is…she's in St. Louis and I'm sure she wouldn't mind if Mrs. Buchanan were to borrow it."

"McSween, eh?" Dolan squinted at her. "So you're working for Mac, are you, Miss Gates?"

"The lady's a schoolteacher," Noah spoke up. "She's here to teach kids how to read and write."

Snake sidled along the counter. With one dirty finger he prodded Noah's arm. "What I want to know is why you didn't do yer shoppin' at Tunstall's store, Buchanan."

"I reckon you'd know the answer to that, Jackson."

"And what's that supposed to mean, huh? You sayin' I done the Britisher in?"

Noah smiled. "I'm saying you'd know we couldn't shop at Tunstall's because it's shut down this morning. I didn't say you killed him. *You* did."

"Why, you—"

"All right, hold it there, now!" The voice of young Billy Bonney snuffed the argument as the Kid strode through the front door, followed closely by the town constable.

"We've come with a warrant," the constable announced.

At that, the store erupted. Guns drawn, men on both sides of the room rushed toward the fray. Susan screamed. Isobel grabbed her friend's hand and was making for the counter when Noah bundled both of them in his arms and drew them against his chest.

"Heads down!" he growled. Barreling between two Dolan men, he kicked wide the counter's swinging door. He huddled Isobel and Susan against the side of a three-foot-high black iron safe. "Stay here. Don't move till I come back for you, hear?"

As he drew his six-shooter, Noah gave the women a last glance. Cradling Susan's head in her lap, Isobel gazed at him, her eyes deep. For the first time in his life, Noah realized, someone else's life meant more than his own.

Wishing she had a gun, Isobel held the sobbing young woman. She scanned the rows of dry goods on the shelves behind her head. Black Leaf sheep dip. Tobacco paste. Pride of Denver soap. Glass lamp globes. Tins from the National Biscuit Company. Red Cross cough drops. Chase & Sanborn's packaged teas. She spied guitar strings, corsets, union suits, gloves and shoes. But no guns.

"Hold on!" a voice bellowed over the rest. "I got a warrant here, and you boys better calm down and listen to it."

Isobel peered over the countertop.

"This here warrant," the constable announced, "is signed by Squire Wilson for the arrest of James J. Dolan, Jesse Evans, Jim Jackson—"

"What fer?" someone shouted.

"For the murder of John Henry Tunstall."

Voices rose again, drowning out the constable. Isobel searched for Noah among the mob, but he was nowhere in sight. If only she had her pistol.

"As sheriff of Lincoln, I'm arresting you!" Sheriff Brady shouted. "All of you!"

"You can't do that, Sheriff!" the Kid protested. "We came in here to arrest these fellers. You can't turn around and arrest us."

"I sure can and do."

"On what charges?"

"Disturbing the peace."

The momentary burst of laughter was followed by a sudden scuffle. A gun went off. Susan shrieked. Isobel scrunched down, covering Susan's head in her lap. Not far from the safe where they hid, she spotted a derringer tucked at the back of a counter behind a cigar box. No doubt Jimmie Dolan had placed it there, but Isobel knew she could put it to good use herself. An ironing board leaned against a shelf, and she dragged it closer and propped it against the safe to form a makeshift barrier.

"Forgive me for leaving you, Susan," she whispered, "but I must have a weapon."

Crawling across the dusty floor, she reached for the gun. But when a hand clamped over her wrist, she let out a gasp.

"Isobel," Noah hissed. "What do you think you're doing?"

"A woman of honor can end a *lucha* between cowards like these filthy vaqueros!"

"You're crazier than a bedbug, lady. Let go of that thing." He pried her fingers from the pistol and tossed the weapon into an open drawer filled with packets of Putnam's fabric dyes. "Where's Susan? I've got to get the two of you out of this place before it blows."

"Here I am, Mr. Buchanan," Susan whimpered.

"It's okay, Miss Gates," he assured her. "Give me your hand, and we'll head out the back way."

Isobel crossed her arms and watched in distaste as Noah escorted the red-haired schoolteacher from the hiding place. Tears streaming, Susan buried her head against his shoulder.

"You'll be all right now, Miss Gates. Come on." Noah cast a warning frown at Isobel, then jerked on her arm and hurried the two women toward the back door.

The hubbub grew behind them as Dolan's men swarmed to help make the arrest. The closing door silenced the commotion inside the store.

"Let me go!" Isobel snarled, twisting against Noah's grip as he hurried her and Susan down the muddy road. "Where are you taking me?"

"Santa Fe. Let that don of yours try to keep his eye on you."

"He's not my don!" she snapped. "You're the man who married me, Noah Buchanan, and I command you to treat me with respect!"

Noah stopped dead still on the road. "If I'm the man you married, Isobel, then you'd better do as I say. That means no pistols, no shooting, no taking matters into your own hands and getting somebody killed. If I'm your husband, I'm the boss. You hear?"

Isobel tossed her head. "What you want is a weak little nobody for a wife, yes?"

"That's right."

"Then you have married the wrong woman."

"You're right about that, too."

"Oh, no!" Susan cried out. "Here comes the Dolan mob with the constable and the others under arrest."

Noah stiffened. "The pair of you head over to Alexander McSween's house and sew Isobel's dress. I don't want to see hide nor hair of either of you around Lincoln Town today."

Simmering, Isobel stared at the towering cowboy who presumed to rule over her by his bartered title of husband. His blue eyes fairly crackled as he met her gaze.

"You got a problem with that plan, Isobel?" he asked.

"I can't take another minute!" Susan sobbed. Lifting her skirts, she ran down the road toward the McSween home. She had just passed the Wortley Hotel when a group of soldiers emerged and surrounded the approaching Dolan mob.

"My only problem on this day is you, sir," Isobel informed her counterfeit husband. "You forget that we made an agreement. You will protect me, and in return I will testify about the murder of John Tunstall. You have no right to treat me like a—"

"You left out part of our deal, darlin'," Noah cut in, pulling her against his chest as the throng of men drew near. "Your job is to be my sweet little wife until Chisum sells me some land."

Isobel tugged her shawl tight and hugged her packet of calico fabric as if it might insulate her from him. "A good wife knows how to protect herself."

"You and Susan were shielded behind that safe. You were perfectly secure."

"Susan. Ah, *sí,* poor Susan who weeps at the sound of gunfire. How happy she was to be taken under your wing like a helpless chick."

Noah's jaw dropped. "You're jealous. Jealous of Susan Gates."

"Jealous? Ha! She can have you, for all I care. I want a man who treats me like a lady."

"Then you ought to try acting ladylike instead of crawling around the floor to get at a gun."

"And allow myself to be shot by some dirty vaquero like the one who killed my father? Never." She lifted her chin. "I should never have agreed to marry you. I can take care of myself. I am good at shooting."

"You're good at a lot of things."

Her eyes darted up, and she read the twinkle in his. Her mouth twitched, and she shrugged her shoulders. "You know very little about me, *señor.*"

"Seems to me I learned a few things about you last night, didn't I?"

At the mention of their kisses, she felt heat suffuse her cheeks. "You know nothing," she managed.

"I know that right now you're starting to look like a blushing bride. So, I'm going to head my pretty little wife over to Mac's house and set you to sewing up your new dress. All right?"

"Oh, yes, my strong, brave husband," she responded, batting her eyes for effect. "I will stitch and bake—and weep for joy when I hear your footsteps on the porch."

"You do that, sweetheart."

Chuckling, Noah tucked Isobel close and strolled with her toward the adobe home. At the warmth of his arm around her shoulders, it occurred to Isobel that perhaps she wouldn't mind being a wife who would sew and bake and wait for her husband to come home at night. What a curious thought.

Chapter Seven

Isobel had never stitched a dress in her life. For that matter, she had never allowed plain cotton fabric to touch her skin—not until the day she wed Noah Buchanan and was compelled to wear one of Susan Gates's simple ginghams. But she had to remember she was no longer Isobel Matas, daughter and heiress of a wealthy Catalonian family. She was Belle Buchanan, wife of a poor cowboy.

All morning, Susan patiently taught her student how to sew. First Isobel learned to thread the black Wheeler & Wilson treadle sewing machine. Using a borrowed pattern that had been the model for nearly every dress stitched in Lincoln Town, Isobel learned to lay out the blue fabric and cut it to size. The bodice took some adjusting, for she insisted on hooks all the way up to her throat. Modesty was a definite requirement these days. She may have succumbed to Noah's charms once or twice, Isobel allowed, but she would not permit such intimacies to become commonplace.

As she snipped and pinned and tried her hand at finishing seams, Isobel thought about those stolen kisses.

What could she have been thinking? She had made a simple agreement with Noah Buchanan. Each would use the other to get what they needed. How then had she slipped so willingly into his arms?

Oh, his kisses… Isobel shut her eyes as the memory seeped through her.

"Are you planning to gather that skirt or not?"

Susan's voice dissolved the memory of Noah's rough stubble against Isobel's cheek. With renewed determination to focus, she resumed sewing. Her feet tilted up and down to work the treadle, while her fingers guided the fabric. The soft cush-cush-cush of needle biting through cotton cloth lulled her. As the full skirt ruffled beneath her fingers and the long hours stretched on, she struggled to force images of Noah from her thoughts.

"How are you and Mr. Buchanan getting along?" Susan asked. Night was setting in and the lamps cast a golden glow over the swaths of fabric that had taken shape during the day. "We've avoided the subject all day, but I can't hold my tongue a moment longer. He seems like such a nice man."

"Nice, yes…" Isobel wet the tip of a thread with her tongue, knotted it and began to hem. "Nice…but common. Like the vaqueros on our hacienda. Strong and powerful but very ill-mannered."

"You still have your sights on Don Guillermo Pascal, then?"

Isobel smoothed the hem and leaned back in her chair. "Noah sent *Señor* Pascal a telegram last night. There has been no reply."

"Maybe he hasn't had time to answer."

"If a man wants to make a woman his wife, he will

do anything for her. He will rescue her from peril. He will care for her at any cost."

"But for all you know, your don is on his way to Lincoln right now."

"He doesn't want me, Susan, and how can I blame him? I have nothing to offer."

"You're pretty."

Isobel laughed. "For a common man, a wife need only be pretty. But in my social class, wealth and land are necessary to forge a marriage."

"What will you do? You've come all this way to marry him."

"I always knew I must find my father's killer first. I must regain my lands and jewels. Then Guillermo will marry me."

"Meanwhile, you're married to Noah, and he's a very good man. You might consider just sticking with him."

"Oh, Susan, what a silly head you have! To think that I would ever consider Noah Buchanan in any serious way is loco. We have an arrangement. He's nothing but a vaquero and so plain. He has no land, no house, no cattle, nothing. His hands are large and rough. A workingman's hands. He's beneath me, Susan. How can I explain it?"

"You just did." Noah's voice echoed off the adobe walls of the little sewing room. Isobel and Susan lifted their heads at the unexpected intrusion.

"Noah," Isobel gasped.

"I came for you. It's almost dark."

She studied the hem of her new dress. Had he heard the horrible things she had said about him? Things she knew were weak excuses to hide the surge of emotion she felt every time she thought of him?

"Isobel learned a lot today, Mr. Buchanan," Susan reported, filling the awkward silence. "She threaded the Wheeler and Wilson. She's fine with a straight seam, too."

"But I sure do hate for the *marquesa* to have to wear such common duds."

Isobel stood, her face hot and her heart thudding. "The dress will suit my purpose. Shall we go?"

Noah shrugged. "Good night, Miss Gates. I hope you have a pleasant evening."

"Mr. Buchanan, do you suppose I might have a word with you? That is, if Isobel wouldn't mind waiting outside a minute."

"But of course," Isobel said.

She watched a pink stain creep up Susan's cheeks as the schoolteacher eyed Noah. Grabbing the blue dress, Isobel bundled it in her arms and stepped out of the sewing room. Why should she care if her friend had cast an eye on Noah? First, Susan was supposedly in love with Dick Brewer, and now she blushed and giggled over another man. Susan, it appeared, was an audacious flirt.

But what difference did it make to Isobel if Susan or any other young lady fancied Noah? She and he both intended the arrangement to end in an annulment. Let Susan Gates have the vaquero.

In a few moments, the sewing room door opened and Noah stepped out into the hall. Without a word, he escorted Isobel out of the McSween home.

"Nice night," he commented as they started down the road.

Isobel chose not to respond. Now that she saw things more clearly, she realized kissing Noah had simply been a result of the madness in this tangled town. But such foolishness was in the past. She knew what she had to do with her life. And she certainly understood Noah's place in it.

"Chilly, though," he said as he opened the front door of the Patrón home. "Mighty chilly."

When they had crossed through the empty front room to their bedroom door, Isobel opened her mouth to speak, but Noah addressed her first.

"Isobel, I heard what you told Miss Gates about me," he said. "I'm a plain, common vaquero. I'm beneath you."

"Noah, wait—"

"Hear me out. Last night I thought maybe we had found something good. I prayed about it all day—half the time asking God to blot you from my mind, half the time begging Him to let me keep you."

"You prayed to God…about me?" The very idea of approaching the Creator of heaven and earth with something so personal confused her.

"Yes," he continued, "and I didn't think I was going to get an answer anytime soon. But a few minutes ago, I heard what you said, and that made things clear enough. I'll give you plenty of elbow room from here on, Isobel."

"But I didn't mean it—what I said to Susan." She gestured emptily, aware that anything tender between them had been swept away by her careless words.

"I may be a common cowboy," he said, "but I've got my pride. Now, if you'll excuse me, I'll head back to Mac's place and bunk down in his barn."

Settling his hat on his head, he strode through the silent living room and left Isobel alone to wonder whether her husband would seek other, warmer arms that night.

In the morning Isobel ate the breakfast Beatriz Patrón brought to her room, then she slipped her new blue-cotton gown over her head. It was not a bad dress, she admitted, though it was hopelessly outdated. But evidently Lincoln Town had never heard of fashion.

What would Noah think of her dress? she wondered. And what did that matter anyway? She had offended him and cast him aside. Why should she give his opinion any credit?

But even as she thought it, she fell to her knees by the bed and buried her face in the blanket. How many times during the night had she slid to the floor, folded her hands and attempted to address God as Noah had—as One who actually cared about her…about Isobel Matas and her insignificant desires.

God was majestic, a Lord who ruled over all the universe. What thought would He spare for a woman who longed to be held and loved and cherished? How could He truly care about a silly, headstrong girl up to her ears in trouble?

He didn't care, of course. God was busy tending to kings and priests, wars and famines, earthquakes and floods. But she needed guidance! Her father was dead, her mother thousands of miles away and her intended husband utterly silent. God would bother Himself with none of that, of course. She was alone.

Rising, Isobel stepped to the washbasin and brushed her hair. As stiff bristles slid through her golden waves, she wondered how to make the best use of this day. She could speak with Squire Wilson about the events surrounding her father's death. She might ask Sheriff Brady, too, though she could hardly trust what such a man might tell her.

Sweeping her hair into a knot, she had just begun to pin it when someone knocked on the door. Dropping the mass of hair, she swung around, fingertips at her throat.

"Yes?"

"Buchanan here."

Annoyed at the flutter that began in her chest at the sound of his deep voice, she strode to the door and pulled it open. Though images of Noah had drifted through her mind all night, she was unprepared for the sight of him. A clean chambray shirt showed beneath the ankle-length canvas duster coat he wore. His denim trousers ended in a pair of black boots. A pistol hung in the holster at his hip.

"We're going on a buggy ride," he informed her. "Bring your shawl. It's cold out."

Too disconcerted to protest, Isobel wrapped her white shawl around her head and shoulders.

"Straighten the bed," Noah ordered. "Good manners."

Isobel had never made a bed in her life, but she bent over to smooth the blankets. A buggy ride? Where had he gotten a buggy? What did he intend? And where had he been all night? With Susan?

She glanced at Noah. His square jaw gleamed from the morning's shave. His blue eyes glowed with the brilliant hue of the morning sky outside her window.

"Where are you taking me?" she asked.

"You'll see." He took her arm and set off through the house. He paused in the kitchen long enough to bundle a stack of freshly baked tortillas in a white napkin and hand them to Isobel.

"Thanks, Beatriz," he said to Juan's petite wife. "If we aren't back by sunset, send out a posse."

"Sunset!" Isobel exclaimed. "But I—"

"I'll be in Mac's rig, Beatriz," he said. Busy with her housework, the woman waved them on. Noah hustled Isobel across the porch and into the waiting buggy.

A pale yellow sun rose to light the Capitan Mountains as Noah drove the buggy toward the Rio Bonito's narrow valley. Purple shadows faded. Greens began to stand out. Sometime in the night, Noah had made up his mind to take Isobel out of town, where he could talk to her about things that needed to be said. And being so far from civilization, he would have time to calm her down before she did something fool headed. At least he could try.

Noah found he had a hard time keeping his eyes on the dirt track. Isobel looked mighty fine this morning. Her new blue dress with its ruffles and gathers showed off her figure in a way that made it hard for him to concentrate. Though she sat up straight on the buggy seat and held her chin high, she looked as sweet and mild as fresh milk.

But he knew better. Beneath that demure facade lay a woman with a tongue as sharp as barbed wire. He had felt its sting the night before when she had told Susan Gates her opinion of him. It didn't take much to set Noah Buchanan on the straight track. And Isobel had done just that. So much for the daydreams that had been rolling around in his head since the night he had kissed her. Daydreams weren't worth a barrel of shucks.

"Where are you taking me?" Isobel spoke up as the buggy passed the Dolan store, where the group of Fort Stanton soldiers lounged on the porch.

"Out of town."

"I guessed that much," she retorted.

Noah didn't let himself rise to the taunt. He wasn't about to start talking to her this close to town.

As the buggy rolled closer to the river, the barren terrain gave way to cedar shrubs mingled with piñons and junipers. Grama grass and bunchgrass, untouched by cattle or sheep so far from town, had grown thick the past summer. Now a dry gray-brown, it crackled beneath the buggy wheels.

The rig bumped and jolted along the rutted trail until Noah turned the horse into the woods. "I intend to speak with several men in Lincoln today," Isobel said. "I can't be away long."

"Eat a tortilla," Noah told her.

Letting out a sigh of exasperation, she crossed her arms. "Noah Buchanan, I—"

"If you aren't going to eat, hand me one. That Susan Gates is a bum cook. Good thing she's set her mind on teaching." He couldn't hold back a smile at the memory of the men hunkering down for breakfast at McSween's house. "Eggs looked like cow chips. And the bacon… well, a man could break a tooth on the stuff."

"Poor Susan," Isobel murmured.

"But she's a sweet gal anyhow. Whoa, now." He pulled the horse to a stop in a glade at the edge of a stream. "How's this?"

"For what?"

"For talking." He jumped down from the buggy and walked around to Isobel's side. When he extended a hand, she stood, lifted her skirt, and set her fingers on his palm. She was trembling, he noted as he helped her down, and he suddenly realized how unexpected—maybe even frightening—this excursion might appear to her.

"What will we talk about?" she asked.

He looked into her eyes, swallowed and hitched up his shoulders. "I'll put down a blanket, and we can sit a spell."

"Has something happened? Is it about Mr. Tunstall's murder?"

He rubbed a palm across the back of his neck. "I'll fetch that blanket."

She stood unmoving while he unloaded a wool blanket from the buggy and spread it on a patch of grass under a tree. Seating herself, she seemed to melt into a pouf of blue cotton.

"What I have to tell you isn't about Tunstall," he began as he sat down beside her.

"Then who?"

He took a deep breath. "I know who killed your father."

"Who did it? Tell me at once!" She clumped her skirt in knotted fists.

"Before you get bees in your britches, I want you to hear me out, Isobel. Do your best to think straight."

"I always think clearly."

He held his tongue about that comment as he continued. "Last night after I left you at Patrón's house, I went to McSween's place. Dick Brewer and I sat out on the porch jawing about this and that. I led him around to telling me about the day he came across that massacre on the trail."

"And?"

"And Dick let out a secret he'd never told. When he found the coach, the guard who was still alive gave him a good description of the man who shot your father. Dick knew right away who it was. The assassin would be long gone by the time the story came out, Dick knew, so the law would drag him back to Lincoln where no one wanted him. 'Course now he's back in town whether we like it or not."

"Who, Noah?"

"The Horrell Gang attacked your father's party—the same bunch that killed Juan Patrón's dad. But the guard told Dick that the man who pulled the trigger on your father had a heavy jaw, a flat nose and spiked-out red hair. His eyes were narrow slits."

"Snake Jackson," she whispered.

"You'd be hard put to find a man to match that description better than Rattlesnake Jim Jackson. This morning, Juan confirmed that Snake was riding with the Horrells back in seventy-three."

Isobel had shut her eyes, the expression on her face filled with pain. Noah could guess how it felt to learn the name of a man who had murdered someone you loved. He fought the urge to put his arm around the woman and hold her close.

But to Isobel, he thought, he wasn't worthy to give her comfort. He was just a no-account cowboy, and he had to keep his hands off.

"Now, Isobel," he said, crossing his arms to keep from touching her. "Look at this situation straight-on. Snake Jackson murdered your father, but he just murdered John

Tunstall, too. He's in a heap more hot water about that. He already has his eye out for a Mexican woman who saw him put a hole in Tunstall's chest. If he ever pins you as that woman, you don't stand a chance. And if he links you to the Horrell business, honey, your days are numbered."

Her eyes filling with tears, Isobel said nothing. Noah knew that she was remembering the moment Snake Jackson had shot the Englishman…and imagining the same man killing her father.

"Take me back to town, Noah," she said suddenly. "I must kill Jim Jackson."

"Kill him?" It was the last thing in the world Noah had expected her to say. He shook his head. "Lady, I just told you your life is in great danger, and you want to ride into Lincoln and try to hunt down a killer? A man who's in league with Dolan and Evans and the rest of those sidewinders?"

Her eyes flashed. "He murdered my father, Noah. What choice do I have?"

"Choice? Take your pick. You can head for Santa Fe and marry your fancy don—or sail back to Spain and settle down with your family."

She looked away. "I don't suppose you've had a telegram from Guillermo Pascal."

"Not yet, but the Pascals are busy folk. Ranching, politics, you name it. If I were you, I'd go home. I bet your mama would be tickled pink to have you back."

"I'm not wanted in Spain. No more than I'm wanted by Guillermo Pascal."

Noah let out his breath. Here was a fine to-do. She wouldn't go to Santa Fe because the don she'd come all this way to marry didn't seem to want her. She wouldn't go to Spain because her family didn't want her. So what did she plan to do—stay in Lincoln? Who wanted her here?

Not Noah Buchanan, that's for sure. He took off his hat, leaned back against the tree and closed his eyes. He had enjoyed that kiss the other night, but if she thought she could treat him like dirt and still expect him to protect her...

"What do you see?" she asked. "In Lincoln. What makes you stay?"

He studied the vast terrain. "New Mexico Territory has elbow room, fresh air, blue sky and plenty of sunshine. It's a tough land. Tough people, too. I like that."

"I see little about the people to admire."

"Most of them are hard as old boot leather. They've worked hard and lived hard. They're either good or they're bad. It's not hard to tell 'em apart. The way a man's heart is—the state of his soul—starts creeping out onto his face. The older he gets, the more he looks like the person he is inside."

"Perhaps you're right," Isobel said. "My father had golden hair, and his smile was gentle. Dr. Ealy's face is filled with peace. Susan Gates is lovely."

"She's easy on the eyes."

"You should marry her."

Noah sat up straight. "Marry Miss Gates?"

"She likes you. She would make you a good wife."

He gave a snort. "You've got two problems with that little notion. One is that Miss Gates has her cap set on Dick Brewer, and he's returning the compliment. Last night when we were alone, she asked me about him. I had only good things to say, of course. I don't imagine it'll be too long before we hear wedding bells."

"A wedding? But they barely know each other."

"They know enough—for sure more than you know your don."

"Don't speak of Guillermo Pascal," she said, knotting her hands in her lap. "It's not your concern."

"But the second hitch in your scheme to marry me off to Miss Gates *is* my concern. I'm already married—in case you forgot."

"I didn't forget," she said.

"Neither did I."

Their eyes met for a moment. Isobel swallowed and glanced away. "How do I look to you, Noah?" she asked. "Does my face show a hardness of heart?"

He took her hand from her lap, opened the fingers and studied them for a moment. "When I first saw you hiding behind that juniper, I thought you were a mite chilly looking. All those shiny green ruffles. Now I have you pegged as hardheaded, afraid of tying yourself down, scared to trust folk. That shows on your face, Isobel. It does."

She lowered her head.

"On the other hand," he continued, "being strong minded and gritty serves a woman well here in the West."

Taking a breath, she spoke in a gush. "Noah, last night you heard me say harsh and cruel things about you. They were lies. All of them. You're the best man I have met since the death of my father. You're gentle but also strong. And brave, intelligent, kind…"

"Whoa, I seem to have improved."

She smiled. "You are a good person. Noah, I'm sorry. What I said last night was wrong. I'm so sorry."

He studied her for a moment. "Isobel, if you didn't mean what you told Miss Gates, why'd you say it?"

Nervous, she lifted the hair from the back of her neck. Her long eyelashes fluttered as she struggled to voice her feelings. "I...I can't allow myself to think too well of you, Noah."

"Because I'm low class?"

"That has nothing to do with it. What is here for me? Nothing. I have no future. My paths to Santa Fe and Spain are blocked. My only hope now is to find Snake Jackson and get my land titles from him. I have nothing. I am nobody. How can I allow myself to look at anything but *revancha?*"

"Listen, Isobel, you can forget about revenge. I'm not letting you near Jim Jackson. The man wants to kill you, and he wouldn't think twice about it."

"What will you do with me?"

"After Tunstall's funeral tomorrow, I'll take you to Chisum's ranch. That's final. No arguing."

"And then? What then, Noah? What is to become of me? You can't hold me there forever. You don't want me any more than Don Guillermo or my family and—"

"I want you, Isobel. I don't understand why, but ever since I first laid eyes on you, I've cared about you. The future is in God's hands, but one thing's for sure. Everything's about to blow sky-high in Lincoln. I've got to get Chisum out of jail and keep Snake from getting his hands on you. All I can think about is right now. And right now, what I know I can't deny. The only truth I can see is that I want you."

Isobel let out her breath slowly. "If you want me, Noah, hold me. Kiss me now."

Chapter Eight

He could hardly believe she had said it. But she was a temptation, and at this moment, Noah could not resist. A woman who looked as Isobel looked, who spoke as she spoke, could not be ignored.

Thoughts of the uncertain future went clean out of his head as he bent to kiss her cheek.

"Isobel, darlin'," he murmured. "What are you doing to me?"

She stared up at him, her face filled with tenderness.

With a sigh, he took her in his arms and kissed her sweet lips. And kissed them again. A cool breeze playing off the stream mingled with the warm sunlight shining on this patch of green grass. In the silent haven Noah felt as if he was a world away from the fear, bloodshed and anger pursuing them.

When her arms came around him, he knew they were in dangerous territory. Gritting his teeth, he drew back and forced his breathing to steady.

"I haven't had much schooling," he told her, "but I learned one thing a few years back. Put a hungry man and a willing woman together, and you've got trouble. I've read the Bible cover to cover a few times, and I figured out the smart thing to do is stick with God's plan for a man and a woman to get married before they do too much kissing."

Isobel relaxed in his arms, her cheek on his shoulder, her dark gold hair soft against his chest. "I have read many books, but never the Bible. The Scriptures are read to us in church. For me, such things as prayer, the Bible, the sacraments are of the old ways—respected but insignificant. Religion is a guide, not a law."

This surprised Noah. Most of the Mexicans and Spaniards he knew took their faith seriously. "Without those *old ways,* I'd have made a heap more mistakes than I did. Fact is, I don't put a foot out of bed every morning without praying first. I try to never make a decision unless I check it out with God first."

"You married me very quickly. Did you check with God?"

He shook his head. "Nope, and that's how come I'm as tangled up as a bull with its horns caught in a barbed wire fence. Only thing I can do now is pray that God will reach down His hand and untangle me."

She fell silent for a moment. "Noah." Her breath stirred his skin. "The day we met, you searched Dick Brewer's cabin for paper."

He tensed. "Yeah…I did."

"What do you write, Noah?"

His touched a strand of her hair, his fingers tracing the golden waves as he pondered her question. Finally he let out a breath. "Not much yet."

"The moment I first saw your hands—when you saved me from the bullet's path that day on the trail—I knew you were more than a vaquero. I knew you were an artist. Your hands are those of a poet."

He smiled at that. "I'm no poet, Isobel."

"Tell me what you write. Please, Noah."

"Just stories, mainly. They're all up here. In my head. Stories about life on the trail. About things that can happen to a man when he's living off the land, when he and God and the cattle are his whole world. Yarns the men spin while they're sitting around the fire after a long day." He sighed. "It's probably a crazy notion."

"It would be crazier not to write down your stories."

"Maybe so, Isobel."

A white butterfly drifted over their heads. Noah watched, wondering how it had emerged from its cocoon so soon. Too soon. An early frost would likely end its life before summer. The white wings trembled, and the butterfly alighted on Isobel's shoulder. She didn't notice. Noah smiled.

He liked Isobel this way, he mused. She was soft and feminine in a way that made him want to do things he'd tried to put clean out of his mind. Things like protect, honor and provide for her. He wanted to keep her at hand so he could touch her hair and brush his lips across hers. He'd like to know her sweet arms were waiting for him at the end of the day.

"You must take me to town now, Noah," she cut into his daydream. "I must find Jim Jackson before dark. I cannot be denied *la venganza*."

It took him a moment to sift through the sunlit imaginings that had spangled his reality. *"La vengan—"*

"I must avenge my father's murder and retrieve the land-grant titles this Snake stole from the *familia*

Matas. I know the name of the assassin, and I have no choice."

Noah stiffened and eased Isobel's shoulders away until she was at a safe distance. "I want you to hear me once and for all, girl. You're not a Matas any longer. You're a Buchanan. I swore an oath to keep you safe, and I always abide by my word. I'll go to Tunstall's funeral tomorrow, and the minute it's over, I'm taking you to South Spring River Ranch. No arguing. And none of this revenge nonsense, understand?"

"I understand, Noah," she said.

She would not obey him, he thought to himself. Not at all.

That evening in Lincoln, Isobel eagerly listened to Juan Patrón's account of the day's developments. He was worried that Dolan's gang would attend the funeral the following morning. With Alexander McSween's party there—along with Tunstall's friends and employees—violence could be expected.

As predicted, McSween had demanded Squire Wilson charge Sheriff Brady and his bunch with the unlawful appropriation of property for using Tunstall's hay to feed Fort Stanton horses.

Brady was arrested and bound over to the grand jury for the coming term of court. Everyone in town, Juan explained, knew that the sheriff now sided squarely with Jimmie Dolan.

After dinner Noah insisted on patrolling Patrón's home and store. He circled the house through the night, checking windows and doors. Isobel could not sleep. She listened to his footsteps until dawn.

When breakfast ended, they joined the crowd gathered

for the funeral. McSween had selected a burial plot east
of Tunstall's store, just behind the land for the church
that Dr. Ealy planned to build.

"John Henry Tunstall," Dr. Ealy said to begin the
solemn service, "a mere twenty-four years of age, met
an untimely death. The son of John Partridge Tunstall
of London, England, our friend was brother to three
sisters, whom he loved with an extreme devotion. Many
are unaware that John was blind in his right eye, but he
overcame this difficulty with the determination of the
gentleman he was."

Isobel studied the row of heavily armed men who
made up the Dolan faction. Snake Jackson was not
among them. They stood beyond a pile of newly turned
earth beside the open grave. The casket, a simple pine
box, sat unopened on the ground.

As the service began, Noah slipped one arm around
Isobel. She glanced at Dick Brewer standing protectively
beside Susan Gates. Like all the McSween men, they
rested their fingertips lightly on their holsters.

The detachment of Company H, the Fifteenth Infan-
try, from Fort Stanton kept watch at a distance. Isobel
surmised that Lieutenant Delany had instructed them
to be a respectful but obvious presence. No doubt the
soldiers were the only thing preventing a clash between
the two angry groups.

"My text today is from the Gospel of St. John, Chap-
ter eleven, verse twenty-five." Dr. Ealy cleared his throat
as he opened the heavy black Bible. *"Jesus said unto
Martha, 'I am the resurrection and the life; he who
believeth in me, though he die, yet shall he live.'* We
are to understand by these words that those who believe

in Jesus Christ unto salvation will abide with Him in heaven after their earthly death."

Recalling Noah's declaration of absolute faith in God, Isobel reflected on the beauty and grandeur of the New Mexico Territory. At such a display, who could discount the power of the Creator?

"I'd like to ask now," Dr. Ealy said, "that we close this service with a hymn. Noah Buchanan, I'm told you're blessed with the best voice among us. As we stand here by the Rio Bonito, would you lead us in singing 'Shall We Gather at the River'?"

Isobel glanced at Noah in shock as he began to sing. Yet another surprise from this man. His deep voice drifted over the stream and across the grassland toward the distant mountains.

"Shall we gather at the river, where bright angel feet have trod," Noah sang, "with its crystal tide forever, flowing by the throne of God?"

The entire company, even the Dolan men, joined in the chorus.

"Yes, we'll gather at the river,
The beautiful, the beautiful river;
Gather with the saints at the river
That flows by the throne of God."

Not knowing the words as the others did, Isobel shut her eyes and absorbed the vibrations in Noah's chest. Though it was a funeral, at this moment she felt more peace than she had known in the entirety of her life. She was folded in the arms of a man who had sworn to protect her. Sweet golden sunlight warmed her. The

anger that had driven her to this land faded, leaving in
its place the gentle lull of tranquillity.

"Soon we'll reach the shining river, soon our pilgrim-
age will cease," Noah sang.

> "Soon our happy hearts will quiver
> With the melody of peace.
> Yes, we'll gather at the river,
> The beautiful, the beautiful river;
> Gather with the saints at the river
> That flows by the throne of God."

Dick Brewer was weeping, his head bowed and his
curly hair resting against Susan's. Alexander McSween
mopped his eyes with a white handkerchief. When the
song ended, the lawyer cleared his throat and announced
that he had a message from Billy Bonney.

The Kid, Isobel recalled, was still in jail. A murmur
of discomfort rippled through the crowd as McSween
began to read. "Though I cannot be present for the burial
of John Henry Tunstall, I want it known that he was as
good a friend as I ever had. When Mr. Tunstall hired
me, he made me a present of a fine horse, a good saddle
and a new gun. He always treated me like a gentleman,
though I was younger than him and not near as educated.
I loved Mr. Tunstall better than any man I ever knew.
Signed, William Bonney."

McSween folded the letter and placed it on the casket.
As the pine box was lowered into the ground, Noah
turned Isobel away from the scene.

"There's a meeting at McSween's house," Dick Brewer
whispered. Noah had left Isobel's side for a moment to

confer with his friend. "Folks are spitting mad that Sheriff Brady won't arrest anyone for John's murder. I think we ought to ask Brady outright what he means by it."

"I'm with you, Dick, but I can't stay for the meeting. I've got to get Isobel out of town. I told her about Snake Jackson murdering her father, and she's hot for blood. The woman's a spitfire, Dick, and—"

"Noah!" Dick grabbed his friend's shoulder. "Over by the tree. It's Snake. He's talking to Isobel."

Noah swung around, fingers sliding over the handle of his six-shooter. "Snake!" he shouted, half-sick with fear. "What do you think you're doing, talking to my wife?"

The heavy-jawed man straightened. "Buchanan, this Mexican ain't your wife."

"She sure is." Noah reached the tree just as Isobel opened her mouth to speak. He grabbed her arm, stopping her words and pressing her toward Dick, who hauled her quickly out of earshot—and pistol range.

"You stay away from my woman, you hear?" Noah growled. "If I see you near her again, I'll bore a hole in you big enough to drive a wagon through."

"Forget it, hombre. The jig's up with your little Mexican *chiquita* now. This morning the stagecoach dropped a pile of fancy trunks at the hotel. The name on 'em was Miss Isobel Matas. Later on, that uppity Mexican so-and-so Juan Patrón came a-wanderin' into the hotel. He took one look at the trunks and then, all sneaky-like, he wrote a new name on 'em. Mrs. Belle Buchanan."

Snake gave Noah a triumphant smirk. "All through this sorry funeral, I been studyin' your so-called wife. She's the *señorita* who was in the woods the day Tunstall got laid out, ain't she? She was wearin' this Mexican veil."

He shook the fragile white mantilla in Noah's face. "And you know what your woman just told me? She thinks I'm the man who done in her Mexican papa a few years back. Well, guess what?"

Noah glanced behind him at Isobel. She was staring, white-faced, her eyes luminous with rage. "What have you got to tell me that I don't already know, Snake?"

"Just this. I'm the man who made her papa a free lunch for the coyotes. And I'm the man who's got what she came to Lincoln lookin' for—her package of fancy papers. And I'm the man who's gonna pull her picket pin the minute your back is turned. So get ready, Buchanan. The next funeral you sing your pretty songs at is gonna be hers."

"Why, you lowdown—"

"Now, just a minute here, gentlemen." The burly Lieutenant Delany stepped between the men. "Haven't the two of you got better things to do this morning? Especially here in the presence of the dearly departed."

Noah glanced at Tunstall's grave. It was nearly filled with dirt now, and the reality of it was a punch in the gut.

"Listen up, Lieutenant," he barked. "This man shot down John Tunstall in cold blood."

"Now, you don't know that, Buchanan," Delany countered. "You weren't even there."

"I was there, all right. And I've got a witness who'll swear the man who pulled the trigger on Tunstall was Jim Jackson."

"Aw, Buchanan, quit your jawin'." Snake laughed. "Tunstall's own men swore out a statement about who was at the killing, and your name weren't on it, nor the name of your witness. If Tunstall's men didn't say neither of you was there, how you gonna convince a judge of it? Huh?"

"Don't sell me short, Jackson," Noah retorted.

"Go on your way, Mr. Buchanan," the lieutenant spoke up. "You, too, Snake. Captain Purington charged me with the protection of life and property around here. Now, get along, the both of you."

Chuckling, Rattlesnake Jackson lumbered across the clearing. He gave Isobel a sideways glance and formed his hand into the shape of a gun. As he walked past her, he aimed at her heart and pulled the imaginary trigger. Tossing his head back in laughter, he sauntered along the side of Tunstall's store toward the Dolan Mercantile.

"If you know something about him, Buchanan," the lieutenant said, "watch your back. He used to run with the Horrells. Now he's in deep with Jesse Evans and the Dolan bunch. Steer clear of him, that's my advice."

"Thanks, Lieutenant." Noah tipped his hat and headed for the Tunstall porch, where Dick stood guarding the women.

As Noah neared, Isobel stepped out from behind Dick and ran to meet him. Noah caught her and pulled her close. "Why'd you tell him, Isobel? Why'd you tell Snake you knew he shot your father?"

"I was so frightened when he came suddenly from behind the tree. He put his hand around my neck!" Tears filled her eyes. "He called me unspeakable names. He told me that a Mexican had murdered his parents in Laredo, and now he would kill every Mexican he could lay his hands on. He said if I tell what I saw in the forest, he will strangle me. Oh, Noah, I was so afraid, and then my fear became anger, and I told him I knew he had murdered my father."

She bent and buried her face in her open hands. Sobbing, she allowed Noah to fold her into his arms. "I have no choice," she choked out. "I must kill that man before he kills me."

"You can't go after Jackson, honey," he murmured. "You're a woman. And a woman's place is somewhere safe and quiet."

"The pair of you better get out of Lincoln fast," Dick said, joining them. "Snake means what he says."

Susan touched Isobel's arm. "*Señor* Patrón told me your trunks came this morning. They're at the hotel."

"My trunks…" She looked at Noah.

"I'll borrow a buckboard from McSween. Dick, will you help me load up?"

"Count on it."

The women started down the covered wooden porch in front of Tunstall's store. Dick set off after Susan, but Noah stood back a moment.

Not far away, men stomped down the mound of soil that covered John Tunstall's grave. Odd, the peace he had felt as he had lifted his voice in song. He could easily imagine the joy he would feel standing with the saints at the river that flows by the throne of God.

But Noah wasn't ready for heaven yet. For the first time in his life he had touched the fringes of serenity. He had found a haven in the sweet kisses and warm embrace of Isobel Matas. He wasn't ready to let that promised land slip away. Not yet.

It took four days to drive the loaded buckboard to John Chisum's South Spring River Ranch. Concerned that Snake might ambush them, they bumped and jolted southeast along the edge of the Rio Bonito before making the slow climb over the foothills that bounded the Rio Ruidoso. They passed the Fritz ranch, and Isobel asked whether they might spend the night there. Noah shook his head.

"Emil Fritz died nearly four years ago, and the wrangle over his estate started the mess in Lincoln," he explained. "The Fritz family hired Alexander McSween to settle the will. Emil had once been Jimmie Dolan's business partner, so Dolan claimed the Fritz money was owed to his store. McSween refused to give up the inheritance. So Dolan accused him of stealing it."

"Everyone has accused everyone else," she said with a sigh. "One man arrests another...and then is arrested in turn. Both claim to be in the right."

"The main thing is that you and I have no part of either side," Noah said. "We'll settle at Chisum's ranch and bide our time until the trouble blows over."

"And what about Rattlesnake Jackson? Am I to let him escape justice?"

"You have no choice, Isobel." Noah set his hand on hers. "If Dolan's bunch wins this feud, Snake will have the law on his side. If McSween's group comes out on top, they'll lock Snake up without needing your testimony. Snake reminded me that the affidavits sworn after Tunstall's murder don't mention us."

Isobel fell silent. She was held hostage by a man who deserved the worst fate she could wish upon him. Ensnared, yes, but a cornered animal—one with spirit to live—didn't lie down and die. It fought. It snarled and clawed and bit. And perhaps...perhaps it won its freedom.

A silver pistol was nestled in the folds of her green silk gown, packed in a trunk on the buckboard. Isobel knew how to use that pistol. She had the skill and the desire. Now all she needed was the opportunity.

Focusing on the large brown hand that covered hers, she noted the fingers hardened with callus. This was a good hand. It held the promise of protection, nurture, passion.

Isobel knew Noah wanted her to be at peace. He hoped to mold her into the sort of woman to whom a simple blue-calico dress and white shawl might belong. He believed he could hide her away and erase the pain in her heart.

As darkness settled over the road, she studied his profile beneath the black felt Stetson. His face was outlined in the last ribbons of golden light. As the days had passed, Noah somehow had shed his common, dusty vaquero image. Isobel had almost forgotten the dark-bearded cowboy who had swept her onto his horse. In his place she saw a human being, a man who held hopes, dreams and desires in the palms of his rough hands.

It frightened her to think how much of herself she had given him, yet how little she knew him. Perhaps Noah was right to insist she step out of the fray and let someone else give Snake the fate he deserved. But this was not the way she had been brought up.

"Noah," she said as they rode on through the darkness. "You told me I have no choice but to abandon the revenge that calls me."

"No choice at all. You just give up the notion, like any woman with a thread of common sense would."

"What do you know about my people? About Catalonia?"

"Not much more than could fit in a thimble. I reckon it's part of Spain. That means everybody speaks Spanish—"

"We speak Catalan." She saw his brow furrow. "The Spanish government forbids us to speak our language, but we speak it anyway. We are fierce, artistic, political people. Catalonia leads the rest of Spain in the production of textiles. Barcelona has grown far beyond its fifteenth-century walls. We dream of autonomy from Spain."

"Autonomy? You folks want civil war—like the one we went through a few years back?"

"Why not? The rest of Spain is poor and ignorant. But we are a high-minded, cultured people. We have the Jocs Florals, our famous poetry contest. We have painting schools and choral societies. We love fraternity and liberty."

"Those sound like revolution words to me," he grumbled.

"In Catalonia, we do not sit and wait for our future. We have a heritage of progress. Change. We will fight for our freedom."

"So, you're one of these high-minded, revolutionary Catalonians. Is that what you're telling me?"

"What I'm telling you is this," she said in a voice so low the rattle of the buckboard wheels almost drowned it. "I am a Catalan. I have a noble spirit and blood of fire. My father has been murdered and our family heritage stolen. These are crimes I cannot allow to go unpunished."

"Now, Isobel—"

"I must prepare myself, Noah. I must find Jim Jackson. And then I must kill him."

Chapter Nine

Noah wasn't much in the mood to chat by the time the buckboard pulled into San Patricio. It was almost midnight according to the moon-silvered hands on his pocket watch. The little town lay in the valley where the Bonito and Ruidoso rivers joined to create the Rio Hondo was shut tight. Noah directed the buckboard into a wooded copse and set the brake.

Isobel sat shivering while he built a fire. They spoke little. She knew Noah regretted yoking himself to a Catalan firebrand. She was pondering the mule-headed vaquero she'd married. By the time they'd eaten the supper of tortillas and roasted meat Beatriz Patrón had packed, both were feeling positively hostile.

"Shall I sleep in the buckboard?" Isobel asked after washing the plates in a chilly stream while Noah banked the fire.

"Unless you'd rather pack a rifle and stand guard over your fancy dresses all night," Noah shot back.

Isobel tossed her head. "Better to appear foolhardy and defend one's possessions than to be so concerned for safety that one loses everything. To run is cowardly."

"Who're you calling a coward, woman?"

"Certainly I'm not the one who chose to flee danger."

"No, you're the one who was so scared she blabbered every secret we were trying to keep under wraps."

Isobel could hardly argue there. She had collapsed in front of Snake Jackson. But with the clarity of reflection, she realized she should have stood her ground with Noah and insisted they remain in Lincoln.

"A brave person may have a moment of weakness," she asserted, "but it is your stubbornness that prevents justice."

Without another word, she climbed onto the buckboard and settled in a pile of blankets in the midst of the trunks.

"Me stubborn?" Noah grumbled as he tended the horses. "She's so ornery she wouldn't move camp in a prairie fire. Spanish hothead."

Isobel pulled a blanket over her head.

"Thinks she's going to kill Jim Jackson," Noah muttered.

But as Isobel drifted to sleep, she heard him singing in a low, almost inaudible voice.

> "On the margin of the river,
> Washing up its silver spray,
> We will walk and worship ever,
> All the happy golden day.
> Yes, we'll gather at the river,
> The beautiful, the beautiful river;
> Gather with the saints at the river
> That flows by the throne of God…."

* * *

The sun was blazing high overhead when Noah drove down the trail to the home of John Simpson Chisum. Isobel descended from the buckboard, her face aglow with pleasure at the sight of the rambling adobe house built around a central patio.

"This is lovely!" she exclaimed.

"And well built." Noah slapped the side of the house with a gloved hand. "Long planks are buried inside the walls so no one can saw through it with a horsehair rope."

"The roof has a *pretil*," Isobel whispered.

"A parapet," Noah corrected. "That wall can protect a lot of armed men from attackers. The place is a fortress. And it's where I aim to keep you safe from Snake Jackson."

Isobel looked at him fully for the first time in many hours. "Is this where you stay, Noah?"

"My house is a few miles north. It's not near as fancy as Chisum's."

"Take me there. I want to see your home."

Noah's brow lifted. "You're not leaving Chisum's for a minute, hear? And while I'm on the subject, I've got a few things to tell you."

"Are these the thoughts that have made you scowl at the world today?"

Noah took off his hat, eyed it a moment, then spoke. "Until John gets out of jail, Isobel, we don't need to pretend we're married. Which is good because I don't want to let things get out of hand."

"You're unhappy because you kissed me?"

"Yes. Well…no." He met her gaze. "It's not good. Kissing. It *is* good, but it's wrong."

"Pardon me?"

He stuffed his hat back on his head. "We made this arrangement, and we plan to end it one day, right?"

"Yes," she answered. But it came into her mind as she spoke the word that she could not imagine the day when Noah Buchanan would ride out of her life as swiftly as he had ridden into it.

"So," he was saying, "I'm going to check on my place while you stay here. You'll be safe. Nobody can get into John Chisum's house."

"Or out?" Anger flared. "You intend to imprison me."

"I intend to protect you. When John comes home, we'll act married again. After he sells me the land and we've found out what's become of Snake Jackson, we'll go our separate ways."

"And you'll be rid of me."

"You'll be rid of me, too, darlin'." He touched her chin with the tip of one finger. But he drew away quickly. "I'll take your trunks inside and then head upriver."

From the nearby corral, three men wandered over to the buckboard, and Noah greeted them by name. Isobel stood aside as Noah directed the removal of her trunks. Noah carried himself with a quiet authority that Isobel had never noticed. In his long coat, black hat and leather boots, he resembled a military officer. Tall and powerfully built, he stood well above the other men. But it was the confident air with which he gave orders that revealed his true position among them.

Isobel watched, trying to memorize him, yet trying to accept the truth that their marriage was a sham. The moments of tenderness meant nothing to Noah, and she must not forget that.

She walked toward the house, past the rosebushes, willows and cottonwoods. As she stepped into the front room, a voice called out.

"Mrs. Buchanan?" A small, plump woman extended a hand. "I'm Mrs. Frances Towry, Mr. Chisum's house-keeper. My husband and I moved here from Paris, Texas, a while back. He runs the harness and saddle shop. Our son works on the range. He's a good friend of your husband. 'Course, I don't know a soul who ain't fond of Noah. You got yourself a mighty fine man, Mrs. Buchanan."

"Thank you," Isobel said, mustering a smile.

"Welcome to South Spring River Ranch. And this here's our cook." She gestured to a chocolate-skinned man. "Pete, say howdy to Mrs. Buchanan."

As they greeted one another, Isobel began to see that John Chisum enjoyed the same lifestyle in which she had been reared. The house was large, cool and well-appointed with furniture and plush carpets. Mrs. Towry prattled on as she led Isobel to a fine bedroom.

"I'm gonna put you and your husband right here in Mr. Chisum's room. Now, don't look so shocked. See this beautiful bed?" A mattress, feather tick and bolster rested on an elaborately carved bedstead. "He won't touch this. Every night, he sets up his camp bed."

"But why?"

Mrs. Towry smoothed a hand over the embroidered shams. "Says it's too much trouble to fold up the bed-ding." A twinkle lit her gray eyes as she glanced at Isobel. "Mr. Chisum is known for pulling jokes. So... if he don't like his own bed, I'll settle you and your husband into it. See how that suits him."

Isobel didn't see how such a joke would endear her

to John Chisum. Before she could protest, Noah entered the room, and Mrs. Towry scuttled out.

"Everything okay?" he asked, jamming his hands into the pockets of his denims, as though fearful he might touch her.

"It's good," she said, trying to smile.

"I'll be back in a couple of days. Don't go anywhere."

"Where would I go?"

"You've threatened to chase down Snake Jackson."

"If I leave, everyone will know I'm not Belle Buchanan. That would ruin your plan to buy land from Mr. Chisum."

"Isobel." He stepped closer. "I'll get my land one way or another. That's not why I want you to stay away from Lincoln. Snake will kill you."

She shrugged. "If I'm dead, you won't have to bother with me."

"Listen, woman." He clamped her shoulders in his hands. "I swore to protect you, and I'm not backing down on that."

"You also swore to be my husband."

"I'm not your husband. Don't tempt me, Isobel."

"How do I tempt you? Tell me."

"Your eyes…your hair…your lips." He drew her against him.

"Noah," she murmured. "I, too, decided some days ago that I must look to my own future."

"That's right." His blue eyes searched her face.

"We are very different. And we want such different things from life."

"Isobel…"

"Kiss me once, Noah. Before you go."

"Isobel…" But his lips pressed hers in a kiss that broke the flimsy barriers of restraint. She slipped her arms around him as she had dreamed of doing. But in a moment, he broke away.

"I can't do this," he said, his voice strained. "No. It's not right."

"Then go, Noah Buchanan. Go to your safe little house. Run away from me. Run from every danger in your life."

"I'm no coward, girl. But steering clear of calamity is how I keep myself alive long enough for my dreams to come true."

"And going *mano a mano*—hand to hand—with calamity is how I make dreams come true."

He shook his head. "Isobel…Isobel."

"Goodbye, Noah." She turned away lest he see the tears brimming in her eyes. This was the last time he would ever hold her, the last time their lips would touch. Their destinies called them in opposite directions, and each had to obey the beckoning whisper.

By the time the moon rose Noah had settled into the four-room adobe *jacal* he had built at the edge of the Pecos River. He checked on the old milk cow and dozen hens he kept penned in a roughshod barn. His neighbor downriver, Eugenio Baca, looked after the stock when he was gone.

By lantern light Noah meandered down to an old cottonwood tree and dug up his pail of money. It was all there—ten years' worth of scrimping and saving. More than enough to buy the acreage adjoining his home. As he reburied the pail and shifted the heavy slab of limestone back into place, he couldn't help but smile. He had the money. He had the wife. And pretty soon he'd have the land.

He slept well. The following morning, he swept and mopped, gathered eggs, milked his cow. Woman's work, but he was used to it. He couldn't imagine Isobel doing the common chores that made a house a home. She would expect servants to obey her every command. Good thing she was settled at Chisum's place.

The next day, Noah unpacked his pens and ink and started writing a story that had been tickling his thoughts ever since Tucson. Working hard, he stayed up half the night, his thoughts racing and the precious oil in his lamp burning. He could hear the men talking inside his head. He could smell the acrid tang of gunpowder and taste the dry dust in his mouth with each new sentence, each paragraph, each page.

He wrote all day Thursday. Almost forgot to milk the cow. Forgot to chop wood. Snow began to fall outside his window, but Noah didn't see it. He was out on the prairie, sun beating down on his shoulders, sweat trickling from his brow. He was shooting wild turkeys and riding a fiery black stallion and bunking down at night with an Indian blanket twixt him and the ground. Stars by the million twinkled overhead. The smell of blooming cactus filled his nostrils by day. The low of the cattle made music in his ears. Amazing how writing could transport you to another time and place.

Around three o'clock in the morning, Noah fell asleep at the kitchen table. His lamp flickered out. Snowflakes slipped in under the front door. Frost crept up the new glass windowpanes.

"Noah? Are you in there?"

He lifted his head. Running a hand across his chin, knocking ice crystals from his beard, he scowled at the shuddering door.

"Noah Buchanan! Open this door at once!"

No mistaking that voice. "Isobel," he croaked. "What in tarnation are you doing here?"

"I've come with my furniture, Noah."

What was that supposed to mean? he wondered as he tried to stand. Oh, no, must have forgotten to light a fire. He stepped to the door, suddenly aware he felt hungry enough to eat a saddle blanket.

"Isobel, what do you…" He was growling as he dragged the door open, but the sight of her stopped his words.

Oh, the woman was a beauty. Dressed in a royal-blue wool cloak with the hood pulled up, she stood like a queen on his porch. Her red gloves and red boots were the only spots of contrasting color, save her bright pink cheeks and lips. Her hazel eyes flashed as one eyebrow lifted.

"You have been drinking, Noah Buchanan," she announced.

Pushing past him with a sweep of her hand, she stepped into the icy room. At the sight of rumpled blankets, dirty dishes and the table piled with papers, she gave a cry.

"Shame, Noah!" She stripped off her gloves and headed for the woodstove. "I let you out of my sight and you become a *borrachón*. What have you been drinking? Whisky? Rum?"

Noah watched dumbfounded as she clanked open his stove door and began to build a fire. A lopsided effort that would smoke up the house before it caught flame.

"I had hoped we might never see each other again," she was saying. "I knew you planned to keep me from my appointed task."

"Killing Snake Jackson is not your appointed—"

"Unfortunately, my furniture arrived."

A prickly feeling wandering up his back, Noah looked out the front window. Two oxcarts loaded with crates waited by the porch.

"You brought the furniture here?"

"Storing it for me is the least you can do, Noah, since you have refused to help me go after Snake Jackson."

They stared at each other.

"Well, you look good anyhow, Isobel," Noah told her.

"You look terrible." Her glance fell on the table littered with reams of paper and inkwells. "You have been writing!"

"Finished my first story last night." Suddenly enthusiastic, he grabbed the sheaf of paper from the table. "'Sunset at Coyote Canyon.' That's the title. You wouldn't believe the ending. There's a no-good skunk of a fellow who sneaks up, and then…well…"

"And what happens?" Isobel settled on a chair, water from her cloak puddling around her feet as the room warmed.

"Well…" Noah fumbled. "Aw, never mind…"

"Is it ready to mail to New York? I'll take it to the post office when I return to Lincoln."

He studied the pages—scrawled handwriting, blotches of ink, scribbles where he'd added ideas that had come to him. "No, it's not near ready."

"I shall cook breakfast," Isobel announced. "You will read the story to me."

Without giving him opportunity to protest, she shed her cloak, rolled up her sleeves and set to work. "Read, Noah!" she commanded.

He cleared his throat, settled into a chair and began to speak aloud words that once had been only in his mind.

Isobel smiled as she tapped a spoonful of grease into the black iron frying pan.

"Up on the ridge a coyote began to howl," Noah read, "a sound that blended with the whine of the wind and the owls' soft hoot."

Isobel cracked six eggs, one by one, into the sizzling grease.

Chapter Ten

"Opal stood between Travis and Buck. In her arms she carried the newborn babe." Noah's voice lowered as he read the words. "She looked into the eyes of the stranger who had come to kill her husband. 'You'll have to shoot me first, Buck Shafer,' she said. 'I won't be parted from the man I love.'"

Isobel was absently stirring the third batch of scrambled eggs she had made that day. Eyes closed, she listened to the final pages of Noah's story.

They had eaten eggs for breakfast, lunch and now supper, and she had burned them the first two times. But she could do nothing but listen as his words transported her into the tale.

"Travis gazed into the face of his wife," Noah continued, "and at the sweet expression of his newborn son in her arms. 'We're all right,' Opal whispered as they stared at the man who lay dead on the floor. Then Travis and his family stepped outside into the flaming orange sunset of Coyote Canyon.'"

Noah placed the last page upside down on the rest of his manuscript. "In my mind, it came out better. The story flowed like water down a ravine. On paper it got jumpy."

His words drifted off, and he sat staring at the table as though he felt sick. "Just a bunch of scrambled words," he muttered, "like those eggs you're cooking."

From behind, Isobel slipped her arms around his neck. She pressed her damp cheek against his. "It is a good story, Noah."

"You're crying?" he whispered.

"If I read this story in Catalonia, I would know that canyon. I would see those people."

"What about Opal? You probably think I should have let her blast Buck Shafer to kingdom come, like you would have done."

Isobel came around Noah and knelt beside his chair. "Opal did what was right. She protected the baby."

"Isobel, why did you come here?"

"My...my furniture, of course."

He shook his head. "You're in quite a tangle. You want to be bold, shoot-'em-up Isobel Matas. But somewhere inside there's a Belle Buchanan who likes fixing up a house and cooking for her man. There's a woman who cries when a story comes out right. And there's a woman who can't stay away from the man she loves. The man she needs."

"You flatter yourself. I don't need anyone."

"You need me." He touched her cheek with a finger when she started to shake her head. "Yes, you do."

"No," she said, but her eyes again filled with tears. "Oh, Noah."

"There'll be other men for you, Isobel. Men who'll fit into your schemes better than I do."

She knew he was wrong. Not only was she a spinster,

but in the days apart from him she had realized she wanted no one else.

"Isobel, you have to go back to Chisum's," he was saying. "I've got chores. And the cow—"

"The cow, the chores!" She pushed away from him and stepped to the stove. "Excuses. The truth for you is the same as for me. You love me."

"But I never let my heart take control. If I'm angry, I give myself time to cool down. If I care for a woman who's no good for me, I back away."

"I'm no good for you?"

"You're so good I can't stand to be this close and not touch. But, Isobel, what could come of it?"

"Then we shall bring in my furniture," she replied, striding to the door. "Stop gawking like a schoolboy and come along."

As Noah dragged the last velvet-upholstered chair across the dirt floor of his house. He had never seen so much furniture in his life. A huge wooden bed sat in pieces to reassemble. A settee and three chairs were lined up by the fireplace. Rolled carpets lay stacked in the bedroom. Dishes and fine linens cluttered the floor. An enormous, gold-framed mirror almost filled one wall.

Heading out the door to check on his cow just before midnight, Noah could hear Isobel singing Spanish ditties as she filled cupboards with her brightly painted plates and cups. How had he gotten into such a mess? A hot-blooded *señorita* determined to gun down Snake Jackson. A head full of stories that wouldn't hush until he wrote them down. A boss in jail, and a best friend sitting on a keg of dynamite in Lincoln. And now a house full of frilly velvet furniture.

As he returned to the house he heard a strange sound—*clickety-click-click, clickety-click, ding, clickety-click.*

What now? He shouldered into the front room. Isobel was bent over a small machine on his pine table. Her fingers darted around *clickety-clacking* on the machine as her eyes scanned his manuscript.

"What are you doing?" he asked.

"It's my Remington!" She swung around and laughed aloud. "It makes letters—like a printing press. I used my typewriter to keep records for our hacienda, but it came from America. See? E. Remington and Sons of Ilion, New York."

Frowning at the contraption, Noah studied the springs, ratchets and levers jumbled among a pair of spools and an inked ribbon. "What do you aim to do with it?"

"I aim to put your story into type before we post it to New York. Look, the first page is finished."

She held up a sheet of white paper with capital letters marching in a straight line across the top. SUNSET AT COYOTE CANYON BY NOAH BUCHANAN.

He whistled softly and sat down beside her as she began to touch the keys again. "Reads pretty good," he murmured as his story began to appear at the top of the unrolling paper. "Well, how do you like that."

"I like it," she said. Her slender wrists moved back and forth in a graceful dance. "When we send it to New York, they'll like it, too."

A smile playing at her lips, she *clickety-clacked* until a second page rolled out of the Remington. Noah leaned one elbow on the table and watched. He felt off balance.

Hadn't he planned to stow Isobel safely at Chisum's house? Hadn't he decided there was no future in wooing her? She didn't want to be hooked up with a dusty cowboy for the rest of her life. He had never planned on a wife and family.

So why did her fancy Spanish furniture somehow feel just right in his adobe house? Why had it warmed his heart to walk in the front door and find her seated at his table?

He studied the gold ringlets that fell from the bun at the back of Isobel's head. She was wearing the blue dress again. The one she and Susan Gates had made. Little ruffles clustered around her neck. Little cuffs clasped her slender wrists.

"This part about the coyote I like very much," she said softly. "It makes me shiver."

The scent of her skin drifted over Noah while she spoke. Unable to resist, he trailed kisses up her neck. The *clickety-click* faltered. When his lips met her ear, the typing stopped altogether.

She faced him, her face a mix of tenderness and frustration. "Noah, you said you didn't…"

"But…I do."

"I'll type your story tonight and leave for Chisum's in the morning. You're tired. Go to bed."

He took her shoulders and turned her toward him. "I know what we said about the marriage, Isobel. And I know we meant every word. But there's no way I can be near you and not start thinking about what it's like to kiss you. You feel it, too, Isobel. I know you do."

"When you left, I sat alone in the big house of John Chisum and thought about my life, my future." She lifted her head and met his eyes. "Death runs close behind me. I feel its breath on my skin."

"Isobel, I'm going to take care of you."

"Listen to me, Noah. I have nothing to claim as my own. Nothing. My own death or the killing of a man—perhaps both—these are my only paths. My heart is desperate."

"You're making this worse than it is. Don't you know God has a good plan for you?"

"God? The God who permitted my father's murder? You put your faith in a tale no more true than this one." She pointed to his manuscript. "My future is in no one's hands but my own. Put yourself in my place, Noah. What would you do?"

He let out a breath. "I'd go after the man who stole my land. I'd track down Snake Jackson. But you don't have to do that. You can go back to Spain."

"Once I was a noblewoman. Betrothed to a don, I was a lady of high breeding and exquisite taste. Now, my heart has been turned upside down. I care nothing for that life."

"It's this land—New Mexico. The mountains and streams."

"It's you, Noah." Before she could think clearly, she slipped her arms around him and kissed his lips.

"Mercy, Isobel," he murmured. Taking her in his arms, he held her close. "Isobel, no matter what we said, I'm not ever going to let you go. I hope you know that."

She shut her eyes and nestled against his shoulder. "Perhaps, Noah. Perhaps."

They set up the new bed in the front room. Isobel slept alone, her dreams tangled and frightening. Noah kept mostly to his room when he was in the house. For three days, no word of past or future was spoken between them. A gale of wind ushered in the first days of March. Snow quickly melted, dry leaves whisked away, shoots of green grass along the Pecos River pushed upward.

While Isobel continued unpacking and arranging her things, Noah went hunting. There was no scarcity of wild game along the river, and in no time flat he had bagged a brace of rabbits.

"Oh, Noah," she cried, her eyes bright with unshed tears as he laid them out. "They're bunnies!"

"They're food, darlin'."

He handed her a knife and taught her how to skin and dress the rabbits. With a kettle of simmering water, a handful of turnips and carrots from the root cellar and a dash of salt, he taught her to make stew.

As the aroma drifted through the *jacal,* Isobel lined the edges of Noah's cabinets with ribbons of white lace she had brought from Spain to wear in her hair.

"Curtains," she said aloud, musing on the glass windowpanes. "We must have curtains."

Noah straightened from the bowl of cornbread batter he was stirring. "What for? Nobody's around to look in."

"A home must have curtains. They let in the light just so…."

Noah rubbed his chin where he'd shaved that morning. "You know, when Mrs. Allison passed away a few years ago—"

"She's dead? Your Mrs. Allison?"

He nodded. "Some kind of a fever got her. Just like the one that got my mother." He fell silent for a moment. "Mr. Allison sent me a trunk from Texas. Things Mrs.

Allison wanted me to have. I took one look inside and shut it quick."

"But why?"

"Aw, it was just the kind of stuff Mrs. Allison loved. I think I saw some fancy curtains in there, pictures of pink roses, silver spoons. It made me sad to look at them, being as they were Mrs. Allison's prized possessions."

Isobel watched the flicker of pain that crossed his face and realized the childless Englishwoman had been the only mother Noah had known. "Please show me the trunk, Noah."

Leaving the cornbread, he led her into a back room where he kept his stores. He raised the trunk's domed lid, and Isobel caught her breath.

"Lace curtains from Nottingham in England." She lifted the soft fabric and hugged it close. "Oh, they're exquisite."

A small grin tugged at Noah's mouth. "Exquisite, huh?"

The trunk was filled with treasures—a silver tea set, porcelain cups and saucers, bone china candlesticks. The heavy linen napkins and tablecloths were evidence of the woman's wealth, and her love for Noah.

Isobel lifted a heart-shaped pewter box and peeked inside. "Here's a letter. It's for you, Noah."

"Me?" He took the envelope on which his name had been written in a fine hand.

"Dear little boy," he read aloud. He cleared his throat as he glanced at Isobel. "Mrs. Allison always used to call me that—*dear little boy*."

For a moment he couldn't read. When he began again, his voice was low. "I pray for you each day as you ride the cattle trails for Mr. John Simpson Chisum. Do be careful. These things I am sending will not fit well with your trail life, but they are all I have. Dear little boy, please remember our sunny afternoons reading books in the library. I have saved every letter you wrote me, one every…every week you have been gone. Dear little…"

Noah swallowed. He gazed at the letter, the muscles in his jaw working as he fought for control. "Dear little boy," he whispered, "I love you so much. Mrs. Allison. Jane."

He folded the letter and slipped it into his shirt pocket. Clearing his throat, he looked at Isobel. "I'd be pleased to hang those curtains for you now," he said.

Sunday morning as Noah sat reading his Bible at the pine table, he couldn't remember a time he'd felt so downright happy.

Not to say that Isobel wasn't more than a mite stubborn and sassy. But he didn't care a lick. In fact, he liked the way she took charge of the house. She unearthed the copy of *Beeton's Book of Household Management* that Mrs. Allison had given him the day he set out for New Mexico. Before he knew it, the young *marquesa* was elbow deep in cleaning and cooking.

Studying the array of bottles and jars she had turned upside down to dry on the fence posts, Noah smiled. As she finished the dishes, she mentioned how nice it would be if he would plow a patch of ground outside the kitchen.

Did the highfalutin *señorita* really mean to plant a garden? The idea of her staying on at his place sat well with Noah. Especially if she could forget about the things that had driven her to New Mexico.

They had spent only three days together, but the words

that ran ragtag around inside his head were sounding better all the time. Mr. and Mrs. Buchanan. The Buchanan family. Well, well. Could you beat that?

Monday morning shaped up to be the prettiest day of the year thus far. The sun appeared over the hills, the wind died, buds began to unfold. Isobel had finished typing Noah's manuscript, bound it in cloth and sewed the packet shut for mailing. She was laundering their clothes on the ribbed washboard and tub on Noah's front porch. He had saddled the horses in preparation for a ride out on the range to show Isobel the land he intended to buy.

Her hair slicked back in a tight bun, Isobel had just bent over the washtub when a raucous holler rippled down the river valley. Chilled, she straightened. Noah came charging out of the barn, his six-shooter drawn.

"Isobel, get inside the house!" he shouted.

"I'll bring the rifle!" But she halted as Billy the Kid's horse thundered up the bank, followed by those of Dick Brewer and a slew of other McSween men.

"Hey, Buchanan!" Billy reined in his horse and swung down. "Looks like you and the *señorita* are gettin' mighty homey round here!"

He let out a hoot as the rest of the men joined him on the porch. Noah had holstered his gun, but Isobel felt a sense of growing dread. She should fetch the rifle by the door.

"Last I heard, you were in lockup, Kid," Noah said.

"Aw, they didn't have nothin' to hold me on. Got out the day after Tunstall's funeral."

"Things are bad, Noah," Dick spoke up. "McSween wrote his will and made Chisum executor without bond."

At this, Isobel realized that, even though Noah's boss was still in jail, McSween's action deeply involved him. No doubt whose side Chisum and Noah would take.

"McSween went into hiding on Tuesday," Dick continued. "We thought he might hunker down at Chisum's, but we went by this morning, and he's not there. Mrs. McSween left for Kansas."

"What about Dolan?"

"No one has arrested any of Tunstall's murderers. Snake Jackson and some other fellows are at Dolan's cow camp down the Pecos. We aim to round 'em up and see they get what's coming to 'em."

"You've formed a gang, Dick?"

"That's right. I'm the leader of the Regulators. Each man took an oath to stick together no matter what. We'll make arrests but we won't shoot on sight. Once we take Snake, Evans and the others into custody, they'll be tried when court sits in April."

"Squire Wilson made Dick a constable and the rest of us deputies!" Billy hooted.

"We want you to join us, Noah," Dick said. "We need you on our side."

Isobel's dreams—lace-curtained windows, a packet of pages bound for New York, a spring garden—began to fade. Noah kicked a heel against the edge of the step.

"I made Isobel a promise, Dick," he said finally. "I've got to stay here and protect her like I swore I would. If Snake gets his hands on her—"

"We'll both go with them, Noah," Isobel cut in, slinging his rifle over one shoulder.

"Isobel, what in thunder do you think you're doing?"

"Five years ago, Snake Jackson rode with the Horrell Gang," she told the men. "Five years ago, he killed my father and stole my land-grant titles. My desire to bring him to justice is as great as yours. I shall ride with you."

"Hold on now, Isobel," Noah began.

"We can't have a woman in the Regulators," Billy protested.

Isobel stepped to the edge of the porch. Inside her heart, she battled the urge to run to Noah's arms and release the past that haunted her. But she smothered the impulse. The last few days had been only a wonderful holiday from reality. With the arrival of the Regulators she understood at last that she would never be free…not until she freed herself.

Shouldering the rifle, she took aim at a bottle drying on a fence post. It exploded in a spray of glass.

She held out her hand. There was only a moment's hesitation before Billy the Kid set his own six-shooter in her palm.

"One, two, three," she counted as she calmly blasted more bottles.

No one moved. A faint breeze lifted white smoke from the end of the revolver. Billy let out a low whistle.

"The *señorita* can ride at my side any day," he said.

Noah was glaring at her. "Why?" he asked. "Why, Isobel?"

"How can I have a future when my past haunts me? I must go with them, Noah. I have no choice."

He shook his head and settled his hat lower on his

brow. "Looks like you've got yourselves a couple more Regulators," he said, his voice resigned. "Now, Dick, if you'll excuse me for a minute, I reckon I'd better go take the cornbread out of the oven."

Chapter Eleven

The Lincoln County Regulators—eleven men and one woman strong—set out from Noah Buchanan's house on Monday, the fourth day of March, 1878. Each horse packed a heavy supply of arms and ammunition. Food was plentiful along the Pecos River, and spring was creeping across the New Mexico Territory. The Regulators planned to make camp each night in the hills, where they would be well hidden.

Two days passed without incident. That night, they camped a few miles up from the Rio Peñasco crossing.

"Noah," Isobel whispered from the folds of her blanket.

He lifted his head. "What is it? You hear something?"

"No." She touched his arm. "Noah, I'm…I'm thinking of dying."

"Dying?" He frowned. "What in thunder are you thinking about that for?"

"If I'm killed, and if my lands are ever recovered from Snake Jackson, I want you to have them."

"Great ghosts, Isobel, you're not going to die. I promise you that."

Ignoring his avowal, she propped herself on one elbow and gazed into the intense blue eyes. He looked haggard, his hair mussed from the day under a hat and lines deeply etched in his face.

"Noah," she whispered again. "You are a good man."

He reached out and stroked her hair with the tips of his fingers. "It'll be all right, Isobel. Go to sleep. I'm watching over you."

The next morning's travel was uneventful. But at midafternoon, the Regulators had just crossed the Peñasco when they rounded a hill and came upon five of Dolan's men.

"It's them!" Billy the Kid shouted.

Hearing the familiar voice, the Dolan five wheeled their horses, broke into two groups and took off overland at a gallop.

"After 'em, men!" Dick hollered. "They're Tunstall's killers."

Weapons drawn, the Regulators gave chase. Isobel caught no sign of Snake in the group, so she spurred her horse after the others. Noah's horse matched hers neck and neck. They rode over a ridge, skirted a patch of yuccas and thundered toward the river. Mud flying from their hooves, the horses pounded along the soft bank.

They'd ridden about five miles when one of the Dolan group's horses stumbled and fell in a tangle of thrashing legs. The rider cried out for help, but his two companions rode on.

"Leave him!" Dick shouted. "He wasn't in the posse that shot Tunstall. Stick with the others, men!"

Oddly pleased at being referred to as one of the men, Isobel lowered her head and guided her horse in a leap over the prone figure who had fallen. Grinning, she turned to Noah.

"Yeah, just watch where you're going, hothead!" he called, giving her a wink.

Soon their horses, too, began to flag from the long chase. As they ascended the brow of a low hill, they realized the other men were no longer in view.

"They've given out!" the Kid crowed. "I bet they're hiding in that patch of tule. Who's going in with me?"

Dick's riders followed Billy down a gully toward a large clump of thick-stemmed grass. As the Regulators closed in, an arm waving a dirty white handkerchief rose out of the tule.

"Hold your fire, men!" Dick shouted.

"Brewer, we give up! Don't shoot!"

"Come on out. We won't shoot. You're going back to Lincoln to stand trial."

As the pale faces of the three men appeared, Billy released the safety on his rifle. In the gully, the click sounded as loud as a gunshot.

"Put it down, Kid!" Noah grabbed the barrel.

"C'mon, fellers, we've got three of Tunstall's murderers," Billy argued. "Let's plug 'em and be done with 'em."

Dick assessed the skinny, bucktoothed boy. "To tell the truth, I'm sorry they gave up, too. If we'd shot it out, we could have finished 'em. But we took an oath, Kid. I promised to transport any prisoners I captured to Lincoln. Alive."

Billy spat. "I say shoot 'em between the eyes and save the court's time."

"No, Kid. I'm not gonna let you do it." Dick nodded to Noah and the others. "Take their weapons, men. Let's ride for Lincoln."

The party spent the night at Chisum's cow camp near the Pecos River. It bothered Noah that they had failed to capture two of the men. The Regulators' position was tenuous. A word from any of those two, and Dolan's men would ride after them.

As he watched Isobel sleeping, Noah wondered how he had made such a big mistake. If Dolan's bunch came to rescue their men, he honestly didn't know how he would fare at protecting his own hide, let alone Isobel's. She was good with a gun, but being hunted by heartless desperados was a lot different from shooting glass bottle targets.

The only thing he could think to do was pray. At Mrs. Allison's feet, Noah had formed a deep faith in God. He was far from perfect, but he tried to follow the Bible's principles. Isobel had no such regard for her Creator. In her quest to avenge her father's death, she was oblivious to the scripture Mrs. Allison had made him memorize: "Vengeance is mine, sayeth the Lord." Maybe Isobel had never heard it.

Was she a Christian? He studied the beautiful woman who had stolen his heart. The idea that a Dolan man might kill her sent a chill through Noah. Losing her would be torment. But then a lifetime wondering if her faith had been enough to see her into heaven? That would drive him loco.

He was still awake when the sun slid over the Pecos

and roused the others. With their prisoners riding near the front of the line, the Regulators wound their way back up the Pecos toward South Spring River Ranch. At Chisum's place they learned that Dolan had organized a band of twenty men—and the posse's sole aim was to hunt down the Regulators.

"You think Dolan's posse might be planning to ambush us and rescue their men?" Dick asked as they rode toward Lincoln the following day.

"If we take the main road into Lincoln," Noah said, "we'll play right into their hands. I say we follow the trail through Blackwater Canyon."

"Good idea." After clapping his friend on the shoulder, Dick rode ahead to inform the others.

As the riders left the road, Isobel sensed a strange certainty that she had come home. The New Mexico Territory was not her beloved Catalonia, but here the sky was large and blue, the trees grew tall, rivers rushed through gorges, deer and jackrabbits nibbled grass damp with morning dew. Here rattlesnakes sunned on gray limestone slabs, and coyotes cried out to the moon.

Oh, she enjoyed her fine furnishings and silk gowns, but they could hardly compare to a land as raw and untamed as the spirit that flamed in her heart. With her hair braided and tucked under one of Noah's black Stetsons, her riding boots hooked in the stirrups and Noah's leather belt and holster at her waist, she felt she had found herself.

"I never got to thank you for typing my story," Noah said, leaning toward her. "I put it in my saddlebag so I can mail it when we reach Lincoln."

Isobel gazed into his warm blue eyes. "I enjoyed the typing. I liked your home very much, Noah."

He smiled. "We had a good time there."

As he reached to take her hand, gunshots rang through the canyon. Noah whipped his six-shooter from its holster. His left hand reached to shelter Isobel as he spurred his horse ahead of hers.

"Kid!" Dick shouted toward the front line. "Who fired?"

Noah and Isobel rounded a bend in the trail moments after Dick. On the ground lay three men spattered with blood.

"Who did this?" Dick barked. "Billy, you responsible here?"

The Kid shrugged and glanced at the other men riding with him in the front flanks.

"Speak up, Billy," Dick demanded. "We promised to bring back prisoners—and now we got three dead bodies."

Isobel slid from her horse. Once again, death. Barely breathing, she walked among the horses toward the corpses. As she took off her hat, her golden braid tumbled down her back.

"Isobel..." Noah took her arm, but she pulled free and knelt beside the latest victims of Lincoln County's violence.

"Here's what happened," Billy was explaining. "I reckon they was arguin'. One of 'em shot this feller, and then him and the other one took off. That's what happened, ain't it, boys?"

"Yeah," the others mumbled in assent.

Isobel stood and rubbed her bloodstained fingers together. "This man was shot in the back nine times."

"Like I said," Billy went on, "he was tryin' to git away. 'Course we shot him in the back."

No one spoke as they stared at the three dead men. Isobel felt sick inside. At least two of them had helped kill John Tunstall, but she didn't feel the expected sense of triumph at seeing his murderers slain.

"Fine way to regulate the law in Lincoln County," Noah spoke up, his voice tight. "Makes a fellow proud to be called a Regulator."

"What's the matter, Buchanan? You been lookin' at the world through lace curtains too long?" Billy jeered.

Noah stared at him a moment before turning away. "C'mon, boys, let's get these men buried."

The three Dolan men had been shot in Blackwater Canyon. Dick Brewer paid a group of Mexicans at a nearby cow camp to bury the bodies. His mood dark, the Regulators' leader said nothing as his posse traversed the canyon trail.

As night fell, Billy Bonney announced that he and the other men responsible for the three deaths would ride to San Patricio and hide in the hills until Dick had conferred with the law in Lincoln. When all was clear, the Regulators could regroup and make new plans.

Noah and Isobel elected to remain with the original party. He had no intention of leaving Dick to face a possible Dolan ambush. The winding canyon trail took another full day to navigate. As the three tied their horses to a post outside Alexander McSween's house, Isobel mentioned that exactly one week had passed since the Sunday Noah had read his Bible at the pine table in his home.

"So much has happened since that peaceful morning,"

she murmured. With a sigh, she stepped onto McSween's porch.

"Isobel!" Susan Gates flew through the door and embraced her friend. "Is it really you? Why, I took you for a man in that getup. Oh, Isobel, I thought I'd never see you again! And what has become of…of…" She scanned the faces. "Oh, Mr. Brewer… How nice to see you."

Susan clearly struggled to contain her joy at finding Dick alive and well. The handsome cattleman made no such pretense. He took two strides toward the woman, took her in his arms and kissed her full on the lips.

"Miss Gates, I'm back," he announced. "I'm here to say in front of all this company that I love you, and if you'll have me, I aim to marry you."

"Mercy!" Susan's eyes lit up as she clasped her hands at her breast. "Why, yes, Mr. Brewer. I'll have you. Indeed, I will."

"Thank you kindly, ma'am. And if you'll excuse me, I need to talk to a good lawyer."

"Reckon I'll do?" A tall man stepped from the shadows of the doorway.

"McSween?" Noah queried. "I didn't expect to find you here."

"Figured no one would shoot me in the back with Governor Axtell in town. Come on inside, Dick." He set a hand on the young man's shoulder and led him into the house.

"Felicitaciones," Isobel said to her friend.

"You couldn't have a finer husband, Miss Gates," Noah added as he brushed past her to follow the other men.

"My stars, what a shock!" Susan giggled as she

gestured toward two wicker chairs on the porch. "Come sit down, Isobel, and tell me what brought that on. I've never seen Dick so bold."

"Dick Brewer is a brave man, Susan." Isobel settled on a weathered cushion. She summarized the events of the past days as Susan listened, the smile on her face fading as Isobel recounted what had befallen the Regulators.

"So what did happen to the three Dolan men out there in Blackwater Canyon?" Susan asked at the end of the tale. "Were they really trying to escape? Or did Billy just up and shoot them?"

"I don't know," Isobel acknowledged. "I think we may never have the full truth."

"You need to know what's happened here in Lincoln while you've been away," Susan said softly. "Governor Axtell came down from Santa Fe to investigate the troubles. He's Jimmie Dolan's good friend, so you can imagine how it all came out. Axtell refused to interview anybody on our side. Mr. McSween even risked his life to come back to town, but the governor wouldn't see him."

"Has Axtell done anything about the situation?"

"I'm afraid so. He voided Squire Wilson's appointment as justice of the peace."

Isobel reflected on the man whose careful record-keeping had helped her trace the events of her father's murder. "That's a great loss to the town," she said.

"The governor also declared that no one can enforce any legal process except Sheriff Brady and his deputies."

Isobel stood as Noah stepped onto the porch. Leaning one muscled shoulder against the doorjamb, he spoke. "Governor Axtell has outlawed the Regulators."

She gasped. "Then Dick had no authority to round up those men?"

"Not as of March eighth, the day they were shot in Blackwater Canyon. We're outlaws," he said. "Every last one of us."

"Oh, Isobel!" Susan cried out.

Noah took a step closer. "Isobel, you need to decide what you want to do. You can ride for Santa Fe tonight, or you can stay here under Alexander McSween's protection."

"And you?"

"Dick and I are heading for his farm on the Ruidoso River. We'll stay until court convenes April eighth."

"But that's three weeks away. I'll go with you."

"No, you won't, Isobel." His words left no room to protest. "I can't protect you there. Stay here or ride to Santa Fe. Your choice."

Isobel gazed into his blue eyes and knew she was not ready to leave them. Not yet.

"I'll stay in Lincoln," she told him. "I'll wait for you."

Isobel settled at Alexander McSween's house along with the Ealy family and Susan Gates. They had been her companions on the trail to Lincoln, and she was glad to rejoin them. But she knew the arrangement set them all squarely in the Tunstall-McSween camp.

Susan and Dick had spent not five minutes alone together before he and Noah set off. But that was enough to convince Susan that he wanted her for his wife—and the sooner the better.

Isobel tried to be interested in planning her friend's wedding. The two women studied the array of fabrics inside the closed Tunstall store. "The green, do you think?" Susan would ask. "Or would pink make a better wedding gown?"

But Isobel's thoughts were on a man whose face was imprinted on her soul. Dressing each morning, she recalled his admiration of her blue gown. Brushing her hair, she remembered him lifting a tress from her shoulder, turning it this way and that. Helping Mary Ealy prepare breakfast, she heard the clatter Noah had made as he'd searched for bowls, a frying pan, spoons.

Isobel had only to gaze out the window, and the scene brought Noah to her mind. Riding into town that first evening and sliding from her horse into his arms. Crossing frozen streets on the way to Juan Patrón's house. Lincoln had become a part of her life. Her life and Noah's, together.

"You love Mr. Buchanan," Susan declared almost a week after the men had ridden away. "Don't you, Isobel?"

She gave a weak smile. "The last time I told you how little Noah meant to me, he was standing just outside the door. Now…oh, how I wish he were here again."

Susan reached out and covered Isobel's hands with her own. "In the eyes of God, you and Noah are married. It's all right to love him. Do you want a husband? Do you want Noah?"

"I tell myself I want to capture Snake Jackson," Isobel said. "I want to regain my land titles. I want to marry Don Guillermo. But…Noah is the only man I've ever wanted in this way. I cannot imagine my life without him now."

"I've got news!" Dr. Ealy strode through the back

door, his coattails flying in the March breeze. "It's about Jesse Evans—one of the men who shot Mr. Tunstall."

"Have they caught him?" his wife asked.

"Evans and some of the others have been hiding out in the Sacramento Mountains. A few days ago they sneaked over to a spread near Tularosa to loot it. They were having a merry time of it, but then the owner showed up. He grabbed a rifle and started firing."

"Was anyone shot?" Isobel had realized at once that Snake Jackson often rode with the Evans bunch.

"Killed one and wounded Evans. Shot him in the wrist and the lungs."

"Lungs!" Mary Ealy exclaimed. "Oh, he can't last long."

Dr. Ealy snorted. "Guess again. Evans escaped to friendly turf in the Organ Mountains. Just this morning he decided to give himself up to the commanding officer at Fort Stanton. So there he lies—safe from the Regulators and receiving the finest medical attention in these parts. Save for my own skilled hands, of course."

"Is Evans a free man at the Fort?" Isobel asked.

"He's under arrest until court convenes in April. They'll try him under one of the old warrants he racked up—horse and cattle rustler, murderer, robber." Dr. Ealy shook his head. "And here's the humdinger of it all. Evans swore it was another man in the bunch who pulled the trigger on John Tunstall."

"Another man?" Isobel exploded. "But I saw Snake Jackson and Jesse Evans kill him!"

Clenching her teeth, Isobel turned away and stepped outside. Never mind about Evans. The real object of her mission was Jim Jackson.

If she could have no part in Noah's life…no station

as a doña in the Pascal family…no rights to her father's land in Catalonia…then she had only one path.

She must find Jackson.

And only one man would know where he was hiding. Gazing up at the rolling green hills that rose above the river, Isobel made her decision. She would ride for Fort Stanton at once.

Chapter Twelve

Isobel knew Dr. Ealy and his wife would forbid her to leave McSween's house. Instead she took Susan aside and explained the situation. If she confronted Jesse Evans while he was under arrest at Fort Stanton, he would be forced to tell her where Snake Jackson was hiding.

"And what then?" Susan asked, panic in her voice.

"Then…only God knows."

Susan's protests did no good. Isobel's revenge would be complete only with the recovery of the land that belonged to her family. Vengeance was her only hope of peace.

Clad in borrowed denim trousers, chambray shirt and leather coat, Isobel set Noah's black Stetson over her gold braid and mounted her horse.

Reaching down, she took Susan's hand. "I shall return in a week. If not, you must write to my mother. Tell her I tried."

"Oh, Isobel!"

"And tell Noah…tell him that I loved him."

Fort Stanton was nine miles from Lincoln. Once under the authority of Kit Carson, it was now commanded by

Captain Purington. The towering snow-covered peak of Sierra Blanca dominated the horizon on one side of the stone bastion. On the other rose the mountains of El Capitan.

Entering the fort with little notice from the guards, Isobel scanned the barracks, irrigation ditches and spaded garden plots. Homes dotted the enclosure, and she noted more women and children than she had expected.

Troops of the Ninth Cavalry Regiment—one of four black brigades organized after the Civil War—were stationed at the fort. Highly respected by area settlers, the soldiers protected them from Apache attacks.

Noah had told Isobel that five years earlier, Jimmie Dolan had been the fort's primary supplier of goods. Accused of defrauding the government, his services had been terminated. She assumed this meant the commanders would oppose Dolan in the Lincoln County conflict.

She was wrong. Noah had said the garrison's orders lay with the law in New Mexico. And the law upheld every move Jimmie Dolan made. Determined to speak to Jesse Evans, Isobel tied up her horse and entered a building that served as the fort's store, hotel and post office.

"Help ya?" The voice came from a row of mailboxes where a man was sorting through a stack of envelopes. "Name's Will Dowlin. I'm the trader and postmaster here."

"I want to speak with a medical prisoner."

"Jesse Evans? He's under guard at the hospital. Go to headquarters and ask for the officer in charge." The postmaster turned toward her. "Will you be needin' a room for the night…ma'am? Or, is it sir?"

"My name is Isobel Matas Buchanan. I seek Jim Jackson, the man who murdered my father. And no, thank you, I won't need a room."

As she prepared to step outside, Dowlin called to her. "Miz Buchanan, I wouldn't go tellin' folks you're lookin' for Snake Jackson. He's liable to start lookin' for you."

She tipped her head. "I certainly hope so, Mr. Dowlin."

Captain Purington was frustrated with the War Department, he told Isobel, and tired of being fettered in his efforts to control the troubles in Lincoln County. Fearing more problems, he at first refused her interview request. But after much pleading, he said if she was fool-headed enough to hunt down a man wanted for murder, so be it.

Late that night, Isobel was ushered into the Fort Stanton hospital. Dr. Appel, the physician who had been paid a hundred dollars to examine John Tunstall's body for the Dolan faction, pointed out Jesse Evans. The outlaw lay on a camp bed, his wrist and chest bandaged.

As she stepped to his side, she touched the place on her thigh where Noah's six-shooter had hung. The holster was empty, the gun confiscated by the guard.

"Hello, Mr. Evans," she said, her mouth dry.

The man stared at her, saying nothing.

She swallowed. "Mr. Evans, I'm looking for Rattlesnake Jim Jackson."

"Snake?" he wheezed. "What fer?"

"He murdered my father, Alberto Matas." The words

came easier now. "It happened five years ago, when Snake rode with the Horrell Gang."

"Aw, not you again." Evans began to cough. He spat a globule of bright blood onto the white sheet.

Isobel saw that none of guards intended to move. "Here," she whispered, blotting his chin with a towel.

"Snake aims to kill ya, miss," he grunted as she tucked the towel around his neck. "Hates Mexicans."

"I'm from Spain."

"Don't matter. When he was a kid, some of your people done in his whole family. Besides, Snake seen you in the woods that evenin'."

"When you shot John Tunstall? Yes. I saw it all."

Evans coughed again. "If I tell you where Snake is and you go after him," he gasped out, "yer gonna git killed."

"If I were dead, I certainly couldn't be a government witness against you."

"Well, now…that sits purty good." He lowered his voice. "Snake's at the L. G. Murphy ranch, about ten miles northwest of the fort near White Oaks."

Isobel stood. "Thank you, Mr. Evans. I wish you a speedy recovery."

"Good luck, *señorita*. Yer gonna need it."

Isobel dismounted as dawn cast a pink light over the mountains. The Murphy ranch house sat atop a small grassy knoll in the distance. At this hour no one stirred.

Perspiration broke out on her temples as she drew her gun and crept through the scrub piñon and oak brush. What would Noah say if he knew what she was doing? No doubt he would berate her for taking matters into her own hands. One of his Bible verses would accompany the rebuke, of course. As if God even noticed a lone Spaniard stalking her father's killer.

It wasn't as though she really wanted to shoot Snake. If she could capture him and take him to the fort, Captain Purington would hold him with Evans until court convened in Lincoln. Then the law could hang them both.

Her breath sounded loud in the crisp morning air as she knelt beside a rail fence. No matter how distant and unfeeling God was, she needed divine help. Leaning her head against a post to whisper a quick prayer, she saw the faces of her father, her mother, her brother… and the gentle smile of Noah Buchanan. *Oh, Lord, keep him safe. Always.*

Cradling her pistol, she flipped open the chamber and counted the six bullets. As she clicked it back into place, a gloved hand clamped over her mouth.

"Don't scream. Don't move."

Fear knotting her throat, she struggled, twisting to see the man who held her. A dark hat, a bandanna, shadowed eyes. Gripping her hard, the man turned her to face him. Strong nose…unshaven chin…blue, blue eyes.

"Mule-headed woman," Noah breathed. "What're you doing out here?"

"How did you know I was gone?"

"Susan Gates sent for me."

"But…but I told her—"

"Enough's enough, Isobel. You're coming back to Lincoln with me."

She caught his arm. "Noah—look!"

The front door of the Murphy house swung open. Scratching his rumpled hair, Jim Jackson wandered onto the porch, a rifle in his arms. He wore only a red union suit, its buttons half undone. As he leaned the rifle against a porch post, Isobel wrestled free of Noah's grip.

"Jim Jackson!" she cried out. "Where are the titles to my land?"

"Get down, Isobel!" Noah hissed, drawing his gun as he tried to push her to the ground.

"I am the daughter of Don Alberto Matas—a man you murdered five years ago," Isobel shouted. "Where have you put my family's land titles and jewels? The ones you stole from my father's coach."

With a loud croak, Snake reached for his rifle, but Isobel cocked her pistol.

"Hold yer horses now, *señorita!*" he yelled.

"Shall I shoot you dead? Or will you talk?"

"Why should I tell you anything, *señorita?*"

"Tell me where you put the titles, or I'll blast off your head!"

"And I'll blast off yore sassy head!" Snatching up his rifle, Snake crouched just as Isobel pulled the trigger. The bullet hit the front door. As she squeezed the trigger a second time, Noah grabbed her by the waist and hurled her to the ground. A bullet zinged past her head and buried itself in a tree trunk behind them.

"Someone's firing from upstairs!" Noah shouted.

"You made me miss my shot!"

"Head for that arroyo."

As Noah dragged her toward the protection of the nearby ditch, Isobel aimed at a face in an upper window and fired her third bullet. A return shot struck a fence post, causing a spray of sawdust and splinters to explode beside them. Isobel took aim at Snake as he scampered around the side of the house.

"Asesino!" she hollered, pulling the trigger. "Murderer! Thief!"

A slug plowed into the dirt beside her. Another hit a rock and ricocheted. As Noah was tugging her down into the ditch, she squeezed off her two remaining rounds.

"Oh, if I could only get my hands on that man—"

Her words hung in her throat as she caught sight of a crimson stain spreading across Noah's sleeve.

His blue eyes darted back and forth as he scanned the landscape. "C'mon—this way!"

"You're…you're wounded!"

"That's what happens when folks shoot at you, darlin'. Follow me."

Running in a crouch through the low shrubbery, they approached the road. The fire in Isobel's blood still pumped like lava through her veins. Yet the man she loved had been shot defending her.

"Get on now!" Noah lifted Isobel in his arms and slung her onto the horse. Swinging a leg over his own saddle, he shouted, "Go, Isobel! Ride like the wind!"

Pistol drawn, Noah rode just paces behind Isobel. If Snake and his cronies gave chase, it would be close. Noah's arm was on fire, and he knew that spelled trouble.

"Are you badly hurt, Noah?" she called over her shoulder.

"I'll live."

"Then we should circle behind the house. They won't expect it. *Por la venganza!"*

As she spurred her horse, Noah reined his. Busy

thanking the Creator for a relatively safe exit, he hadn't quite caught her drift. Maybe it was the loss of blood, but his head didn't feel right. Hadn't he just rescued Isobel? Hadn't he just dragged her to safety as bullets flew around their heads? Hadn't he just gotten himself shot trying to get her away from Snake Jackson?

"Isobel!" he bellowed, goading his horse. "Isobel, get back here!"

A branch raked his hat from his head as he followed her horse's flying hooves through a thicket. Stifling a curse, he gritted his teeth.

"We'll take cover there," she cried, wheeling her horse around. "Behind the privy."

"Isobel!"

But she was off again. When her horse galloped across a stretch of open ground, shots rang out from the Murphy house. The horse shied, dancing sideways as Isobel fought for control.

Jaw clenched, Noah started across the clearing after Isobel. Bullets seemed to come from every direction. Feeling vulnerable without his hat, he hunkered down low.

"Isobel!" he called over the commotion.

"Noah—to the outhouse. My horse will follow yours. I can't leave now. I'm too close!"

"Close to getting yourself killed," he growled. "Get out of here, darlin', and I mean now."

Hostility bordering on hatred flashed from her eyes as she swung her horse away from the privy. He followed, this time steering clear of the road in case of an ambush. When they had ridden a couple of miles without hearing pursuit, Isobel reined her horse to a stop.

"Where are you taking me?" she demanded.

"Home."

"I have no home—and you just made certain of it."

"Snake Jackson won't give up those titles, Isobel, even with you shooting at him from behind a privy."

She shook her head and looked away. "How little you understand me, Noah Buchanan."

"You can say that again."

"At Fort Stanton, I will recruit soldiers. They'll be brave enough to fight by my side against Snake Jackson."

Noah snorted. "We're not stopping at Fort Stanton, Isobel. Or in Lincoln. I'm taking you to Chisum's ranch."

"You will have to keep your gun on me, vaquero, because I mean to return to the Murphy house. I know my mission."

"So do I, *señora*."

Cradling his wounded arm, Noah reached for his hat, then remembered he'd lost it. He ran a hand across his damp hair and let out a sigh. No hat. No breakfast. A hole in his arm. And one crazy spitfire. This arrangement was turning out to be some kind of fun.

As angry as she felt at being deterred from her goal, Isobel was worried about Noah's wound. She insisted on bathing his arm in the clear, icy water of the Rio Bonito.

"It's a clean wound," she informed him as they sat under a tree near the stream. "The bullet passed through. God was with you."

"He's always with me. You, too."

"How can you say such a thing? He is God! If you

saw the churches in Spain, you would understand His majesty."

"Honey, I see it just fine in the New Mexico sky. Majestic as He is, God told us, 'I will never leave you nor forsake you.' He loves us, Isobel."

"If God loved you, He would not have let a bullet go through your arm." As she bound his forearm with a strip of cotton torn from her petticoat, Isobel struggled against her own guilt. Noah had been injured protecting her. She didn't like it that such a man could be hurt. He had seemed so strong, so invincible. Like her father.

Noah brushed a strand of hair from her forehead. "Didn't your daddy ever let you do anything wrong, so you'd learn from your mistake and be a better person?"

Isobel thought back to the first time she had taken her horse over a fence. Though her father had warned her not to do it, he had stood by and watched as she disobeyed. When she'd fallen, he had been the first to her side.

"Why do you reject Him, Isobel?" Noah asked.

She tugged a necklace from inside her blouse. "I carry God with me, you see. You can never accuse me of rejecting Him."

Noah lifted the gold crucifix with his fingertips. "You carry Him, but you won't let Him carry you. You keep Him on this cross so He won't interfere with your plan to wreak vengeance on Snake Jackson. You think you can direct your own life, Isobel. But you're wrong."

"You know nothing about me or my plans. You treat me like a child—forcing me to run when I should stay and fight. You are a coward."

He turned his head, blue eyes piercing. "A coward?"

"That is what I said."

He gave a little grunt. "I must be slipping. I used to be a commonplace vaquero. Now I'm a coward."

"If you had stood by my side—"

"But you're right. We should have fought it out with Snake and his pals from behind the privy. Then, when Dick came to claim our rotting bodies, he could say, 'Yup, these two are dead as doornails, but they sure were brave.'"

"I have no intention of dying at Snake Jackson's hand," Isobel shot back.

"You have some kind of holy halo to keep bullets away?"

"Mock me if you will. I shall never run from my destiny, Noah. I am not afraid of death."

"Well, you and death can get together and have a little tea party one of these days. But until our arrangement is over, you're staying right here."

They set out again without speaking, and it was not long before they arrived at the gate to John Chisum's spread. Isobel caught her breath as they neared the house. Rosebushes had leafed out and were beginning to bud. Once dry grass had brightened to a soft green. The stream ran high and swift through the valley.

Isobel softened as she recalled the sweet days she had spent with Noah on this land. Now he had brought her here again. If she went to his house, she would fall into that dreamworld again and surrender her quest. Or was a life with Noah her true quest?

She studied him as he unlatched the gate. It seemed forever since her hands had slipped over his broad shoulders. Since his arms had held her close.

"Noah," she said, "when will our arrangement be over?"

His eyes were soft as he regarded her. "When things calm down in Lincoln. When I'm sure you're safe from Snake Jackson. When I convince Chisum to sell me some land."

"I see," she said, trying to imagine the day he would look into her eyes and bid her farewell.

"Howdy, Buchanan!" A slender, mustached man with deep brown eyes and thinning hair strode toward them. "Where's your hat, partner?"

"Looks like we may end our arrangement sooner than we thought," Noah spoke under his breath. "Here comes John Simpson Chisum."

Chapter Thirteen

John Chisum took Isobel's hand and kissed it. His thick brown mustache—each end waxed into a curly point—brushed over her bare skin.

"Hey there, you old coot," Noah said as he and Chisum embraced.

But the older man drew back with a frown. "What did you mean leaving your new bride at my place, Buchanan? I was mighty ashamed of you when Mrs. Towry told me about it. Especially when I realized that your wife had taken to sleeping in my new bed and hanging her shiny silk dresses in my wardrobe."

Noah turned to Isobel, who blushed a deep red. She lifted her chin. "But Mrs. Towry said—"

"Buchanan," Chisum cut in, "don't you know I've been cooped up in a Las Vegas jail for three months? Eating grub that ain't fit for man nor beast. Sleeping on a hard prison cot. Why, I've been living for the day I could get back here and stretch out on my pretty bed."

Mortified, Isobel spoke up quickly. "Oh, Mr. Chisum, please, I—"

"Now I reckon I'll just have to sleep on my old camp cot."

"Sir, I—I'm terribly sorry," Isobel stammered. "I had no idea. And certainly Noah never intended to offend you."

At this the cattle baron slapped his knee and burst into a gale of hearty guffaws. "Oh, I got you good there, didn't I, Mrs. Buchanan? I had you thinking your husband was in a heap of trouble, right? Camp cot—why, that's where I always sleep!"

Noah tucked Isobel under his arm and gave Chisum a punch on the arm. "You had us plumb tongue-tied, you old joker. I should have guessed what you were up to the minute you started in on her."

It took a moment for Chisum to control his laughter over the grand prank he had pulled. Isobel saw little humor in the situation.

"Don't you mind me, now," Chisum said. "Everyone knows I love a joke. Welcome to the family."

She mustered a smile. "Thank you, sir."

"Noah Buchanan," Chisum said as his sharp brown eyes studied Isobel. "I never would have figured you to settle down. But now that I've seen your enchanting bride, I understand. You folks come on into the house."

As Isobel and Noah followed, he turned and fixed them with another frown. "You know how I feel about gun fighting, Buchanan. A six-shooter will always get you into more trouble than it'll get you out of."

Without waiting for a response, he strode into the cool shadows of his front room. Isobel had already decided that John Chisum was the most eccentric man she had ever met. He swaggered when he walked. His speech was peppered with sarcasm and loud hoots of laughter. He loved practical jokes that were funny only to him.

But as Isobel entered the cattleman's opulent home for a second time, she was reminded that, as odd as he might be, Chisum was also a shrewd businessman.

"Two hundred miles along the Pecos River," he boasted as Isobel gazed out the front window. "Largest ranch in the territory. I dug those irrigation ditches between the roses and the orchard. Clear water. One hundred rosebushes. We'll have watermelons this summer. You and Noah come over for some *sandía*."

"I would like that," she replied.

Chisum fiddled with the waxed end of his mustache. "Tell me about yourself, Mrs. Buchanan. Your kinfolk. Your friends. What possessed you to up and marry my best trail boss?"

Isobel spotted Noah talking to Alexander McSween across the room. Evidently the lawyer had sought refuge at Chisum's ranch.

"My father owned land," Isobel replied, reminding herself to make Chisum believe that Noah was a happily married man. "Noah reminds me of him."

"You married for love?"

She glanced at Noah, whose blue eyes were on her. "I love my husband," she murmured.

"Reckon you'll like living in the territory?"

"I already do."

"Reckon you'll manage to settle ol' Buchanan down?"

"I already have."

"Then how'd he wind up with that bullet hole in his arm?" Chisum asked, leaning closer.

Isobel was ready. "He was protecting me, as a good husband should."

Chisum grinned beneath his mustache. "I like you, Miss Goldilocks. You're spunky. We'll get along fine."

He clapped his hands, and the room fell quiet. Isobel noted that others had entered the room, but she recognized none of them.

"Noah Buchanan, Belle," Chisum began, "I'd like to introduce you to Alexander's wife, Sue McSween, just in from St. Louis."

A small woman with mounds of curled chestnut hair and almond eyes stood to greet them. Her small lips beneath a prominent nose turned up in a smile. An elegant violet brocade gown trimmed in white ruffles hinted at her husband's wealth.

"And here are Mr. Simpson, Mr. Howes and Dr. Leverson," Chisum continued. "Dr. Leverson has come down from Colorado to establish a colony here."

Isobel stared at the man and wondered at the ill-fated timing of his arrival in Lincoln County. When the guests resumed their chatter, Noah started for the front door.

"Buchanan, where are you off to in such a hurry?" Chisum asked, blocking his path.

"Thought I'd check on my place." Noah nodded in Isobel's direction. "I'll leave Belle with you, if you don't mind. She'll be safer here."

"I certainly do mind." Chisum glanced at Isobel. "Not that I wouldn't appreciate the company of such a lovely creature, but she's *your* wife. You'll need someone to tend that bullet hole of yours. Adios, partner."

Laughing heartily, Chisum hailed McSween across the room and swaggered off, leaving Noah gazing at Isobel.

* * *

"You make one move to escape, and I'll hog-tie you to this rail," Noah vowed as he and Isobel wrapped their reins around the hitching post outside his adobe home.

Isobel decided not to respond to such a vulgar comment. When she pushed open the front door and stepped into the familiar room, her annoyance wavered. The house smelled wonderful—crisp starch in the lace curtains, old leather coats hung on pegs, the charred remains of their last wood fire. From the kitchen wafted the aromas of ground coffee, cinnamon, lye soap. From the bedroom, the eucalyptus and lavender Isobel had packed among her clothes mingled with the bay rum cologne Noah sometimes wore.

She shut her eyes and stood for a moment, swept away by memories…laughter, as she and Noah hung curtains, giggles over too many onions in the rabbit stew, the soft *swish-swish* of the straw broom, the *clickety-clack* of the Remington.

"I mailed your story to New York," she said when she felt Noah moving behind her.

"Thank you, Isobel."

She turned to him. "It seems we go in opposite directions, Noah. You are for the quiet life. I am for *la venganza*."

He studied the oriental carpet beneath the velvet sofa. "I remember when you seemed happy with the quiet life, Isobel."

"I remember, too." Again, their eyes met.

"I've lived a rough life, Isobel," he said. "A man's life—rounding up cattle, warding off rustlers, going without decent food. My gun has sent three men on to their rewards—two cattle rustlers, a horse thief. Despite what you think, I'm no coward. But I've got to follow my dreams. It's time."

Noah gazed at her face, and she began to fear he could read her longing, her passion. Did he know how deeply she cared for him? Did he sense that she loved him?

"Then we'll keep apart," she said quickly. "Do as you wish. I'll do the same."

"Good. In a few days I'll talk to Chisum about the land I want to buy. As soon as we hear Snake is in jail, you can get on with your own business."

"Yes," she said in a low voice. "I understand."

But as she began removing her shawl, Isobel knew that every word she had spoken was a lie. She didn't want to stay away from Noah, though he had no use for her. He understood her quest, but he would never help her. When the time was right, he wanted to be rid of her.

Isobel slipped into Noah's life again as though it were something they had planned. He slept in the barn while she returned to the bedroom. Every morning when he walked into the house and smelled the eggs frying and the coffee bubbling, his heart lifted.

And there she always was—Isobel. Freshly scrubbed from her morning bath. Dressed in her blue cotton dress or one of the fancy Spanish outfits she'd refashioned. Her hair gleamed like sunshine, and her lips were always ready with a smile.

As they ate their breakfast at the white-clothed table, her plans spilled out in a gurgling stream. The house soon wore a new coat of caliche whitewash. The windowpanes sparkled. The floorboards squeaked of fresh wax. Noah repaired his fences and gave the barn a coat of red paint.

He sensed that Isobel was channeling her urge for revenge into labor as she spaded the deep, rich river soil beside the kitchen. In his storage bins she found seeds for corn, beans, peas and chilies. She cut the eyes from old cellar potatoes and planted them in rows beside the onion bulbs. Then he taught her how to dig irrigation channels from his ditch to her garden.

In the second week, Noah woke one morning with the idea of taking Isobel out to see the land he hoped to buy. He had no illusions that she would want to stay on with him. Many a sunset he had seen her standing on the back porch and looking in the direction of Lincoln Town. She kept her pistol beside the bed, and he knew if she could, she would ride out again in search of Snake Jackson and *la revancha*.

"Can you leave your laundering for a day?" he asked that morning as they cleared the breakfast dishes. "I thought we might go riding."

"To Chisum's?"

"No." He hung the iron frying pan on its hook. "Thought you might like to see the land I want to buy."

She scrubbed the entire kettle before nodding.

As the horses cantered through belly-high green grass, Isobel was sure she had never been so happy. Dressed in her riding skirt, shirtwaist and boots, she had placed one of Noah's old hats on her head.

She watched him riding just paces ahead, his shoulders broad above the straight line of his back. The wound in his arm had almost healed, and his hair had grown too long. She had considered asking if he would like for her to trim it, but they had not touched each other since returning to the house. The thought of lifting his hair in her fingers was… No, she could never cut his hair.

"I own a few head of cattle," Noah said, beckoning her. "They range with Chisum's herds. Now and again I round them up, see how many calves have dropped and send a few beeves to the railhead. I've saved a little money. Enough to buy a spread, anyway."

"A small one, like Dick Brewer's?"

"Smaller. Chisum staked his claim on this land, and he's fought off rustlers too long to let it go easy." He surveyed the rolling grasslands dotted with wildflowers and yuccas. The turquoise sky spread overhead like a clear lake. "Sometimes, I almost think I can look straight up into heaven and catch a glimpse of God."

"I have never seen my land," Isobel responded.

"Good country around Santa Fe. You'll like it."

Isobel nodded, though she knew she would never own that land unless she fought to reclaim it.

Noah led them beneath a tall tree and they dismounted. "This is a cottonwood," he said. "Remember what I told you last month?"

"You said the leaves in the wind would sound like a river."

"Listen."

She stood beside him in silence, head bowed, eyes shut. For a moment the only sound was the thudding of her own heart. Then she heard it. Whispering, rushing— the gurgle of cool, clear water.

"Yes," she whispered. "Yes, Noah."

She lifted her head and let the winds play across her eyelids. Dappled sunlight warmed her cheeks. Grass swished against her riding skirt. A warm mouth covered her lips.

"Noah!" Her eyes flew open, and she stepped backward.

"Isobel, wait," he said, catching her around the waist. "This has been too hard—you and me together like this. I've prayed day and night, and all I can see to do is ask you to stay here with me. I'll protect you, I swear it. I can't promise much, but I'll give you what I can. I'll give you a home."

"A home? Is that what you think I want from you?"

"It's better than what you've got now. It's better than nothing."

"Oh!" Pushing away from him, she walked around the cottonwood tree and leaned against the trunk. How could he be so blind? Didn't he see the longing in her eyes as she cooked for him? Didn't he feel it in his freshly polished boots, in the ruffles of white lace lining his kitchen shelves, in the neat rows of the garden? Didn't he know she wanted his heart?

Noah's love was her only hope of healing. Without it, her pain would drive her toward a violent destiny.

"Now, Isobel," Noah was saying, his head lowered like an angry bull's as he circled the tree. "I just offered to make good on this crazy marriage of ours. I offered you a home and all that goes with it. Can you tell me what gives you the all-fired uppityness to huff in my face and go marching off like I've insulted you?"

Her heartbeat pulsed in her throat as she watched his blue eyes roam her face. She sensed the power in him, and the need. His stance—shoulders set, legs spread, feet planted firmly—said nothing would get past him now. He wanted honesty. He wanted answers. And he wanted her.

She lifted her chin. "You think a destitute woman has

no choices. She must surrender her dreams in exchange for security."

"So, I'm not good enough for you. Is that it?"

"I want more in my life than a house and food."

"Well, what is it you want?" he asked.

She stamped her foot and tossed her head. "I want passion!"

"Passion? Why didn't you say so?" He bent and kissed her. When he lifted his head, his eyes were deep pools. "I've been pussyfooting around you so long I'm about to go stark raving loco. Now, come here and kiss me."

Before she could stop them, her hands slipped around his neck and her fingers threaded through his hair. She stood on tiptoe, pressing her lips to his again and again.

Noah smiled down at her. "We can make it work, darlin'."

"I'm so weak in your arms. How can I say no when you do this to me, Noah?"

"This is why we're good together. This and everything else that's happened between us in that little house."

She kissed him again, and when she drew back, his blue eyes grazed over her. "Oh, Isobel," he breathed. "Oh, darlin'…"

She sighed, her eyelids heavy. "Noah, how can I ever leave you?"

"Don't leave me, Isobel. We'll head for Chisum's right now, and I'll get him to sell me the land."

She studied the nodding heads of silver grass in the distance. "Why not?"

He ran a finger down the side of her neck. "Not a reason in the world."

* * *

Arriving late that afternoon at South Spring River Ranch, Noah and Isobel walked hand in hand up the steps of the front portal. John Chisum opened the door before they could knock.

"Why, it's Goldilocks and Papa Bear!" he chortled. "Come on in! Plenty of guests here—two more won't hurt."

Clearly in no mood for Chisum's nonsense, Noah took his boss's shoulder and spoke in a low voice. "John, I want to talk to you."

"Sounds serious."

"It is."

Chisum held out a hand in the direction of the hall. "Kindly excuse us, Mrs. Buchanan," he said.

Isobel nodded, watching them go and wondering whether Noah's dream would come true at last. Dusting her skirt, she sat on the edge of a blue sofa.

"I don't suppose you've heard the news," Sue McSween said.

"News?" Isobel looked around her at the earnest faces of the woman, her husband and three other guests. A chill slid into her stomach.

"Rumor has it," Sue said, "that Sheriff Brady is threatening to place my husband in confinement."

"Jail," Alexander McSween clarified.

"The jail in Lincoln is no more than a hole underground." Sue glanced at her husband. "Some say the sheriff intends to run water into the jail and drown Mac."

"You cannot allow yourself to be taken," Isobel told the lawyer.

"I'm duty bound to be in Lincoln for the opening of court on April first—three days from now."

"But I was told the opening was April eight," Isobel declared.

"It's been garbled," Sue said. "We think District Attorney Rynerson, that great hairy ape, may have switched it deliberately so that in the confusion Mac could be arrested. Or ambushed and shot."

"No!" Isobel rose to her feet. "Not another good man. We won't allow it."

"We're all riding with Mac, Mrs. Buchanan," another of the guests put in. "Mrs. McSween, Mr. Chisum. All of us."

Isobel looked at McSween's protectors—every one of them soft-handed and pale. None wore a gun.

"Well, Miss Goldilocks," Chisum said as he stepped into the room. "Looks like you and your husband are landowners—soon as Buchanan produces the pot of gold he claims to have. Congratulations!"

Noah wore a broad smile. "I'm a mighty blessed man," he said. "A beautiful wife. Land. Good friends."

"I'm so happy," Isobel murmured as he drew her close.

Noah smiled. "Let's head for home, honey. I've got some digging to do."

"Noah," she said with a sigh. "First we must escort Alexander McSween to Lincoln Town. Sheriff Brady plans to kill him."

Chapter Fourteen

While Isobel recounted her conversation with the McSweens, Noah studied the determination in her face, the hope in the eyes of Sue McSween, the fear in the posture of Alexander McSween and the others.

"You go on home, boy," Chisum said. "Plow your land. Start a family. We'll watch over Mac. Some friends of yours are...uh...taking care of things in Lincoln Town. The Regulators."

"What about Dick Brewer? Is he with them?"

"No, I reckon Dick's still at his farm, mending fences and keeping a sharp eye on his own back."

Noah could never knowingly allow an innocent man to ride into an ambush. "I'll go with the rest of you," he announced. "You'll need protection."

Chisum shook his head. "Buchanan, you just spent a good quarter of an hour in my library explaining how you planned to lay down your six-shooter and start a family. How you're a loyal husband now. How you want to be a peaceful rancher. You're not changing your mind, are you? I'd hate to have to change mine."

Noah bristled. "I will lay down my gun, John. And

I do mean to ranch. But I'll never let the bunch of you ride into Brady's trap without my protection."

"All right, calm yourself." Chisum clapped Noah on the back. "You can ride with us—you and your wife. We'll make it a jolly jaunt, how's that?" Turning about, he leaned in the direction of his kitchen. "Mrs. Towry, we've got more company! Tell the cook to add two extra places to the dinner table!"

Early on April first, Noah and Isobel rode into Lincoln ahead of the others. They would make sure the Regulators were in place to guard the arrival of the McSween party.

"What do you think of Sue?" Isobel asked him.

For most of the journey, the two women had ridden together, surrounded by the men. Noah watched them talk and hoped they were forming a friendship.

He shrugged. "Never gave her much thought. Folks say she's got money smarts."

"Am I very much like Sue?"

"Sure you are. You're smart. You're determined."

"I'm also angry, opinionated, unforgiving."

"Whoa, now," he said. "I've seen those in you, but you have good qualities, too."

"Noah," she whispered. "I don't like Sue McSween."

"Aw, she's not so bad. Give her time."

"But you don't understand…." Her words trailed off. "In Sue, I saw a mirror of myself—a woman driven by a desire for land, power, wealth. I saw a bitter woman, Noah."

He reached over and took her hand. There were a lot of things he could have said—quick assurances, shallow denials—but he was beginning to appreciate what he saw in Isobel's face. A softness was growing, a melting of anger, a gentleness.

"I have been praying," she said as they rode past Juan Patrón's house. "Praying as you do. I may…it's possible I may have been wrong about God.… I think He might be listening to me after all, and I need His help. I want to wipe away the reflection I saw. I want to change."

Before he could reply, Noah spotted Sheriff Brady. A rolled sheet of white paper under his arm, the sheriff stepped into the street. Four armed deputies accompanied him, two at each side.

"I wonder where they're headed," Noah said under his breath. "Courthouse, I'd bet."

"Maybe it's the mix-up in court dates," Isobel speculated as they rode past the *torreón*. "What time is it? No one's out."

Noah opened his pocket watch. "Nine o'clock."

An uneasiness seemed to hang over the street. The usual morning scents of piñon smoke and baking bread were absent. No children laughed or played outside. No women bustled toward the stores.

"Do you see any of our people?" Isobel asked. "Dick or Billy?"

"Squire Wilson hoeing his garden yonder. His son is out in front of the Wilson house. But—" Noah stopped short as a Winchester barrel appeared atop the adobe wall of John Tunstall's corral. Billy the Kid's face emerged behind it.

"Isobel, look out!" Noah shouted. A row of rifles bristled up from behind the wall, followed by the men holding them—all Regulators. A fusillade of gunfire shattered the quiet. A hail of bullets slammed into Sheriff Brady. For a moment he hung in midair, mouth open.

Then he toppled to the street. One of his deputies staggered toward the courthouse, moaning for water. The other three fled.

Noah drew his six-shooter as he tried to steady his horse. "Get off the street, Isobel!" he roared.

In shock, she stared as Ike Stockton ran from his saloon with a mug of water for the bleeding deputy. Billy the Kid jumped the adobe wall and dashed into the road where Brady's body lay. He bent to grab a fallen rifle.

"This is *my* gun!" he snapped at the dead man before tearing open the sheriff's coat and searching the pockets.

"Billy!" Noah yelled. A shot cracked from the window of a nearby house, and a bullet tore through the Kid's left thigh. Yelping, skipping for cover, he left a trail of blood across the dirt road.

"Noah—it's Squire Wilson!" Isobel cried, observing the man lying in his garden patch.

"Isobel, take cover!" Abandoning his horse, Noah sprinted across the road. The squire lay in a fetal curl, his hands wrapped around the backs of his thighs.

"I was hoeing onions," he moaned. "In this godforsaken town, can't a man even hoe his onions in peace?"

Noah rolled the man over, passing a hand across the wound where a bullet had ripped through both his legs.

"It's all right," Isobel whispered to the squire's son.

Noah frowned to realize she had followed him. Scooping up the fallen man, he started for the squire's house, where his hysterical wife stood in the doorway. She grabbed her son's arm and jerked him inside.

"Oh, is he gonna die?" she shrieked as Noah carried

Wilson through the door. "My son, my son, are you all right?"

In moments, Noah deposited the squire on a bed and headed back outside again. "I told you to take cover!" he barked at Isobel. "I can't lose you, girl!"

Taking her arm, he rushed her through McSween's gate and onto the porch.

Susan Gates threw open the door. "Isobel, did they shoot you?"

"She's fine," Noah growled. "Now, get her inside and keep her safe. Tie her up if you have to."

Susan took Isobel's shoulders as Noah started out. But he stepped aside just as Billy Bonney staggered into the house. Face ashen, upper lip glued to his buck teeth, he gripped Noah's arm.

"Buchanan, I need Doc Ealy," he huffed. "I'm hit."

Noah had half a mind to let the Kid take what he deserved for pulling a dirty game on Brady and the deputies. But he slipped a supporting arm around the youth and helped him into a back room where Isobel huddled with Susan and the Ealy family.

"Billy took a bullet in the leg," he informed the women. "Where's Doc?"

"He went to help the squire," Isobel told him.

A skinny young man holding a rifle stood. "Dr. Ealy asked me to keep watch over the women."

Noah recognized him as Tunstall's store clerk. "Well, boy, I hope you're ready. The law is sure to come looking for Billy."

Everyone in the room gathered around as Noah laid the Kid on the bed. "Don't never get shot, ladies," he told the two little Ealy girls. "Hurts like fire."

"Kid, you did a fool thing gunning Brady down," Noah growled. "Ambushed him. What was that about?"

"It's not how it looked, I swear. All us Regulators snuck into town last night to keep an eye on things for Mac." Billy grimaced as Mrs. Ealy began cutting away the lower half of his trousers. "When we seen Brady headin' our way, we knew he was gonna arrest Mac and then flood the jail and drown him. Brady organized the posse that murdered Tunstall, you know, and he never arrested nobody for the killin'. As sheriff, he weren't never gonna get his dues, so we settled the matter ourselves."

"And then went through Brady's pockets," Noah said.

"I was lookin' for the warrant for McSween's arrest. I knew Brady had it with him, but I didn't find it before them Dolan dogs shot me."

"The Regulators were at South Spring the other day," Noah said. "Did McSween and Chisum order you to ambush Brady?"

Before the Kid could answer, Dr. Ealy hurried into the room. "George Peppin just declared himself sheriff," the doctor puffed, jerking off his spectacles and cleaning them with the tail of his frock coat. "A Dolan man, of course. They're saying McSween's behind the ambush, even though he's not in town. Peppin sent a message to Captain Purington to bring troops from Fort Stanton. They've sworn to arrest McSween and the Regulators, and they're coming after Billy first."

"Why me?" Billy hunched up onto his elbows. "A whole passel of us shot at Brady."

"Oh my!" Dr. Ealy seemed to see the youth for the first time. He peered at the wounded leg. "I don't like harboring a criminal, but Christian duty binds me. Mary, fetch my bag."

While Noah looked on, Dr. Ealy drew a silk handkerchief through the raw hole in Billy Bonney's leg. Isobel and Susan mopped the trail of blood from the back door to the bed. Mary Ealy kept an eye on the window while the store clerk sawed a hole in the floor of an adjoining room.

"Here comes George Peppin!" Mary cried out. "He's got some deputies and a bunch of others. They've followed the blood in the street. Oh, what shall we do?"

With Peppin pounding on the door, Dr. Ealy hastily bandaged Billy's leg. The doctor and Noah helped the wounded man into the next room and lowered him into the hole in the floor. They handed him a pair of pistols before replacing the boards. The women placed a carpet and a rocking chair over the spot.

With Noah standing watch, Isobel settled into the chair, and Susan took a stool nearby. The two Ealy girls crawled onto their laps.

Taking the Bible from a table, Isobel began to softly read. *"The Lord is my shepherd, I shall not want. He maketh me to lie down in green pastures. He leadeth me beside the still waters. He restoreth my soul."*

Peppin stomped into the room, his boots thudding on the wood floor. "We seen the trail of blood leading to the door, Buchanan, and we aim to find out where Billy Bonney has got to."

"You're wasting your time, Peppin," Noah answered. "My wife is reading the Good Book to calm the children."

Peppin snorted as his deputies began overturning furniture, tossing pillows to the floor, ripping curtains in their search for the Kid. Isobel kissed the cheek of the girl on her lap, and continued.

"Yea, though I walk through the valley of the shadow of death, I will fear no evil, for Thou art with me."

She rocked on the loose floorboards while the intruders tore up the house. If Sue McSween was unhappy with Dolan's men before, Noah realized, she was going to be furious when she saw what they had done to her home.

It was all he could do to stand by while the men smashed china plates, tore velvet upholstery and uprooted ferns. Isobel stroked the little girl's golden hair and kept rocking. As the vandals stormed out of the house, Isobel's voice continued.

"Surely goodness and mercy shall follow me all the days of my life," she read. *"And I shall dwell in the house of the Lord forever."*

The McSweens' home was raided two more times that day in search of Billy the Kid. The final inspection was undertaken by Captain Purington and twenty-five cavalrymen from Fort Stanton. Billy stayed hidden with his six-shooters under the floor, beneath Sue McSween's carpet and the Bible-reading Mrs. Belle Buchanan.

Isobel tried to calm her fears as Noah left to intercept the McSween party as they got to Lincoln. Later, Noah reported that Isaac Ellis, a McSween sympathizer, had put the group up in his house on the outskirts of town. Peppin, Captain Purington and his soldiers wasted no time in arresting McSween on the warrant retrieved from Sheriff Brady's body.

"Mac refused to surrender," he told Isobel that evening

as they sat on a bench on Juan Patrón's back porch. "He said Brady's death canceled Pippin's status as deputy and didn't make him sheriff."

"But you told me Mac turned himself in," she said.

"He surrendered to Captain Purington on the condition they take him to the garrison and hold him in protective custody until court convenes next week."

"Such lawless men, all of them."

"You should have heard the shouting match between Purington and Mac's buddy Dr. Leverson. He's English, but he's got friends in high places. Says he knows the secretary of the interior, Carl Schurz. And he's pals with Rutherford B. Hayes."

"The president of the United States?"

"Yup. Leverson accused Purington of ignoring the Constitution by searching the house without a warrant," Noah explained, chuckling. "Finally the captain cursed the Constitution and Leverson for a fool. So Leverson started urging the soldiers not to obey a captain who would show such contempt for the Constitution. By that time, Purington was mad as a rattler on a hot skillet."

Isobel shook her head. "Everyone in Lincoln is so angry. I'm…I'm afraid, Noah."

He slipped his arm around her and kissed her forehead. "I'm here with you, darlin'. Nothing's going to happen to either of us."

"Who told the Regulators to assassinate the sheriff?"

Noah pondered for a long time. "I don't know. I'd like to think our men are better than that. But, Isobel…I'm just not sure."

"Will it calm down now that the soldiers are here?"

"Captain Purington's got a twelve-pound mountain howitzer and a Gatling gun at Fort Stanton. Fear of him bringing them to town ought to keep folks in line. District court will bring a lot of people to town—people who don't want to get shot at."

Isobel leaned into Noah's embrace. "I don't know where Snake Jackson and my land-grant titles are. I saw two more murders today. That makes six since I came to Lincoln County."

An image of Noah's adobe house filtered through her thoughts. She wondered how the cow and the hens were faring. Would the corn and beans have sprouted in her garden? How high was the river flowing? Had it rained?

Her sigh drew Noah's attention, and he cuddled her closer. "Isobel, I've got my land, and I've got you beside me. I'm not going to let those slip away. Not for anything."

"But what will happen next?"

"This evening when one of the boys sneaked into the McSween's house to fetch Billy out from under the floor, he told me Dick Brewer had called a meeting of the Regulators. Brady was a Dolan man, but he wasn't a bad fellow. The Regulators are going to be unwelcome in Lincoln Town."

"Do you think Dick wants to disband the group?"

"Probably. He's never been a man for violence." Noah brushed a strand of dark gold hair from Isobel's shoulder. "I'd like to hear what he has to say. I trust Dick's judgment. I'd lay down my life for that man."

"Let's go to the meeting," she whispered.

"It's a good safe distance from Lincoln," Noah assured her. "At a place called Blazer's Mill."

* * *

To reach Blazer's Mill, Noah, Isobel and the Regulators rode through friendly territory. Dick Brewer joined them at his farm. As they journeyed west, they picked up five new sympathizers.

Noah and Dick insisted Isobel ride close to them. Dick was furious about Brady's murder. The killing betrayed the true purpose of the Regulators, he said, which was to bring law and order to the county. He wanted to disband the group but the Regulators were still needed.

Members of the posse who had shot John Tunstall roamed loose—at least two hid near the little town of Tularosa, not far from Blazer's Mill. A huge number of Tunstall's cattle had been stolen and driven to San Nicolas Spring near the Organ Mountains. The spring, too, could be reached from Blazer's Mill. Worst of all, Dolan had put a bounty of two hundred dollars on any Regulator. If the group dispersed, bounty hunters could pick them off.

Isobel studied the two men, one slender and finely carved, the other massive, as if hewn from stone. Noah and Dick were notches above the other Regulators. They were clean men, their guns polished, their horses groomed. Both were intelligent and skilled, yet they avoided violence.

As she rode the grassy trail along the Rio Ruidoso, Isobel began to see a picture of the future. At first her thoughts seemed childish, but soon she began to pray her dreams could become real.

She and Noah would live as husband and wife in the adobe house beside the Pecos River. They would own land and run cattle. She saw their children scampering through the front yard or wading in an irrigation ditch… little girls in pigtails…little boys with scuffed knees. A lush garden grew beside the house, rich with peas, beans, corn, chilies. Laundry flapped on a line, the New Mexico sun bleaching the linens a pure, brilliant white. Chickens scratched in the dust. The aroma of *biscochitos* drifted from the kitchen window. Lace curtains billowed in the breeze.

Dick and Susan Brewer would visit, their buckboard full of children. Laughter would fill the house as the families ate together. Isobel and Susan would discuss children and recipes. Noah and Dick would linger on the porch after the little ones had gone to bed. They would speak in low voices about their land and livestock.

"Billy was a good kid till they killed Tunstall," Noah was saying. "Now he's angry, reckless, hotheaded. He never thinks about the future. All he wants is revenge."

Dick glanced behind at the youth—little the worse for the shot that had torn up his leg a few days earlier. "Billy and Tunstall were pals. Tunstall was the first man to accept the Kid and try to help him."

"I'll talk with him after lunch." Noah checked his pocket watch as the group rounded a pile of logs beside the mill, then entered a corral near Dr. Blazer's four-square house. "Maybe I can make him see sense."

Isobel's usual fire-and-ice demeanor seemed to have suddenly melted, Noah noted as they dismounted. She wore a peaceful, faraway gaze. It worried him.

That morning, she had pinned her hair high on her head, all swooped up in curls and waves. Gold tendrils danced around her neck and forehead. Isobel had already earned the Regulators' respect for her shooting and riding. Today her beauty had won their devoted admiration.

Noah grunted. Those poor, female-starved cowboys wouldn't know how to behave around a woman like Isobel. But they flirted and made eyes at her all the same. Some in the bunch were said to be downright handsome. Ladies thought the Kid was a charmer. He could dance better than any man Noah knew, and when he felt like it, he could be amiable—so long as a person didn't stare at those buckteeth and droopy eyes.

Most of the Regulators had been in the woods the night of Noah's wedding and knew it was a sham, but Isobel made it plain she belonged with him. She slept near him each night on the trail. She rode at his side. She followed him with her eyes.

Now, at Blazer's Mill, she was introducing herself to Mrs. Godfroy, the wife of a government agent who rented the house from Dr. Blazer.

"I'm Mrs. Noah Buchanan," Isobel said.

The woman smiled. "Would you and your friends like some dinner?"

Dr. Blazer, a dentist, had leased his house as head-quarters for the Mescalero Indian Agency. Mrs. Godfroy was known for serving a fine meal, and the men looked forward to eating there before hunkering down to talk things over.

They were settling around the table for a meal of stew and cornbread when Noah glanced out the window. A small cloud of dust drifted up from the road the Regulators had just ridden. Now Noah spotted a lone mule and rider—a small man, loaded down with pistols, cartridge belts and rifles. He carried his right arm at an odd angle.

A wash of ice slid down Noah's spine. "Boys, looks like we've got a visitor," he said. "Yonder comes Buck-shot Roberts."

Chapter Fifteen

"Buckshot Roberts was in the posse that shot Tunstall!" Billy Bonney shouted, grabbing his rifle and angling toward the window. The other men pushed away from the table and went for their weapons.

"Roberts is a bounty hunter," the Kid said. "He'll be after that two hundred dollars Dolan put on our hides."

"Hold it, boys!" Dick called. "I've got a warrant for Buckshot's arrest. Let's get him to surrender."

"Surrender," Billy muttered. "I'd rather put a bullet through him."

"Frank, you know Buckshot Roberts pretty well." Noah addressed one of the two Coe brothers. "Why don't you talk to him?"

"No problem." Frank buckled on his six-shooter and left the room.

Noah handed Isobel a Winchester. "Buckshot Roberts is almost too crippled to lift a rifle," he said in a low voice. "But he's fought Indians and Texas Rangers, and he'll stand up to all fifteen of us if he's pushed. I want you to stay close to me."

She nodded, disconcerted to see these armed men in a dither over a single bounty hunter riding a mangy mule. What could one man do against so many?

Frank Coe had begun talking to Buckshot from the porch. Watching from a window, Dick shook his head. "Frank just stepped out of my line of vision. Three of you boys go arrest that little varmint."

Mrs. Godfroy was in a tizzy. "Mr. Brewer, you can't shoot your guns around this place! Those men are standing by a door that leads to Dr. Blazer's storage room. He's got a Springfield and a thousand rounds of ammunition in there."

"Roberts, throw up your hands!" A voice outside the window cut off Mrs. Godfroy's warnings.

"Hold on," Buckshot Roberts shouted back.

A blast of gunfire followed. Mrs. Godfroy screamed. Everyone inside the house raced for the back door. Noah grabbed Isobel's hand and ran behind a water trough near the corral. They crouched there, breathing hard as they loaded their Winchesters.

Isobel peered around the trough and gasped. "Buckshot's wounded!"

Noah jerked her back to cover, his blue eyes flashing. "Careful, Isobel. The man is a deadeye shot."

"But he was hit—his stomach was covered with blood."

"Gut shot." Noah took off his hat and wiped his brow. "He won't last long."

Just then, Charley Bowdre and George Coe dashed around the water trough. "Loco little spitfire!" Bowdre spat. "He drew on me, so I shot him—but he won't quit! He blew off my cartridge belt and mangled George's finger."

Muttering curses, George Coe bound his hand with a bandanna. "Blasted off my trigger finger right at the joint, ornery little—"

"Buckshot hit Billy," Bowdre cut in. "I don't know where he is now."

Isobel peered around the trough at the crippled bounty hunter who had managed to shoot four men. In the doorway to the storage room, he lay stomach down on a bloodstained mattress. His rifle was aimed at the trough.

Perspiration trickled down Isobel's temples as she took cover again. "Dick's coming our way."

As he slid in next to Noah, Dick yanked off his hat. "How many shot here?" he asked.

"Two. George Coe and Bowdre," Noah answered. "They'll live."

"A shot skinned Billy's arm—says it matches the one he took in his leg the other day."

"How's Mrs. Godfroy?" Isobel asked.

"Screaming that Buckshot's in a room full of ammo. I'm going to that stack of logs near the sawmill to get a better look. If I don't talk him into surrendering, he'll die on that mattress."

Noah grabbed Dick's arm. "Let me talk to him."

"I'm leading the Regulators, Noah. I'll do it."

Without waiting, Dick ran in a crouch toward the pile of wood a hundred yards from Buckshot Roberts. Noah handed ammunition to Bowdre, whose gunbelt had been shot off.

"Dick's behind the logs," Isobel reported. "He's trying to get a better look at—"

"No!" Noah roared.

Too late. Dick lifted his head just above the line of

logs. Buckshot took aim and fired. The bullet struck Dick between the eyes, and he toppled over.

"No!" Noah's cry echoed. "No!"

He started for his friend, but Bowdre and Coe dragged him back. Trembling, Isobel sank against the trough.

"He's gone, Noah," Coe barked. "Let's get out of here before Buckshot kills us all."

As he grabbed Isobel's arm with his bloody hand, a hail of slugs splintered the trough, causing water to stream out the holes. As soon as the shooting paused, the three men hustled her toward the corral.

The remaining Regulators were already on their horses. Several men blocked Noah to keep him from heading back to his friend. As the group sped away from the mill, Buckshot continued firing.

"Dick," Noah groaned. "We've left Dick."

"Brewer's dead, Buchanan," Billy Bonney said. "The Godfroys will bury him."

Noah lapsed into silence. But when Isobel gazed at the man she loved, she saw his tears.

For almost two days Noah said nothing. When the Regulators arrived at Dick Brewer's ranch, they gathered on the porch to talk. Isobel joined them, but she noted that Noah sat a short distance away, hat in hand as he studied the ground.

"We need a new leader," Billy declared. "With Dick dead, we got even more reason to blast them Dolan snakes to kingdom come."

"You want to be leader, Kid?"

"Sure!"

A disgruntled muttering followed, then Frank Macnab

spoke up. "I'll put my name in the ring, boys. Everybody knows I'm a cattle detective. Makin' war on rustlers is my job, and the Dolan bunch is no better than a pack of thieves. I reckon I can get myself deputized easier than any of you."

"He's right," Charley Bowdre said. "Macnab is used to trackin' folks down. I'd stick by him as leader."

"Me, too," Frank Coe added.

"Aw, nuts," Billy said, flinging down his hat.

Noah stood. "I'm going to round up Dick's cattle and take them to Chisum's ranch for safekeeping," he said. "I'll cast my lot with Macnab."

"You stickin' with the Regulators, Buchanan?" Bowdre asked. "Nobody'd think you was yeller if you wanted to leave. With Dick gone—"

"With Dick gone, I've got a job to do," Noah spat. "It's called revenge."

Without a glance at Isobel, he stalked off the porch and headed for his horse.

Isobel heard Noah's boots on the porch of Dick Brewer's cabin. After the Regulators left, she baked a batch of biscuits and cooked a thick cream gravy. It wasn't much of a meal, but she knew Noah liked it.

Head down, he entered the front room and hung his lariat on a nail by the door. Without looking at Isobel, he sat on a stool and took off his boots.

"Noah," she tried, his unfamiliar reticence distressing her. "I…I made your supper."

He stepped to the table and sat in one of Dick's rickety chairs. Isobel split the biscuits with a fork and ladled gravy over them.

As he ate, she turned over memories of the first hours they had spent alone together. Here in Dick's cabin, Noah had taught her to wash dishes, their hands touching in the warm, soapy water.

But Dick's death had changed Noah into this unspeaking, angry bull of a man. A man who frightened her.

"Will you have more biscuits?" she asked.

He shoved his plate at her.

"How many days will it take to round up the cattle?" she asked as she filled it.

He chewed a bite so long she thought he wasn't going to answer. Then he lifted his head. "You were right all along. When someone you care about gets killed, you don't stand back and let things take their course. You don't wait for the law. Not in Lincoln County."

"Noah, what are you saying?"

"I'm saying that Dick Brewer got killed—as fine a man as any to walk God's green earth. Buckshot Roberts deserves to die for killing Dick. Jimmie Dolan, Snake Jackson, Jesse Evans—the whole passel of them—deserve to die. And I aim to bring them to justice."

"You mean you'll try to kill all those men yourself?"

"I mean I will kill them." He pushed his plate back and stood. "I understand you, Isobel Matas. Finally, I understand."

He went into the bedroom. Isobel sat at the empty table staring at the chipped plates and blinking away tears. Her vision of a little adobe home on the Pecos faded. The kitchen garden would never bear fruit. There would be no laughing children, no laundry flapping, no *biscochitos* baking. Susan and Dick would never visit. The dream was ashes.

* * *

Dick Brewer had not owned many cattle. Even so, the drive from his place to Chisum's South Spring River Ranch exhausted Noah and Isobel. At night, they took turns sleeping and guarding the herd. During the day, they worked to keep the cattle out of the river and move them east.

Caring for Dick's cattle was the least Noah could do for his friend. After meeting Susan Gates, Dick had told Noah about his desire to raise a ranching family on the vast New Mexico range. He had confided that he hoped every one of his children would have Susan's red hair and gray eyes.

Choking down the knot in his throat that rose every time he thought of Dick, Noah studied Isobel from a distance. Her riding skirt was dusty from days in the saddle. Her white shirtwaist hung loose. The long gold curls that turned men's heads were shoved beneath one of Dick's old hats.

Isobel had buckled on one of Dick's holsters, and her pistol now hung at her thigh. A leather cartridge belt studded with bullets girdled her hips. Noah would have figured her for a tough trail hand if not for the soft glow in her eyes each time she looked at him. Where was her fire?

As they camped each night, she cast sweet smiles Noah's way. Her hands gently spread his blanket on the thick grass. She never tried to make him talk as they sat beside the campfire. Instead she cooked, dusted his Stetson and read aloud from his Bible.

Her tenderness was almost enough to weaken him to the point of shedding tears. But when he lay alone in the dark, he saw Dick rising from behind that stack of logs…a bullet slamming into his forehead…his body jerking backward…crumpling.

No! Dick's death demanded justice, and Noah was the man to deliver it.

Noah and Isobel drove the cattle onto Chisum's spread and left the herd with the hired hands. They found Chisum's square ranch house empty of guests. But Mrs. Towry, the housekeeper, knew all about the shoot-out at Blazer's Mill.

"Buckshot Roberts died the day after you left," she said as they sat on the sofa in Chisum's front room.

"Gut shot," Noah mumbled.

"Major Godfroy and Dr. Blazer sent to Fort Stanton for a doctor. I don't know why they wanted to save that rotten bounty hunter. Dr. Appel drove down from the fort, but it was too late. They buried Buckshot Roberts right beside Dick Brewer."

Noah clenched his teeth to suppress a curse and stared out the window.

Mrs. Towry continued. "Mr. McSween is at Fort Stanton. District court was to start in Lincoln this morning. Everyone thinks Judge Bristol will be staying at the fort for protection. Soldiers will stand guard every day at court. The town should be safe now."

Isobel glanced at Noah. "I'm going to Lincoln," she said. "I want to be there for the trials."

Noah frowned but made no move to dissuade her. "Fine. We'll go."

Mrs. Towry took in a breath. "But Mrs. Buchanan has been on the trail for days with those reckless Regulators. Herding cattle like a common cowboy. It's plain indecent the way you've treated your bride. Why don't you take her home? The fellow who looks after your place told me a coyote got into your chicken coop. Your milk cow got scared and broke loose. Court will go on for weeks, and if I was you, I'd check on my place."

"Well, you're not me, Mrs. Towry," Noah said, standing and slinging his saddlebag over one shoulder. "I have business in Lincoln."

"It is one thing," Isobel said, throwing open the guest-room door, "to mourn your friend. It is quite another to be rude."

"What did you say?" Noah emerged from behind an ornate bamboo screen, his shirt in his hands and his face dripping wet.

"You were impolite to Mrs. Towry." Isobel tried to keep her eyes on his face. "She was trying to help."

"And I was trying to make my point." He stepped back behind the screen. Amid splashing water, she could hear him muttering. "That house is in the past…crazy idea anyway…writing stories and all that nonsense…"

Isobel marched around the screen. Noah was bent over the washstand, scrubbing his hair with soap. Sputtering, he came up for air. As he blindly reached for the towel, his hand inadvertently touched Isobel's shoulder.

She sucked down a gasp. Taking the linen towel from its brass hook, she handed it to him. For a good minute he rubbed his hair and face.

Then he lifted his head to stare at Isobel. Bright blue eyes shone in a face so haggard and tormented her heart ached.

"Noah," she whispered. "What happened to you?"

"The best man I ever knew got a bullet between the

eyes. And now he's buried next to his killer. If you don't think that turns my stomach—"

"Sit down, Noah Buchanan," Isobel cut in, pointing a finger at the chair near the window. "Sit. Now."

"I'm busy."

"Sit!"

Casting her a black look, he obeyed. She drew a fresh linen towel over his shoulders and around his neck, tying it in back.

"What are you—"

"It's time for a haircut," she said. "My husband may act like a barbarian, but he won't look like one."

She rummaged through a drawer until she found a pair of scissors. "When I was a girl," she said, snipping at his sideburns, "I was afraid."

"Afraid of what? You lived on your fancy hacienda with your rich clothes and your rich parents. What was there to be scared of?"

"Many things." She smiled as she drew the comb through his hair and cut the ends. "I was afraid of my horse."

"Your *horse?*"

"Yes, I was terrified of him. One day my father took me aside and brushed away my tears. He said, 'Isobel, *mija,* you must change your fear into anger. Anger will make you strong. And with that strength, you will control your horse.'"

She snipped the back of Noah's hair. "From that time, I hid my fear behind the curtain of anger. No one, nothing, could frighten me. I have pursued revenge with that anger—never letting anyone see my fear."

"Are you afraid of Snake Jackson, Isobel?"

"I'm afraid of losing the ones I love."

He reached up and took the hand that held the comb. "You lost your father. I lost Dick. You hide your fear. I hide my pain. What's so bad about that kind of anger, Isobel?"

She searched his bright blue eyes. "Once a man taught me that there was more to life than fear and pain and anger," she said. "That man showed me how to laugh at bubbles in dishwater. How to weep over a beautiful story. He taught me that God loves me…that because the Lord is my shepherd, I need fear no evil. That His Spirit comforts me—even in the valley of the shadow of death. Because of you, Noah, I am learning how to really live."

He stood suddenly, knocking back the chair as he moved away from her to the window. Isobel watched as he leaned an arm against the sill, his fist clenched.

Stepping to his side, she laid her hand on his back and ran her palm down the taut muscles. He let out a breath and turned to her, his eyes red.

"That man died, Isobel," he whispered in a hoarse voice. "The moment that bullet hit Dick Brewer's forehead, the old Noah Buchanan died. Buckshot Roberts's bullet blew away that part of me. I feel anger now, nothing else."

"Come, Noah," she said, taking his hands and drawing him near. "Let me remind you of other things."

Isobel shut her eyes as their lips touched. He kissed her cheek, her neck, and she felt protected in his arms. "Noah, we could be so good together."

She slipped her arms around him, but when her fingers threaded through his hair, he stiffened and pushed her away.

"No, Isobel," he growled, his eyes icy, distracted. "I can't. I've got things to tend to."

Pushing away from her, he strode across the room. She heard the door slam as she stood alone, needing her husband.

Chapter Sixteen

On the long ride to Lincoln, Isobel pondered her future. Though she knew Dick Brewer's murder had changed the silent man who rode at her side, she had no doubt that deep in his heart Noah would remain the same. The intense pain he felt over the loss of his friend proved that his gentle nature had not been erased.

"I've been considering," he said as they neared Lincoln. He hadn't spoken more than a few words for three days, and his declaration surprised Isobel.

"What have you considered?" she asked.

"I think it's time we ended our arrangement."

She tried to squelch the dismay that rose inside her. "Why is that?"

"We've pretty much wound things up. I helped you find the name of your father's killer. I protected you from Snake Jackson and the others. You can't testify against Evans and Snake, because the Regulators didn't name you as an eyewitness in their first report. So you're off the hook on that. District court will put an end to Lincoln's troubles. Dolan might go free because of his connections in Santa Fe, but his men will wind up behind bars."

"And I helped you get the land you wanted from John Chisum. So our contract is fulfilled."

"Reckon so."

Isobel nodded, but inside she felt frantic to sort out the real meaning behind Noah's words. Did he want to be rid of her? Did all that had passed between them mean nothing? Or did he love her and fear for her safety as he carried out his plan to avenge Dick Brewer's death?

"What will you do now?" she asked. "Continue as Chisum's trail boss?"

He scowled at the sun-dappled road. "You know what I'll be doing."

"Buckshot Roberts is dead. What more do you want, Noah?"

"I want to bring Jimmie Dolan down."

"Will you ambush him on the street like the Kid did Sheriff Brady? Will you become a bounty hunter like Buckshot Roberts?"

"I'll do whatever it takes, Isobel. Dick wouldn't let Tunstall's death rest. I'm not going to let Dick's death rest. And the man behind both murders is Jimmie Dolan."

"What's to become of me while you wreak your revenge?"

"Look, I didn't take on your entire future the night I married you, Isobel. We struck a temporary bargain. Do whatever you want."

"Then I shall ride with you in pursuit of Jimmie Dolan."

"No, you won't!" He whirled on her, his blue eyes flashing. "I've already lost Dick, and I'm not going to lose…" He bit off his words. "Stay at McSween's house through the trials. Susan Gates will be in a fix over losing Dick. She'll need comforting."

"And what about you, Noah?"

"I don't need your comforts, Isobel. You saw that three days ago."

"Three days ago, I saw a man whose best friend had been murdered. One day you'll wish me near."

"No, I won't. If I need a woman, I'll find one with no strings attached. I don't want to be tangled, Isobel."

"And I tangle you."

"Yes, you do."

"So, you will throw away your stories, take down the lace curtains, let the kitchen garden go to weeds. Those days with me meant nothing. You'll forget our laughter, my burned eggs, the typewriter—"

"Don't. Just don't talk about that, Isobel. I don't want to hear it."

"You said you wanted to make our marriage real. You took me to Chisum's house to buy land for us."

"That was before Dick got killed." He reined his horse and studied her, his eyes dark. "I'm sorry I steered you wrong, Isobel. Sorry I made you think there could be a future for us…like I was good for you."

"You are good for me."

"No. You don't know what kind of people I come from. I told you about Mrs. Allison and her library. But my daddy was a gambler. He left after I was born. My mother sold herself to keep food in our bellies. Then she died of a fever and left all us kids orphans. I'm no better than Snake Jackson. His folks left him an orphan, too. It was only the luck of the draw that got me on as a stable hand with the Allisons."

"Luck? Don't you mean God? Didn't He put you with Mrs. Allison? Are you not the man who reads the Bible and prays each day? The man God shaped to write 'Sunset at Coyote Canyon'? Who was that man, if not you?"

"But I've got my daddy's roving blood, Isobel. I'm a wanderer. Chisum didn't want to sell me land because he thought I couldn't sit still long enough to care for it. I may have fooled you into thinking I was a good man, but the truth is, I've got an outlaw's heart."

Isobel blinked at the tears blurring her vision of Lincoln's dusk-shrouded road. So this was how Noah would end their union.

"It is your choice," she told him. "I am now both Isobel Matas and Belle Buchanan. You are a good man and a rootless drifter. Neither of us can continue to be both. We must choose. Choose well, Noah."

Lest he see the tears that spilled down her cheeks, Isobel dug her heels into her horse's sides and rode for the home of Alexander McSween.

When Isobel arrived, she found Susan Gates very ill. Dick Brewer's death had come as a terrible shock, and nothing Dr. Ealy had tried helped.

While Isobel wept with her friend, she cried her heart out to God. How could Noah let her go so easily? How could he turn his back on what they had begun to build? *La venganza* was not worth such sacrifice.

Days passed, and Isobel saw nothing of Snake Jackson or the wounded Jesse Evans and their bunch. Though the town swarmed with people, she often escaped to sit beside her father's grave. Don Alberto Matas really had died, she accepted finally. She would never see his golden hair or hear his laughter again.

Hoping to catch a glimpse of Noah, she stopped at the courthouse several times. He was nowhere to be seen in the crowded room.

Isobel breathed a sigh of relief when district court concluded on April 18, and that evening Dr. Ealy brought a summary of the news. Most of the trials, he said, had turned in favor of the McSween faction. For the killing of John Tunstall, indictments had been brought against Jesse Evans, Jim Jackson and several others as principals, along with Jimmie Dolan as accessory. But of the principals, only Jesse Evans could be found. He was put under a five-thousand-dollar bond. Dolan was arrested and placed under a two-thousand-dollar bond. The judge continued his case.

For the killing of Sheriff Brady and his deputy, four indictments had been handed down—all to Regulators. For the killing of Buckshot Roberts, only Charley Bowdre had been indicted. Since neither Bowdre nor any other Regulators were to be found, no arrests could be made. The sheriff held the warrants.

Alexander McSween was cleared of criminal charges, and Fort Stanton released him. The grand jury indicted Jimmie Dolan for encouraging cattle stealing.

Sitting in a rocker beside Susan's bed later that evening, Isobel recognized that Noah's prediction of peace in Lincoln had come to pass at last. But when someone began hammering on the back door, she tensed, remembering the day she had helped hide Billy the Kid under that very floor.

Dr. Ealy opened the door. "Noah Buchanan—good to see you again!"

Noah stepped into the room and swept off his black Stetson. "I need to talk to Isobel," he said. His focus flicked to her. "Would you step outside for a minute?"

Isobel glanced at Susan. The ache in her friend's face mirrored what she saw in Noah's. Taking her white shawl from the peg by the door, she stepped onto the back porch and looked up at the sliver of moon hanging just over the roofline.

"I'm riding for Santa Fe tomorrow morning," Noah said. "If you want, I'll take you to the Pascals'."

Isobel ached to feel Noah's arms around her. But she saw that his intentions toward her had not changed.

"Why Santa Fe?" she asked him.

"This afternoon, Dolan left Lincoln headed that way. Rumor has it he's planning to talk to Governor Axtell and Tom Catron, the U.S. district attorney for the territory. Catron holds a lot of property mortgages and loans around these parts. Axtell and Catron are both in the Santa Fe Ring, and if Dolan gets their help, he can turn things to his favor pretty quick."

"And you mean to stop him?"

"Legally, if I can. If not…" He shrugged.

"Why must you be the one to pursue Dolan?" she asked. "Billy is always hot for blood. Let him do it."

"The Regulators are in hiding, and nobody's after me. Besides, I know how to talk to men like Catron."

Isobel pondered the painful consequences of riding with Noah again, bearing his rejection day and night. And what of Guillermo Pascal? Her betrothed had never responded to the telegram sent so long ago. Surely he would not want Isobel to appear on his doorstep like some windblown beggar.

But when she looked into Noah's blue eyes she heard herself whisper, "Yes. I will go with you to Santa Fe."

The sun had not risen when Isobel rode through Lincoln Town at the side of Noah Buchanan.

"Don't let him get away from you," Susan had whispered as she had hugged her friend goodbye. "He's a fine man."

But what good had it done Susan to fall in love, Isobel wondered. Dick Brewer had been killed as easily as Noah might be. Now Susan had to live with loss for the rest of her life.

Loss and rejection seemed to hound the women of Lincoln County. It would not be long before Isobel had to face the rebuff of Guillermo Pascal and his family. She could no longer deny her land grants had been lost forever. She would return to Catalonia with nothing but heartache to show for all her months in New Mexico.

Yet—against all better judgment—Isobel loved Noah Buchanan. She knew she could live without him. She also knew she didn't want to. God had given her one week in which to win the heart of her husband. Would He help her mend the rifts between them?

Noah chose a difficult passage over the mountains to Santa Fe. He hoped Jimmie Dolan might have opted for a longer but safer route up the Pecos River. If Noah had his way, he would beat the Irishman to the capital and speak with Catron first.

Climbing the mountainous trail with Isobel only a few feet behind gave Noah time to think. He wasn't sure what had driven him to the McSween house to propose such a venture. The moment he had stepped through the front door and had seen Isobel sitting on the rocker by Susan's bed, he knew he ought to back right out the door and run.

Great stars, she had looked beautiful that night! Waves of golden hair had hung shimmering over her shoulders. She must have sewn a new dress, a pink confection with ruffles at the wrists and around the neck.

On seeing him, she had risen from the rocker with her hazel eyes shining. When he had taken her out in the moonlight, it had been all he could do to keep from gathering her up in his arms and kissing her the way he wanted to.

He turned around now to check on her. She wore fancy Spanish riding clothes—a black outfit that covered her neck and swung down to her boots. She had swept her hair up into a tight knot high on the back of her head.

But Isobel was no *marquesa* on this ride. Around her waist hung a belt studded with a row of bullets. Dick Brewer's old hat dipped low on her brow, and she looked ready for battle.

Letting out a breath, Noah focused on the winding trail. He had to force away memories of their days in the little adobe house by the river. He had to forget the letter that had come to him in Lincoln saying his story had been passed to a magazine editor in New York.

There was no room for dreams in the real world, and he'd better not forget it. For too many years he had believed people were better than they were. He had prayed for a peaceful future. He had expected to become a writer.

Nonsense, all of it. It had taken the death of his best friend to show him. People were liars, cheaters, murderers. A man in the West could bet his bottom dollar a bullet would put him in the grave.

It was no good getting attached, Noah reasoned—especially not to a pretty Spaniard who made a fellow lose sight of the facts. He clenched his jaw and made up his mind he could last one week on the trail alone with Isobel and not get tangled. He had to.

With the help of the Good Lord, he would keep his mind on the job at hand—bringing Dolan down. He had to resist taking Isobel into his arms…and into his heart.

On the first day of May, 1878, Noah and Isobel caught a glimpse of the Pascal hacienda. As they approached the house in the rolling foothills of the Sangre de Cristo Mountains, Noah struggled to swallow the lump of grit in his throat. The Pascal spread was a grand affair—much grander than his ramshackle home and milk cow. This house had a roof of red tiles and a deep, shady porch. From its perch on a pole near a flowering lilac bush, a green parrot eyed the two riders.

Sleek black horses pranced for their trainers in a nearby corral. Fat cattle, belly-deep in green grass, dotted the foothills. Caballeros in leather chaps and wide-brimmed hats rode among the herds.

As Isobel and Noah dismounted, a man in a blue uniform greeted them.

"I've brought Isobel Matas," Noah explained. "The Pascals are expecting her. I sent a wire from Lincoln almost two months back."

The man's dark eyes swept up and down, taking in Isobel's dusty riding clothes, pistol and battered felt hat.

With a taut smile, he extended a hand. "Won't you come inside?"

Isobel waited on the sofa in a grand salon while Noah paced, his hat swinging in his hand. Through large glass windows he studied the hills. Then he focused on the interior of the elegant home.

"Looks like your dream's about to come true." He halted, his deep voice echoing off the wooden vigas on the ceiling.

"The Pascals have a fine home," Isobel noted.

"I expect you'll be happy. I'll send your furniture and trunks—if you still want them."

She fiddled with the string that bound her holster to her thigh. "How long will you stay in Santa Fe?"

"Don't worry about me. I'll be busy bringing Dolan down…and getting our marriage annulled." He started pacing again. "Just do your best to get this fellow to keep his end of the bargain he made with your father."

"Are you so eager to be rid of me?"

His eyes darted to her face. There was a moment of silence as each gazed at the other.

"This was the plan, wasn't it?" Noah said. "I was to take you safely to your fancy don."

Isobel stood. "But, Noah, that was before—"

"Buenas tardes. Good afternoon." The chocolate-rich voice drew their attention to the doorway. Tall, with slick black hair, a thin mustache and crackling brown eyes, Don Guillermo Pascal removed his hat and gave the slightest of bows.

"Señorita Matas," he said. "What a lovely surprise."

Noah took a long look at the man who soon would be Isobel's husband. And a dandy he was. He wore a brown suede suit with black leather trim and rows of buttons. At his hip hung a pistol with a carved ivory handle. Every inch of his holster and gun belt had been tooled. And on his feet gleamed the shiniest pair of pointed-toe boots Noah had ever seen.

He glanced down at his own leather boots, crusted with dried mud and worn down at the heels. His denims had been washed hundreds of times and were threadbare to prove it. The cuffs of his chambray shirt had frayed so badly there was no point mending them. A layer of dust had coated his hat, and his duster smelled of saddle leather and old horseflesh.

Don Guillermo glided toward Isobel and took her hand. Lifting it to his lips, he placed a kiss on her fingertips.

She smiled.

When the Spaniard lifted his head and saw that flash of white teeth and those full lips, Noah knew right off Isobel had won her man. His eyes sparkling, Don Guillermo bent for a second kiss.

"*Cariña,* you must be exhausted from your journey," he said. "I'll order a servant to prepare your room. You must bathe and refresh yourself before dinner."

Isobel tipped her head.

"You may go, *señor,*" he told Noah. "Señorita Matas will have no further need of your services."

With that he stepped through the door, boot heels ringing sharp *rat-a-tats* on the tile floor.

Noah fixed his eyes on Isobel. Her high cheekbones held a flush that told him she'd been pleased by the attentions of the elegant *señor.* He tried to squelch the image of the man ever touching Isobel again. His prickly mustache poking into her lip as he kissed her. His long, thin fingers toying with her hair.

"Noah—"

"Isobel—"

Their words overlapped. She cleared her throat. He stuffed his Stetson on his head and crossed his arms over his chest.

"You will leave me here?" she said. It was more a plea than a question.

He walked to the door. "Take care, Isobel."

As he crossed the long hall, Noah passed a woman who must have been Guillermo's mother, hurrying to meet their guest. A black lace mantilla billowed behind her.

"*¡Ah, Señorita Matas—que bonita!*" the woman cried. "*¡Bienvenidos, cariña!*"

Noah hightailed it to his horse and rode away, thinking how glad he was to have Isobel off his hands. Yes, sir. No looking out for somebody else's skin. No wild-goose chases after Snake Jackson.

He had to admit they'd had a good time together, all in all. The cowboy and the *señorita*. Memories filtered through his mind—the first moment he saw her in that new blue dress, the night she slipped off her horse into his arms, the way she typed page after page of his story, the hours she spent working that kitchen garden, the way she fit so perfectly against him as he held her....

But she was where she'd always wanted to be—with her rich Spaniard instead of some old dusty...what had she called him?...vaquero.

Isobel didn't need to be out riding the trail, hiding from bad hombres like Snake Jackson and sleeping under the stars. She deserved a fine hacienda, fat cattle, fiestas. She deserved a man like Guillermo Pascal.

Noah reined his horse and looked over his shoulder at the hacienda. He would never forget the woman he loved.

Chapter Seventeen

Doña María Pascal gave her eldest son the privilege of showing their visitor around the house and grounds. Isobel searched in vain for any sign of Noah as she walked down a flagstone path lined with blossoming red roses.

When Don Guillermo extended a hand to assist her over a bridge, she had no choice but to take it. Tucking her arm through his, he drew her close.

"So you came all the way from Catalonia?" he asked.

Isobel nodded. "A telegram was sent from Lincoln. I've been in New Mexico more than two months."

"But *cariña,* you should have come directly to Santa Fe. If I had known—"

"Known what?" she retorted, losing patience. "You knew my father had been murdered and the land-grant titles stolen. My mother sent a letter saying I was traveling to New Mexico—so you knew that, also. What did you not know, *señor?*"

"We speak honestly, I see." He took a breath. "Very well, *señorita.* I did not know you were so beautiful."

The honest avowal caught her off guard. "How can my appearance possibly matter in this situation?"

"It matters very much. To me." Stroking his narrow black mustache, he eyed her. "At my father's death, I became the head of our family, and I lack nothing. Your land appealed to me when your father offered it as part of the betrothal agreement. But I've acquired much property since. If I regain your titles—and I have no doubt that I can—I will absorb the land into my own. The jewels, of course, are of value, as well. Land, jewels… these I have in plenty. But women are scarce in this rough land."

"Especially beautiful women?"

He smiled. "You are a beautiful woman with a quick mind. Our fathers were wise to have arranged our marriage."

"You intend to follow through with it, Don Guillermo?"

"Only time will tell, Señorita Matas."

In the following days, Isobel spent much of each day nosing through local newspapers. Don Guillermo had little patience for her preoccupation with reading and marking the latest events in Lincoln County. If she didn't participate in the activities of the estate, he informed her, he would have the newspapers removed from the house.

Isobel did her best to behave as a future doña in the *familia* Pascal. After all, she had once made a marriage of convenience—why not again? But the answer was obvious. She had grown to love Noah Buchanan with a passion she knew could never be matched. Even so, she wrote a letter to Dr. Ealy, asking where he had registered the hasty marriage and how she might end it with equal quickness.

Guillermo Pascal was not unpleasant, she admitted to herself. His appearance was tolerable. His manners were impeccable. But what attraction could she possibly feel for this self-absorbed, shallow man?

And so, reading the *Cimarron News Press*, she wept over the memorial Alexander McSween had written for Dick Brewer. His glowing praise reminded her of the deep loss Noah and Susan had suffered.

Editorials in the *Santa Fe New Mexican,* the *Trinidad Enterprise and Chronicle* and the *Mesilla Independent* volleyed the situation in Lincoln County back and forth—some writers favoring Dolan, others praising the bravery of McSween and the Regulators.

Jimmie Dolan began to defend himself in the newspapers. Isobel felt his whining letters only revealed his many weaknesses.

A short notice buried in the *New Mexican* brought her hope for Noah's case against Dolan. James J. Dolan & Co. was temporarily shuttering its mercantile in Lincoln due to unstable conditions. Was it possible the outcome in the district court had driven the tyrant from the county?

More good news came when Alexander McSween wrote that he had been authorized by John Tunstall's father in England to offer a reward of five thousand dollars for the apprehension and conviction of his son's murderers. Isobel knew this would improve the reputation of the Regulators, even though they themselves had been outlawed. Bounty hunters would set their sights on Snake Jackson and the rest of Dolan's bunch.

When Guillermo left the hacienda to look after his

properties in Santa Fe, Doña María began joining Isobel on the patio. At first they simply enjoyed the sunshine and fresh air wafting down from the Sangre de Cristos. But soon the elder woman began leafing through newspapers, too.

"This cannot be good for the Regulators," Doña María commented one afternoon as she was browsing the *Cimarron News and Press*. "They're killing again in Lincoln County."

"Who died?" Isobel craned to read the news over the doña's shoulder.

"Somebody shot a man at the Fritz ranch on the Rio Bonito—Frank Macnab."

"Macnab was the leader of the Regulators! Who shot him?"

"The Seven Rivers Gang—from the Rio Pecos."

Isobel tried to breathe. More men had joined the Dolan forces. And they'd murdered Frank Macnab, leaving the Regulators leaderless again.

"Oh, more trouble here," Doña María said, trailing a finger down the text as she read. "George Coe shot one of the Dolan bunch. It says the Fort Stanton soldiers have returned to Lincoln to keep order, and the Seven Rivers men surrendered to them."

"Is Captain Purington holding them at the fort?"

"Colonel Dudley runs the garrison now." The doña turned to Isobel. "You were in Lincoln. Do you favor Dolan or McSween?"

"McSween is good and honest," Isobel answered. "He carries no gun and tries to make peace. Jimmie Dolan used his mercantile to cheat the United States government so badly his business was banished from Fort Stanton. Now he plays games of deceit on the landowners. His men are murderers and thieves."

The old woman leaned forward, brown eyes sparkling. "It's like a bullfight, yes? One strong and brave struggling against another, also strong and brave. Who will win?"

"I don't know, Doña María."

"Together we watch this bullfight, Señorita Matas."

Isobel nodded, feeling the first spark of companionship since her arrival. "We watch together."

The doña laughed and clapped her hands. "*¡Olé!*"

Isobel enjoyed sitting with the matriarch on the portal. But she soon saw that her dreams of helping run the Pascal hacienda were impossible.

No one in the family would hear of her riding out to see the cattle. She was kept inside, fed, pampered and clothed by the finest dressmakers in Santa Fe. She spent the days with the doña—stitching and playing cards.

But no matter how hard she tried to play the dutiful betrothed, she could not erase Noah Buchanan from her heart. Was he still in Santa Fe? Surely not after all this time. What had become of his quest for justice against Jimmie Dolan?

Almost a month had passed since Noah had ridden away from the Pascal hacienda. The newspapers never mentioned his name. Susan Gates wrote to Isobel twice, but she said nothing about the cowboy.

Dr. Ealy sent a letter saying he had registered the Matas-Buchanan marriage with Squire Wilson. When Governor Axtell had voided Wilson's appointment as justice of the peace, it had complicated matters. Wilson was still recovering from his wounds, but he had assured

Dr. Ealy that he would find a way to look back through the records and see what could be done to quickly annul the union.

Feeding sunflower seeds to the green parrot one morning at the end of May, Isobel heard someone join her on the portal. She supposed it was Doña María, for they always sat together at this time of day to read and chat.

Over the weeks, Isobel had weighed her options and decided to return to Spain. After Dr. Ealy confirmed the dissolution of her marriage to Noah, she would rejoin her family as a confirmed *soltera*, a spinster. She had chosen that day to tell the doña about her plan, so she was surprised when Don Guillermo touched her arm.

"Señorita," he said.

She gasped. "Oh, *señor*, you startled me."

"Forgive me, but I must speak with you about our betrothal." He folded his hands behind his back. "I have contacted territorial officials in Santa Fe regarding your family's stolen land titles. It should be little trouble to restore them."

"But my family was told the thief had started transferal proceedings. How have you settled it so easily?"

"I have connections, *cariña*." He gave her a small smile. "I have found it agreeable that we should wed. The ceremony will take place at the end of three weeks."

"Three weeks!"

"Have no concern, Isobel. I have arranged everything. The food, the entertainment, your gown, the church. The first banns were published in this morning's newspaper. You and my mother, I am certain, will peruse the announcement at your leisure."

"But what about my family? My mother?"

"I have written to confirm the details," he continued. "My mother is amenable to the union, as are my brothers."

"And what about me?" Isobel said. "Did you ask for my consent, Don Guillermo?"

"You gave your consent five years ago when you agreed to the betrothal. You confirmed it the day you walked through my door."

Isobel looked away. "Five years was a long time ago. I admit, I have come to care for your mother and your family. Once, becoming your bride was the summit of my aspirations. But, since coming here, I have had time to consider my future. I intend to return to Spain."

"Spain? Certainly not! I won't allow it. Our families signed a betrothal agreement. I have begun proceedings of land transfer from your name to mine. The wedding is arranged, *señorita,* and you will marry me."

"That's not much of a proposal, Pascal."

The deep voice from behind a boxwood hedge startled Isobel.

"Noah?" She caught her breath as the cowboy rounded the hedge.

"Don't draw your gun, *señor.*" Noah leveled his own six-shooter at the Spaniard.

"What is the meaning of this?" Don Guillermo demanded.

"I've come for Isobel."

"Señorita Matas is my betrothed. She will go nowhere."

"I hate to break it to you, but Isobel is my wife. Mrs. Buchanan, to you. I married her the day we met—February eighteenth, 1878, three months ago."

Guillermo turned on Isobel. "Perhaps you can explain what this man is—"

"I've come for you, Isobel," Noah cut in. "We've got urgent business in Lincoln County."

Isobel could hardly speak in the presence of this man she had believed she would never see again. "What happened?" she managed.

"Seems like snakes are always after you, sweetheart."

Speaking to Isobel, Noah holstered his gun, but his blue eyes never left Guillermo's face. "Tom Catron—one of the territory's biggest snakes himself—let slip a little fact the other day while we were chatting. Seems his district attorney's office has been working on behalf of the Pascal family to secure a packet of stolen land-grant titles from a fellow named Jim Jackson."

"Snake?" Isobel's eyes darted to Don Guillermo.

"A couple of years back," Noah explained, "Snake Jackson went to Jimmie Dolan and told him he had the Matas family's Spanish land-grant titles. Dolan took the matter to his pal Catron in Santa Fe. Catron approached the Pascals to see if things could be done under the table in a way that could benefit everyone. Don Guillermo could buy off Catron, Dolan and Snake, get the land he wanted and never have to get hitched to a spinster. I'm told he's been known to enjoy the company of many women."

"But I came to New Mexico and upset your plans," Isobel said to Guillermo. "Then you decided you liked me well enough, after all."

Noah grunted. "Pascal realized he could marry you, get the titles legally and cut the other men out of the deal. With his connections inside the ring, he knew he wouldn't have much trouble."

"The ring?" Doña María's voice was shrill across the garden. "What ring is that?"

"It's nothing, *mamá.*" Don Guillermo held out a hand to keep his mother back. "A little business between Señor Buchanan and myself."

"Business?" Embroidery bag in one hand and newspapers in the other, the doña elbowed past her son to face Noah. "Speak frankly, *señor.* I've heard many rumors about this ring. What do you know?"

"Your son is a member of the Santa Fe Ring, doña," Noah said. "He's in with Governor Axtell, Tom Catron and the other scalawags trying to own New Mexico. Guillermo has doubled the Pascal family land holdings since your husband's death, ma'am. These days, nobody gets land in the territory so easily without connections."

Isobel glared at Guillermo as she recalled his words to her minutes before, *I have connections, cariña.*

The doña's eyes narrowed at Noah. "You accuse my son of illegal dealings, vaquero."

"He's a liar, *mamá,*" Guillermo interjected. "The fool even claims to have married Señorita Matas!"

Doña María turned to Isobel. "Who is this man?"

Isobel knew she could deny everything Noah had said. She could marry Don Guillermo and have her hacienda, horses, gardens, fiestas. Her children would be of pure Spanish blood, a proud dynasty.

Then she looked into the cowboy's blue eyes.

"Noah Buchanan speaks the truth," she admitted softly. "He is my husband. For my protection, we wed in haste. I came here planning to marry your son, but now I understand who he really is. I shall return to Spain."

"But the wedding? And my grandchildren? And what about our newspapers, *mija?*"

"You have been good to me, Doña María," Isobel said, kissing her gently on each cheek. "I thank you."

Her heart lighter than it had been in many weeks, Isobel lifted her skirts and started for the stables. It seemed that God had heard her prayers and chosen to smile upon her after all.

"I made appointments with Governor Axtell and District Attorney Catron," Noah was saying as he and Isobel sat on a blanket beside a flickering campfire. "Then I took a room at a hotel and began to write."

"Another story?"

"An argument against James J. Dolan." Noah paused for a moment, recalling how with each stroke of his pen he had tried to force his longing for Isobel deep inside his heart—with the hope it would stay hidden forever.

"I kept after Catron every day," he continued, "until he agreed to look into Dolan's finances. The more he dug, the more he saw the extent of Dolan's business troubles."

Isobel shook her head. "One man betrayed so many."

"Turns out Catron was endorsing Dolan's notes to the tune of more than twenty thousand dollars. Now Dolan is deeply in debt to the district attorney. A few months back, he mortgaged all his property to Catron as security for the notes, and he got a new note for twenty-five thousand dollars. This month he took out a second mortgage."

"So Dolan's mercantile is bankrupt?" Isobel said. "The man is ruined?"

"Catron was trying to keep him afloat so he wouldn't be saddled with the debts. But Dolan shut down his store, and he's been barred from making deliveries of flour and beef to the Mescalero agency. I reckon if he leaves Lincoln County, broke and defeated, I'll feel like Dick's death has been avenged."

"I'm happy for you, Noah."

He shrugged, realizing nothing could fill the place Dick Brewer had held in his life.

"I read that Macnab was killed," she spoke up.

"Yeah, sad to say. I'm hoping Dolan's bunch will disband and things will settle down in Lincoln. It's what I was trying to accomplish all the time I was in Santa Fe."

"It seems you were successful."

"I nearly let you marry Pascal." Noah flipped a twig into the fire. "When I read the wedding announcement in the paper this morning, I couldn't sit still. I'd already found out enough about Pascal to hook him into the ring. I deduced he was the silent partner Catron said was planning to take your land grants. 'Course, I didn't know for sure till I bluffed him this morning."

"That was a bluff?"

Noah shrugged. "A good guess."

"Noah, why didn't you leave me with the Pascals?"

He stared at the fire awhile before answering. "I couldn't let you marry Pascal, Isobel. You deserve better."

"What sort of man do I deserve, Noah?"

"Maybe you'll find a decent fellow when you get back to Spain."

"In Spain I will be a *soltera,* a spinster. When people learn I broke the Pascal betrothal, my name will be dishonored. Don Guillermo will spread the story of my rash marriage to a common vaquero. Even with an annulment, I will be too old to marry."

Noah couldn't imagine any man in his right mind turning Isobel down. Not one thing about her failed to move him. Her hair lying dark gold on her shoulders. Her smooth neck. Long arms. Long legs.

But there was more to Isobel than beauty. He'd almost forgotten how easily they could talk. She made him laugh and think and create and dream. He loved everything about the woman.

But how did she feel about him? He had given her no promises, no tender words of commitment, no hope for a future with him. Then he had abandoned her to the Pascals.

She might not want to spend her life with a man who still felt his friend's death like a knife in his gut. If Dolan somehow rode out his troubles, Noah couldn't let the matter go. Nothing would change that.

"Now that your *venganza* against Jimmie Dolan is accomplished, how will it be between you and me, Noah?" Isobel asked in a soft voice. "Will it be as before—at home by the Rio Pecos? Or will you drive me away again?"

"Isobel…" It was more a sigh than a word. "Great stars, you make things hard on a man."

"And you make things hard on a woman."

Their eyes met and held. "What do you want?" he asked. "Do you want to try to get your titles from Snake before Pascal gets his hands on them? Do you want to own your own spread up here in the north? Do you want to go back to Spain and live a quiet life, away from all the guns and killing?"

When she didn't answer, he spoke the final option. "Or do you want to be hooked up with a dusty cowboy who can't even promise you a tomorrow?"

Isobel gazed at the fire. "I may never live happily ever after. But I want to live happily today."

"Come here, Isobel." He took her hand and drew her into his arms. "You know, I made a fine show of myself in Santa Fe. Bought some fancy duds, ate good food, slept on clean sheets. Every day I worked to whittle Jimmie Dolan's empire into pieces."

"Were you happy?"

"I was miserable. Walked around looking like a throw-out from a footsore remuda." He shook his head. "I thought revenge would feel good."

"But you taught me how foolish it was to try to steal vengeance from the hand of God. I gave up my quest just as you began your own."

"We've taught each other an awful lot." He slid one hand up her arm. He hadn't touched a woman since leaving her with Pascal. All his desires seemed dead—killed along with Dick Brewer.

Sure, women had made eyes at him in Santa Fe. But he loved Isobel. Only Isobel.

Now, holding her, he felt a rush of need stronger than he'd ever known. Something inside his soul longed to connect with hers. A spiritual ache had resurfaced the moment he had seen her that morning, standing in the garden in Santa Fe.

"Noah," she murmured as she snuggled against him. "I couldn't let Guillermo Pascal come near me. It was impossible for me to think of any man but you."

"The minute I saw your name on that wedding announcement, I grabbed my saddlebag. Didn't give it a second thought. Just got on my horse and headed out to fetch you. I had to have you with me again."

"I don't know how I once thought of you as a common man. Each day I was alone, I ached for you."

"I love you," he whispered, kissing her lips, slipping his fingers into her hair. This was the union, the bonding, the oneness he needed.

"I love you, too," she whispered against his ear.

"I'll stay with you, Isobel. Rain or shine, darlin', you're mine."

Chapter Eighteen

On the journey from Santa Fe to Lincoln, Noah's desire to write came back in a flood. He spent two nights guarding Isobel and roughing out a story on paper he had tucked into his saddlebag. A young orphan boy, a hungry wolf, marauding Apaches, twists and turns. When he read it to Isobel, she declared it even better than his Coyote Canyon tale.

Their final day's ride took them to the little town of White Oaks. While Noah tended the horses, Isobel stopped at the mercantile, where she hoped to learn news of Lincoln from the shopkeeper. She was looking at a length of yellow calico when Noah stepped into the store.

"Isobel, come with me. Now." Taking her arm, he ushered her quickly to the back door.

"Noah? What's wrong?"

"I spotted Dolan at the feed store," he explained as they mounted their horses. "He's back in Lincoln County. And he's brought the Kinney Gang with him. Follow me—and stay close."

When they were safely into a thicket of aspen

trees, Noah pulled his horse to a halt. Isobel drew up beside him.

"Who's Kinney?" she asked.

"Cattle thief, murderer, robber. Roams the Rio Grande Valley—mostly around El Paso. John Kinney is ten times meaner than Jesse Evans or Snake Jackson. Looks like Dolan hired the Kinney Gang to do his dirty work."

Her heart faltering, Isobel lifted up a silent prayer for guidance. Did Dolan's return mean that Noah's efforts to ruin him had failed? Would the man she loved set her aside again in his pursuit of vengeance?

"Let's go back to Santa Fe, Noah," she begged. "We should stay out of the trouble this time."

He took off his hat and wiped his sleeve across his brow. "I have to get to Lincoln and warn McSween. With Peppin as sheriff, Dolan back in town and the Kinney bunch roaming the county, things could get bad for the Regulators."

He slapped his hat against his thigh. "Blast this whole ugly mess!"

Isobel's shoulders drooped as her dreams sifted away. Noah was staring up through the trees at a patch of sky, as if waiting for God to speak. Finally he put on his hat and turned to her. "I'll take you to Chisum's ranch. It's the safest place I know."

"But you won't have time to warn McSween. Noah, I'll go with you."

"No. I'm not going to lose you, Isobel. Not again."

"Don't tear us apart. Please, Noah." She caught his hand. "The safest place for me is at your side."

He shook his head. "All right, I'll take you to Lincoln. But, darlin', I'm afraid things are shot to pieces again."

"We're together, aren't we?" she said, forcing a smile. "How bad can it be?"

Warned by Noah and Isobel, the Regulators rode out of town, shattering Lincoln's newfound serenity with the thunder of horses' hooves. Minutes later, the Kinney Gang rode in.

Isobel and Noah hurried to John Tunstall's store, where Susan Gates and the Ealy family had taken rooms. Isobel talked briefly with her friend while Noah watched through a curtained window as John Kinney rode up and down the street, as if to say, "Look, folks, I'm here and I'm in charge."

Noah was fingering his pistol in frustration when Isobel leaned against his shoulder to kiss his cheek. "Susan is better," she whispered. "She started teaching school. That seems to have taken her mind off her loss."

"I'm glad to hear it." Noah mustered a smile.

Isobel knew his thoughts. Maybe Susan had recovered from the death of her fiancé, but he would never get over the loss of his closest friend.

"Dr. Ealy says I should stay here," she told him. She peeked out the window at Kinney. With a shudder, she took Noah's hand. "I want to be with you."

"Some of the Regulators rode for San Patricio. The others planned to hide at Chisum's. I say we head to Chisum's. If we ride fast, we may be able to catch them."

Once they had agreed on a plan, it took only moments for Isobel to bid her friends farewell. Then she and Noah slipped out to the hitching post where their horses were tethered.

"Kinney and his men are roaming all around here, Isobel," Noah warned. "Stay close to me. We'll ride for the woods and keep under cover until we're clear."

She nodded, her heart hammering at the prospect of impending danger. Noah led their horses down a slope toward the Rio Bonito. Isobel was trailing not five paces behind when she heard a cry.

"It's Buchanan!" someone shouted from the street. "He's a Chisum man! Get him!"

Noah whipped out his six-shooter. "Isobel, ride around me!"

She spurred her mount forward while Noah covered them with his gun. Horses crashed through the underbrush behind Isobel as her gelding charged into the river. Holding the reins with one hand, she pulled her pistol from its holster. Branches raked her arms. A bullet smashed into a tree trunk just ahead. Splinters flew.

"Isobel, ride!" Noah shouted behind her as he fired at their pursuers.

She lowered her head to the horse's neck. On the hill above the stream, the Huff house and the *torreón* flew past. "I'm headed for the hills, Noah! Follow me."

Her horse galloped out of the streambed and began climbing the foothills. She glanced behind to see Noah riding only a few yards ahead of the outlaws. At their head rode a hulk of a man…a man with a lantern jaw and slitted eyes.

Snake Jackson.

Muffling a scream, Isobel watched the outlaw gang break into two groups.

"Rattlesnake, you and your men stay with those two!"

Kinney shouted. "We'll ride for San Patricio and round up the rest of 'em!"

"Keep going, keep going!" Noah flew past Isobel and gave her horse's flank a slap. "Snake's after you."

Anger surged as Isobel buried her head against the horse's neck and rode for her life. With each heartbeat, she saw her father's face, his golden hair, his gentle hazel eyes. She saw John Tunstall in his dapper tweeds. She saw blue-eyed Dick Brewer, curly hair tossing in the breeze. And she saw Snake Jackson. She heard his mocking cries, hoots of derision, jeering laughter.

A bullet splatted into the dirt beside her. She swung around. Noah was returning Snake's fire, his arm stretched behind him and his six-shooter blazing. Chisum's ranch was a three-day ride, Isobel realized. How could she and Noah possibly hold off Snake Jackson and his men? Darkness was hours away. Their horses couldn't keep up this pace much longer. In a moment Noah would be forced to reload.

She scanned the hills for cover. Nothing but scrub piñon and cedar. The horses crashed through evergreen branches, scenting the air with the sweet smell of tree sap. But Isobel's nostrils were filled with fear. She was about to die by Snake Jackson's hand—just like her father. In her besotted love for Noah Buchanan, she had forgotten her true purpose. Now she would pay for her failure with her life.

Gritting her teeth, she turned and fired three wild shots at Snake. The outlaw lifted his head and whooped. "Missed me, *señorita!* But I'm gonna git you!"

"Isobel," Noah hollered, flying past her again. "Stay in front. Let me do the shooting!"

She lowered her head and surged past him. Why had

she let herself grow lazy and sloppy? She and Noah had dallied on the road from Santa Fe. Then she had waylaid them to comfort Susan Gates. Now they would both suffer for her weaknesses.

Her horse pounded around a bend, hooves kicking up dirt and old pine needles. The animal had begun to slow. Noah rode against her again, blue fire in his eyes.

"Find cover!" he called. "Your horse is going down."

She skirted the base of a hill and spotted a stone outcrop halfway up. Pointing so Noah could see without giving them away, she guided both horses through the trees.

Wheezing, foam dripping from its mouth, her horse slowed to a trot. Fear acrid on her tongue, Isobel slid to the ground and began to run. She clambered over a boulder and slid across a rock ledge.

At that moment a burning pain tore through her shoulder, shattering flesh and muscle. She tumbled behind the rock.

"Isobel!" Noah's urgent whisper came from a few paces away.

She clutched at the searing pain in her right shoulder. A warm liquid seeped onto her fingers.

"Snake winged you." Noah was peering between two boulders as he spoke. "They're coming this way. I need your help, darlin'. Please try."

She attempted to sit up, but her stomach turned and bile rose in her throat. "Noah," she groaned.

"Can you load this, Isobel?" He tossed a six-shooter into her lap. "If I can turn Snake and his men back, I'll have time to work on your shoulder. But if we can't hold them off—"

A bullet sent rock fragments flying past them. Isobel clenched her teeth and flipped open the pistol's chamber. With effort, she pried the cartridges from Noah's gun belt. Then she slid the bullets into their slots and clicked the gun shut.

Noah grabbed it and tossed a second empty six-shooter onto her lap. The hot metal burned through the thin fabric of her skirt. As she began to reload, bullets slammed into the stone around their heads. Cries rang out through the hills. Horses galloped past. Isobel continued loading Noah's two six-shooters, his rifle and her own small pistol. Pain fogged her mind. Blood soaked her sleeve and trickled onto her fingers.

Now and then Noah peered at her, his eyes dark blue with concern. "Isobel, darlin', hold on for me," she heard him whisper. "Don't give up on me now."

Then the firing stopped. Smoke cleared. The tang of gunpowder lifted. Warm arms came around her. Noah laid her out across the ground, her head resting on a pile of soft pine needles. Streaks of orange, blue and purple painted the sky. Noah's face appeared.

"Rest now, sweetheart," he murmured. "Snake's gone, and I'm going to patch you up."

She heard her sleeve tear and shut her eyes. Noah's voice drifted in and out. "Dear Lord, help me. The bullet's still in here. Isobel, darlin', I've got to take this thing out. Hold on to me, now."

A searing pain in her shoulder cut through the fog and brought her sharply awake. A scream rose in her throat. Then it faded away with the pain, the knife, the bullet. Blackness swam over her and took her away.

Isobel opened her eyes to find Noah seated on top of the rock outcrop. He had lifted his face to the heavens, but his eyes were shut. His lips moved silently. Brilliant morning sky framed his profile, the straight nose and square jawline, the sweep of dark hair.

Shifting, Isobel tried to ease the throbbing pain in her shoulder. Noah heard the movement and scrambled from his perch.

"Isobel?" He crouched beside her. "Isobel, darlin', are you awake?"

She tried to speak, but her throat felt parched as desert sands. Noah smoothed the hair from her forehead.

"I got the bullet out," he whispered. He dug around in his shirt pocket, then held up a flattened piece of lead. "Take a look at that, would you?"

She tried to grin, but the pain in her shoulder pounded unbearably. Noah adjusted the wool blanket that pillowed her head.

"You've lost a lot of blood," he said. "I need to get you back to Lincoln."

"No!" she croaked. Snake and Kinney would find them there. She wanted to go someplace safe where they could be together and forget Lincoln's trouble.

"Doc Ealy is the only one around these parts who can patch you up right. I've seen gangrene, Isobel, and I'm not going to let that happen to—"

"No!" She grabbed his arm with her good hand. "Not Lincoln."

"We can't stay here. Snake'll be back. And soon. I've got to get you out of here."

"Chisum's," she mouthed. "Please, Noah."

"That's a three-day ride for a fit horse and a healthy rider. I don't imagine you can even sit up straight, and you've been in and out of consciousness all night."

But the thought of being so close to Noah's little

adobe house drove Isobel to struggle up from the pallet. Blood siphoned from her face, but she threw the blanket back.

"All right," Noah said, grabbing her shoulders before she fainted. "I knew you were mule-headed, Isobel, and I can see you mean business. Come on, you'll ride with me."

He tethered her gelding behind his horse and then settled Isobel in his arms. They kept away from the river's edge for fear of ambush and stopped often to drink, rest or tend Isobel's shoulder. In the midst of her daze she could hear Noah growling about Jimmie Dolan and Snake Jackson. In between she heard the soft refrains of hymns.

Once Noah prayed out loud, a fervent plea. He spoke in that tone Isobel had heard so often—as if God were a father with whom a man could talk about his deepest needs.

Somewhere in the feverish mists, she remembered the wedding ceremony in the Lincoln County forest and her fears that God would punish her for such a hasty, selfish union. Perhaps this was God's chastisement—her wounded shoulder, her terrible fears, her hopeless love for Noah Buchanan.

But even as she pondered a rebuking, angry God, she heard Noah's voice. "God is love," he sang.

> "His mercy brightens
> All the path in which we rove;
> Bliss He wakes and woe He lightens:
> God is wisdom, God is love."

Several times each day Noah bathed Isobel's shoulder and changed the dressing. The slightest jolt sent a searing pain that nearly made her scream. Noah fashioned a sling to hold her arm close against her body. She couldn't eat. Only water from the Rio Hondo kept her going.

Their journey took many more than three days, but they could go no faster. Accepting that, Isobel nestled against Noah, her mind wandering from memories of her father to hanging lace curtains, typing pages of a story, galloping along mountain trails, baking *biscochitos*.

Through these memories wove a deep baritone.

> "E'en the hour that darkest seemeth
> Will His changeless goodness prove;
> From the gloom His brightness streameth:
> God is wisdom, God is love."

June was nearly gone when Noah's horse trotted the last few yards down the road to Chisum's house. The scent of blooming roses perfumed the air, and Noah's spirits rose in spite of his fears for Isobel.

About the only words she had said were how much she wanted Noah to stay with her, never leave her, always be near. As hard as it was to acknowledge, he now knew without a doubt that he loved Isobel Matas Buchanan.

In the frozen instant he'd watched her tumble behind that pile of rocks, his heart had nearly stopped. When he'd made it to her side and had seen her life's blood oozing out of that shoulder wound, a red rage had filled him. The fear of losing her had convinced Noah that he loved her.

If Dick Brewer meant a lot to him as a pal and confidant, Isobel meant far more. They could laugh, talk, even cry together. He had told her his dreams of writing, his ambitions and hopes for his land and future. And she shared hers with him. The thought of losing her was more than he could bear.

But the trouble with Snake Jackson would continue unless somebody stopped him. With Jimmie Dolan and now John Kinney fueling his fires, Snake wasn't about to back off. All three needed a dose of strong medicine. Lead poisoning would do the trick, and Noah knew just the man to deliver it.

"Darlin', after I settle you here I'm going back to Lincoln," he whispered into Isobel's ear as they neared the hitching post in front of the Chisum house. "Don't get your feathers ruffled about it. When I'm sure you're in good hands, I'm going after Snake and Dolan."

"Noah, they almost killed me!" Her hazel eyes filled with terror. "Please don't go."

"I'm going *because* they almost killed you." He took her hand. "The way I see it, Isobel, the only way to stop killin' is to kill. You were right about that. My big speeches about being strong enough to stay out of the trouble were like spittin' in the wind."

"Noah, I can't lose you. Not again."

But he was already handing her down to the waiting arms of Mrs. Towry and the men who had rushed to meet the riders. She recognized the faces of several Regulators before she was carried into a cool room, tucked into bed with a damp cloth on her forehead and abandoned.

"Noah!" she croaked. "Noah, please!"

But her voice echoed off the bare walls.

Chapter Nineteen

Noah sat at Isobel's bedside for three days. She was exhausted from the ride, but her pain had eased. Better still, the shoulder wound was healing well.

Mrs. Towry tended Isobel like a mother hen. Tongue clucking, she bustled back and forth, fetching ointments from John Chisum's medicine box, chicken soup, fresh bandages and cool, sweet lemonade. Finally Isobel was able to sit up on her own and then walk about the room while leaning on Noah's arm.

One morning after breakfast he settled on a chair by her bed. "Today's the Fourth of July," he said, his blue eyes twinkling. "Know what that means?"

"A celebration of the day the United States declared its independence from England." She smiled at Noah's patriotism despite the fact that New Mexico was still a territory.

"When I lived in Texas," he said, "Mrs. Allison used to fix a picnic for everybody. Feel up to a picnic today, darlin'? Me and some of the other Regulators thought we'd ride over to the Pecos."

"What about Sheriff Peppin's posse?" she asked. "Aren't they staying in Roswell?"

Isobel had heard that the hastily assembled posse included notorious outlaws known as the Seven Rivers Gang—led by deputies Marion Turner and Buck Powell.

"Aw, they're just a bunch of rascals," Noah said.

"But they're fifteen men, and we have only twelve. Some of ours will have to stay behind to keep an eye on Mr. Chisum's place."

"Regulators have been riding between the Pecos and the ranch without any trouble from that posse. I just thought it would be fun to get you out of the house. You can ride in the buckboard. Take in some fresh air. Think you're up to it?"

A day in the outdoors appealed to Isobel. If she rode in the buckboard, she could wear a dress. Just the idea of putting on a fresh gown, brushing her hair into artful waves, setting her feet in a pair of slippers instead of heavy leather boots—

"I'd love it!" she exclaimed.

He bent over the bed and kissed her cheek. "I'll give you half an hour. Mrs. Towry's fixing a basket. She might come along with—"

"Buchanan!" Billy Bonney kicked open the door and charged into the room. "Buchanan, hit the rooftop! It's Buck Powell and the Seven Rivers Gang."

"What do they want?"

"Who knows? Me and the Coe boys was ridin' back from Ash Upson's store this mornin'." Billy brandished his six-shooter as he spoke. "Twelve of 'em jumped us! It was a runnin' gun battle all the way back to the house. Now they're takin' potshots at the boys on the roof.

You gotta get up there and help afore somebody gets killed!"

Noah glanced at Isobel, but before she could say anything to try to hold him back, he dropped his hat on his head and drew his gun.

"Stay away from the windows, Isobel," he called back as he and Billy ran from the bedroom. "And don't go looking for trouble!"

She watched the door slam shut as their boots pounded down the hall. "I found trouble when I married you," she murmured, settling back against her pillow. "And you found it when you married me."

The shooting went on all day and most of the night. The picnic was abandoned, though Mrs. Towry got a big holiday meal onto the table anyway. The Regulators took turns coming down from the parapet roof to eat before heading back upstairs.

It was clear to Isobel that the Regulators were confident in their position. With Chisum's fortifications and a large supply of ammunition, they were having no trouble holding off Buck Powell and his posse. Isobel and Mrs. Towry spent the night in the central courtyard of the house. If not for the occasional burst of gunfire, it would have seemed idyllic.

Roses in full bloom scented the air. Beds dragged onto the patio offered down comforters, pillows, bolsters, shams and embroidered sheets. But the two women sat up most of the night, speculating on how the battle was proceeding and worrying about the men.

At dawn the following day, Isobel woke with a gentle hand on her shoulder. "Buck Powell and the others have gone," Noah said. "We think they've headed to Lincoln for reinforcements."

"Has anyone been hurt, Noah?" she asked.

"We've had the upper hand the whole time." He gave her the hint of a smile, then his face grew solemn. "I've been talking with the other Regulators, Isobel. We figure we can't end this trouble without all-out war on Jimmie Dolan."

"War?" Isobel whispered.

"Justice, darlin'. Dolan is responsible for too many deaths. Any way you look at it, Isobel, he's got to be put away."

In silence she gazed at the embroidered coverlet, lit pink with the sunrise. She ran one finger over a red rose entwined with green leaves.

"And then there's you," Noah added before she had a chance to speak. "Snake Jackson won't rest until he kills you, Isobel. He's got nothing to lose by pulling your picket pin. And he's got plenty to gain—the land titles, money from Pascal and Catron, elimination of an eyewitness, and one less 'Mexican'—"

"I'm Spanish."

"Isobel!" Noah clenched her hand tightly. "Hear what I'm saying. Your life is in danger."

"I know that," she said, rubbing her shoulder.

"The Regulators will ride to Lincoln this morning. A couple of the boys are headed to San Patricio to round up the rest of the bunch. Everyone plans to meet at McSween's house and decide how to finish this business. Isobel…I'm going with them."

She snatched her hand from his. "What's happened to you, Noah? What has become of the man with gentle hands who lifted me from the path of a bullet? Where is the writer who would rather leave a fight than shoot an enemy?"

"That man is gone."

"Oh, Noah…"

"I've been around a few years, darlin', but I didn't learn what was what until I met you. The fact is, Isobel Buchanan, I love you. I'm not going to let Jimmie Dolan or Snake Jackson or anyone else hurt you. Never again. And the only way to fight fire is with fire. Gunfire."

"Noah, please don't do this!"

"What's happened to my little spitfire? When we met, you were bent on vengeance. If I had helped you instead of trying to stop you, Snake Jackson might be dead right now—instead of wounding you with a bullet. You were right. It's time for revenge."

He stood suddenly, knocking back the wooden chair. "I'm going now." He settled his hat on his head. "Heal up, Isobel, you hear?"

He started across the patio, and she called his name. But he didn't turn.

"I love you, too, Noah," she whispered.

Moments later, Isobel heard the drumroll of horses' hooves as the Regulators rode away. She eased herself to the floor and stood. In the week since the shooting, her arm had grown stronger, and she was able to move it more comfortably now. She made her way into her bedroom and gazed out the window.

A light cloud of brown dust trailed the men, and an overwhelming sense of loss enveloped her. What she had known and loved of life was about to end.

Mrs. Towry crossed the garden near the window, a

basketful of roses on her arm. She waved at her guest. "Shootin's over, honey. It's safe to move around."

Isobel tried to smile. "May I join you in the garden?"

"You still look mighty pale." The older woman shook her head. "Such high talkin' them boys was doin' this morning. I wish Mr. Chisum was here to preach some sense into 'em. They think they're gonna be heroes—shootin' up Lincoln and killin' all their enemies. What next?"

"Noah went with the others, didn't he?"

Mrs. Towry nodded. "Good thing, too. He's the most levelheaded of the bunch. He should be leader of the Regulators. Doc Scurlock ain't a bad feller, but your husband's got horse sense. He reminds me of Mr. Chisum—smart, peaceable, strong. I sure wish Mr. Chisum would hurry back from St. Louis.... Well, honey, come on out to the garden."

A week had passed since the Regulators' departure when Mrs. Towry rushed onto the porch where Isobel was stitching.

"Mrs. Buchanan! Look what come in the mail from Lincoln. I bet your husband sent it."

Isobel grabbed the letter and tore open the envelope. "Dear Mr. Buchanan," she read aloud.

"It is my great pleasure to inform you that your story, 'Sunset at Coyote Canyon,' has been accepted for publication in our magazine, *Wild West*. It will run in five installments, beginning in December. Congratulations. Enclosed please find a check for the sum of fifty dollars. *Wild West* would like to see more of your fine writing, Mr. Buchanan.

Sincerely, Josiah Woodstone, Editor."

Mrs. Towry frowned as she studied the envelope. "This ain't from Mr. Buchanan, is it?"

"Noah's story," Isobel said. "It's going to be published."

"Mr. Buchanan writ a story?" Mrs. Towry muffled a laugh. "Ain't what I expected of a cowboy like him, but here's fifty dollars to prove it's true. That ought to go a good way toward payin' off the land he bought from Mr. Chisum."

Isobel gazed at the letter. Noah's story would be published. His dream would come true. But where was he now, this man with a gift so few possessed? No doubt he was in Lincoln warring with someone who would still his voice with a bullet through his heart.

It was her fault, she thought, tucking the letter into her pocket. If she hadn't been so headstrong, so determined to seek out Snake Jackson, Noah wouldn't be caught in Lincoln's troubles.

When they'd met, he'd been on his way to buy land and write stories. He was the man Mrs. Towry had described—peaceable, gentle. Thanks to his untimely marriage to a selfish Spanish woman, he had tossed away that cloak and assumed the one she had brought—revenge. Now, because of Isobel, he was chasing down Jimmie Dolan with an outlaw's bloodlust.

She had ruined Noah. While he had taught her to find the beauty in life, she had taught him to seek vengeance. From Noah she had learned to cook meals that would satisfy, to plant a garden, to value marriage and home. She had discovered that what she wanted most was love. Noah's love. She ached for him. Nothing else in the world mattered.

Leaving Mrs. Towry to her flower arranging, Isobel hurried to her room, found her saddlebag and groped around inside. Yes—her pistol. She contemplated the weapon for a moment before tossing it onto the bed.

Quickly she changed into riding clothes and leather boots. She transferred Noah's letter from the New York publisher into a pocket. Stopping by the kitchen, she took some bread and cheese, along with a knife and a box of matches. After stuffing these items into the saddlebag, she slung it over her good shoulder and slipped out the door.

Fussing over the roses, Mrs. Towry hummed on the porch. Isobel left the house through a back door. In the corral, she selected a horse that had not yet been unsaddled from a morning's ride. Pain shot through her shoulder as she mounted.

"Now," she breathed as she goaded the horse's flanks. "Take me to Lincoln. I have to save my husband."

Though Isobel knew the trail, travel was more difficult than she had anticipated. Riding alone, she had to be alert for outlaws who roamed Lincoln County's roadways. Perhaps it had been foolish to leave her pistol behind, but Isobel never again wanted to touch a weapon. As she rode she recited the words she ached to say to Noah.

I was wrong! Wrong! Revenge is not the way. Leave it to God, my love. Come home with me to the little adobe house by the river.

Would she ever get the chance to say those words?

Isobel prayed as she had heard Noah pray—the deep and soul-drenching pleas of her heart. "Please, dear God, let Noah live. Let me atone for my errors. Allow me to lead Noah away from violence and into a life of love."

Each night she lay bundled in blankets and listened to the rush of the river. As she gazed at the stars through piñon branches, Isobel recounted her life and its many blessings. Noah Buchanan was the greatest blessing of all. Before it was too late, she had to convince him to leave Lincoln.

Though her shoulder had regained strength and flexibility, she knew how easily the pain could resurface. For the rest of her life, she would bear a scar—a round patch of smooth, tender skin, a reminder of the man who had killed her father and had tried to kill her.

Her fourth night on the trail, Isobel camped at the spot where the Rio Hondo met the Rio Bonito. Lincoln lay only a few miles away, and her sleep was restless.

Early the next morning she rose as dawn was breaking over the mountains. In the pale purple light she took the kitchen knife from her saddlebag and cut off a slice of cheese and a hunk of bread. After eating, she set Dick Brewer's old hat on her head and mounted her horse.

Isobel had not been riding long when she noticed a horse and rider coming toward her on the trail. Her pulse began to pound in her neck and temples. Could it be Noah? The man removed his hat and tipped his head.

"Mornin', *señorita*," he said.

Isobel's breath hung in her throat. "Jim Jackson."

"Most folks call me Snake."

She glanced around for a path of escape, but he was already drawing his six-shooter.

"Me and some of the boys just happened to be passin'

Casey's Mill yesterday," Snake said, casually taking aim
at her heart. "One of the hands mentioned seein' Mrs.
Buchanan ridin' all alone. That's when I realized I hadn't
finished a job I started the other day. Seems yer like a
cat, huh? Nine lives."

"Mr. Jackson, you can see I'm unarmed," Isobel said.
"I'm going to Lincoln to find my husband. I have no
business with you."

"No business with me? What about this here packet
of papers I been carryin' around for five years? Ain't
that yer business, *señorita?*" He slapped his saddlebag
and gave her a wink. "Took it off yer papa, y'know. The
day I shot him dead."

Isobel clenched her jaw. Snake had ridden close
enough now that she could see his eyes set deep beneath
his heavy brow.

"Now, don't deny it," he teased. "You been chasin'
me ever since you come to Lincoln County, *señorita*.
First you seen me do Tunstall in. Then you figured out
I blew yer papa to kingdom come. You followed me to
Murphy's ranch and tried to shoot me. Then back to
Lincoln where you and your Mexican-lovin' husband
tried again to gun me down."

"You chased us from Lincoln," Isobel corrected.

"Aw, well, it don't really matter now. Point is, it's
time for one of us to finish the game. I reckon it better
be me."

"I renounce my claim, Snake. Take my family's land.
Take our jewels. Just let me go to Lincoln."

"What's this? Has the little she-devil lost her fire?"

"Yes, I have. I'm through fighting. I'm going to pass
you in peace and go on my way."

Flicking the reins, Isobel rode toward Snake. Their

horses brushed on the narrow trail. She kept her focus straight ahead and tried to push back the terrible images of blood and death. Don Alberto Matas. John Henry Tunstall. Dick Brewer. Sheriff Brady.

"Oh, *señorita*." Snake grabbed her arm, nearly jerking the wounded shoulder from its socket. As he pulled her backward in the saddle, he released the safety on his six-shooter. "I'm afraid we got unfinished business."

"Let me go, Snake!" she ordered.

"You really thought I was gonna let you ride by me?"

"I hoped you would be man enough to holster your gun." She stared into the slitted eyes. "I have no quarrel with you, so set me free."

Smiling, he raised the gun to her head and jabbed it into her temple. "Yer dumber than I thought, *señorita*. See, I got a lot of killin' to do to make up fer the bunch of Mexicans that murdered my parents."

"I had nothing to do with that," she gasped as cold steel pressed against her head. Pain wrenched through her shoulder where he pinned her against him. "I want only peace. Let me go. Please!"

"Somebody's gotta pay. Might as well be you."

With his last word Snake pulled the trigger. An instant before the blast, Isobel tilted her head and sank into the saddle. The bullet blew off Dick Brewer's hat and slammed into a tree. Both horses bolted, but Snake still gripped Isobel's arm. The horses struggled, turning in circles. With her free hand, Isobel fumbled for the knife in her saddlebag.

Snake muttered a curse. He righted his gun and took aim a second time. Isobel whipped the knife across his arm, and the six-shooter tumbled onto the grass in a spray of blood.

"Curse you!" Snake yelled.

He lunged at Isobel and both riders tumbled to the ground. The air whooshed from her lungs. She rolled, trying to escape, but Snake tangled her legs with his as he pulled his own knife from his belt.

"Now," he growled. "Now we'll see."

Just as he lunged for her throat, she stabbed his back. Her knife sank into flesh and struck bone. Snake bellowed and bolted upright with the pain. Then his knife flashed downward and buried in her arm, not an inch from the bullet wound.

"Stop!" she shrieked, twisting in agony.

"I'll kill you first."

He yanked the knife from her arm and went for her throat a second time. She squirmed and thrust. Her blade buried deep in his stomach. He shuddered.

Barely able to breathe beneath his weight, she tried to jerk her weapon away but lost her grip on it. If only she could escape…now…while he was wounded. She tried to push out from under him.

Snake reared. His eyes flashed with hatred. She grasped at the swinging steel in his hand. The blade nicked her cheek, and she screamed.

Blood seeped from the corner of his mouth and still he grappled with her. He caught a handful of her hair and twisted her head backward, grinding her scalp into the dirt. She could see nothing but trees. Her throat exposed to his blade, she waited for the final slash.

"*Señorita*," he mumbled. As he slumped forward, she felt his knuckles brush her neck.

"Dear God, help me!" Isobel labored to catch her

breath. She lay beneath Snake and listened as the last gurgle of life left his chest. Gasping, she shoved his body to one side and struggled to her knees. At the scene of horror, she cried out.

Snake Jackson lay on the ground, her knife buried in his stomach. His blood puddled on the road. "I've killed him," she whispered. "I've killed him after all."

She buried her face in her bloodied hands. Bile rose in her throat. She staggered up and hung over a tree branch, retching with fear and revulsion. Tears streamed down her cheeks and dripped pink bloodstains in the grass. For a moment she could do nothing but lean against the tree and cry.

How had it come to this? Once she had longed to end the life of Jim Jackson. But now...now that she had killed him...

"God," she murmured. "Dear God, forgive me!"

Weak and in terrible pain, she lurched down to the river, filled her hands with water and splashed her face. Cradling her injured shoulder, she slumped into the grass, stretched out her legs and shut her eyes.

She had no idea how long she lay still. With every breath she saw Snake's face. She had taken his life. She had killed. Covering her eyes with her good arm, she wept more bitter tears. Once, she had imagined satisfaction, even joy, after her revenge was complete. But death was ugly, senseless.

She had to find Noah and turn him from the same path. It was her only hope of atonement.

In time, she struggled to her feet. The two horses grazed side by side near the trail. She studied Snake Jackson's body for a moment, then she touched each eyelid to press it closed before she walked to the horses.

She knew what she must do. She had battled for her birthright with her own life and had won it at the cost of another's. Slipping her hand inside Snake's saddlebag, she found a slender packet. Her father's neat handwriting graced the yellowed envelope. "Spanish Land-Grant Titles," the words read in both English and Spanish. "The Possession of Isobel Matas."

Bowing her head, Isobel held the packet close. Land. With it, she could draw the hand of any eligible man in New Mexico or Spain. She could have Don Guillermo or any other husband she chose. She would be a landowner at last.

But there was only one man she wanted. It was time to find him.

Chapter Twenty

When Isobel rode into Lincoln that night, Sheriff George Peppin met her on the road, his rifle drawn from its scabbard. The middle-aged man, known to many in town as "Dad" Peppin, frowned.

"Mrs. Buchanan? Is that you?"

"Yes, it is." She tucked a wisp of her hair behind her ear, as if that might tidy her appearance. "Do you know where my husband is? It's an urgent matter."

"He's holed up in McSween's house with the other Regulators. Don't you know what's goin' on here, ma'am?"

"I've come for my husband. That's all I know."

"Well, you can't just ride into town and—"

"Who's this?" Jimmie Dolan rode out of the shadows, a dark hat perched on his thick, glossy curls.

"It's Noah Buchanan's wife," Peppin said.

"What happened to you, woman? You're covered in blood."

"Never mind my appearance, sir," Isobel told the Irishman. "I've come for my husband."

"Your husband is camped out with fourteen other

outlaws on the roof of Alexander McSween's house,"
Dolan spat. "They've knocked holes in the parapet and
made the place a firing range."

"I'll go and fetch him, then."

"And my men will shoot him to the ground the minute
he sets foot out of that house. This is war, Mrs. Buchanan. Twenty of McSween's men are inside José Montaño's
store. Nearly as many are over at Isaac Ellis's store."

"I'll speak to Juan Patrón. He'll help me."

"That Mexican grabbed up his family and rode to Las
Vegas like a banshee was after him. Five McSween men
are camped at his house."

"If McSween has taken the town," Isobel said, "how
do you propose to keep me from my husband?"

"Because my men hold the *torreón*," Dolan shot back.
"And now I've got you." He gave Peppin a nod. "Take
this woman to the Cisneros house, Sheriff. We'll hold
her there. Maybe we can use her to bargain with."

"Hold me?" Isobel exploded. "James Dolan, I will
not be made a prisoner—"

"Take her away, Peppin."

The sheriff nudged Isobel with the end of his rifle.
She refused to move.

"Mr. Dolan," she said, "I own the finest land in New
Mexico. I took my title papers from Snake Jackson this
morning. If you'll set my husband free, I'll give them
to you."

"Land, eh?" Dolan squinted at her. "You took those
titles from Jackson? Rattlesnake Jim Jackson? Did you
kill him?"

Isobel looked away. "You'll find his body on the road
to Roswell where the Bonito and Hondo rivers join."

"You're a banshee yourself. Hand over that packet, ma'am," Dolan commanded, drawing his own gun.

"I don't have them with me," she retorted. "You don't think I'm so foolish as to carry valuables into this murderous town, do you? I buried them. But if you'll set my husband free—"

"Ah, just take her away, Peppin. I'll get the titles later. Can't have a banshee roamin' the town, can we?"

"Mr. Dolan, this woman is wounded," the sheriff said. "I'd better take her over to Tunstall's store and let Doc Ealy have a look at her."

"Any woman who could kill Snake Jackson and steal those land titles he's been so proud of all these years can't be underestimated. Especially if she's tryin' to break out one of the Regulators. Give her husband and the rest of McSween's bunch a look at my ace-in-the-hole. Then take her to the Cisneros house. And lock her up tight."

"Yes, sir."

The Irishman rode away into the darkness. Peppin gave Isobel an apologetic shrug and prodded her forward.

"Will you send Dr. Ealy to me, Sheriff?" Isobel asked as they neared a three-room adobe house opposite McSween's. "Jackson wounded me in the shoulder. Please, I need help. Dr. Ealy won't cause trouble. He's a missionary—a man of God."

"I'll do what I can for you, Mrs. Buchanan."

Peppin paraded Isobel past Alexander McSween's house, but it was so dark she couldn't be sure Noah saw her. The Cisneros family had fled Lincoln, the sheriff told her, as had most of the town's peaceable citizens. Dolan had taken the Cisneros house, though it was too small to hold many fighters. Peppin led Isobel to the front bedroom, locked her in and stationed an armed man at the door.

From a curtained window, she could see a row of silhouettes lining the roof of the McSween house across the street. She tried to identify Noah among them, but there was not enough moonlight to see clearly. For some time, she waited in hopes that Dr. Ealy would come— not so much to tend her wounds as to reassure her that Noah was all right.

When no one came, she bathed her wounds in a washbasin and lay back on the bed. Though she had not planned to sleep, the sun was well up when she was awakened by the sound of her bedroom door swinging open.

"Breakfast, Mrs. Buchanan?" Her young guard walked in with a loaf of bread under one arm and a pot of hot coffee in his hand. His other hand rested lightly on the handle of his pistol. "Sorry to bust in on you. If you don't mind my sayin' so, ma'am, you don't look too perky this mornin'."

Isobel attempted to smooth her wrinkled shirt-waist while the guard set the bread and coffee on the dresser.

"Say, did you really kill Rattlesnake Jim Jackson?" he asked, giving her a sideways glance. "That's the rumor."

"Yes, and I'd rather not discuss it," Isobel informed him. "When will I be set free?"

"Soon as things settle down. Dolan sent a letter to Fort Stanton askin' for soldiers."

Isobel studied the young man whose limp, blond

hair hung almost to his shoulders. "Thank you for this information," she said.

He smiled. "I reckon John Kinney and the rest will hightail it up from San Patricio when they hear what McSween's done. Dolan thinks his posse will be here by this afternoon."

"And then?"

"A shootin' match, I'd guess." He backed toward the door, keeping his eyes on his prisoner. "I'll be outside if you need me. Just holler."

"What is your name, sir?"

"Ike Teeters. I'm from Seven Rivers."

"You're in the Seven Rivers Gang?"

He chuckled, showing a row of uneven teeth. "Not hardly. My eyes don't see too good from a distance, ma'am. Truth be told, my shootin's downright pitiful. But I can do guardin' work. I'm fine at that."

"Why don't you wear spectacles, Ike?"

"I ain't got the money. Chisum pushed my family off our land, and it's all we can do to get by."

"John Chisum?"

"Who else? Us Seven Rivers folks is small cattlemen—law-abidin', hardworkin' fellers—and we can't do nothin' against a powerful man like him. We joined Dolan to fight Chisum."

As he was shutting the door, Ike poked his head back in. "I'll see if I can get you a doctor, Mrs. Buchanan."

As he spoke, John Kinney's posse rode into Lincoln and began shooting at the McSween house, their bullets shattering windows and gouging holes in the adobe walls. When the Regulators returned fire, Isobel spotted Noah on the roof. His black Stetson moved back and forth behind the parapet.

The gunfight raged until sunset. As darkness brought an end to the shooting, Ike managed to slip Dr. Taylor Ealy across the street to the Cisneros house. The missionary doctor hurried to Isobel's bedroom with his bag of medications and bandages.

"Dr. Ealy," Isobel couldn't contain herself as he brushed aside her hair to take a look at her shoulder. "Can you get a message to Noah? Please help me save my husband's life!"

"Your *husband?* I see things have taken an interesting turn since that hasty wedding in the forest. Good thing I got nowhere trying to annul your marriage."

"Noah and I are still married?"

"In the eyes of God and the territory of New Mexico you are." The doctor patted her hand. "Now, you must try to rest. With more than sixty gunmen on his side, McSween has the advantage. Dolan's posse numbers just forty."

"Is it all-out war, then?"

"Only God knows," he said as he placed a clean bandage on her wound. "I'll try to speak to Sheriff Peppin about you. If you're being held for the death of Jim Jackson, you deserve the chance to post bail. If Dolan is holding you hostage, it's illegal."

As he prepared to leave, gunfire again erupted on the street. Ike Teeters burst into the bedroom. "Doc, you better get back to Tunstall's store. They're shootin' it out again, and I'm only supposed to protect Mrs. Buchanan."

Dr. Ealy hurried for the door.

"Take my message to Noah!" Isobel called out. But the door slammed behind him. As she crawled into bed, she breathed a prayer for her husband's safety.

She recalled his vivid blue eyes, his bronze skin, his dark hair, his gentle hands. *Dear God,* she lifted up her prayer. *I'm responsible for one man's death. Please keep it from becoming two.*

Dawn on the fifth day of Isobel's imprisonment brought the customary pop of gunfire as the sniping began again. She changed into a dress Ike had found in the house, a simple gown of pale yellow cotton. As bullets slammed into the wall outside, she washed and combed her hair. Then she knocked on her bedroom door.

"Ike," she called out. "I must speak with you."

He unlocked the door and stepped into the room. "Yer lookin' spunky this mornin', Mrs. Buchanan. I've just about got yer breakfast ready."

The loaf of bread and pot of coffee was more food than many people in town would have by now. Supplies were running low, and children would be hungry.

"I can't eat, Ike." She held her aching shoulder. "I must see my husband. Will you escort me across the street?"

"Aw, I can't do that, ma'am. It's against Dolan's orders."

"Please, Ike! After I talk to Noah, you can bring me back here. Hold a gun on me if you like."

The young man scratched his scraggly locks. "It'd be risky. Things is hot out there this mornin'."

"Just let me go—"

"What on earth is that?" At the sound of shouting and horses' hooves, Ike bolted to the window. Isobel rushed to his side.

"What's goin' on, ma'am? I can't see nothin'."

"It's soldiers from Fort Stanton," she cried.

"Wahoo! That means we got the army on our side, Mrs. Buchanan!" Ike did a little dance around the room. "Count 'em for me, would ya?"

"There's Colonel Dudley," she said. "Four officers. Eight…nine…ten…eleven black cavalrymen. More than twenty white infantrymen. And they've brought cannons!"

"It's the howitzer!" Ike whooped as he squinted to see. "Dudley's brung the howitzer! She's a twelve-pounder. And there's a rapid-fire Gatling gun comin' along behind. Dolan's won the war now. Mac might as well give up."

Isobel sank onto a chair and buried her face in her hands. It was too late. Too late. The soldiers had come to obliterate Alexander McSween's forces. Among the dead would be Noah Buchanan.

Chapter Twenty-One

Before Colonel Dudley and the soldiers could take positions, Isobel saw several Dolan men run to Alexander McSween's house and begin pouring coal oil around the wooden window frames.

"What do they mean to do?" she asked Ike, clutching his arm.

"I reckon they're gonna try to burn out the McSween bunch."

"Burn them!" Isobel rose to her feet, but Ike pushed her out of bullet range.

"Don't worry yerself none, ma'am," he drawled. "That house is made of adobe brick. It ain't gonna burn worth a lick."

"But the window frames. And the roof. Oh, Ike, you must take me across the street at once. I have to save my husband."

"Settle down, now. Tell you what. I'll step outside and see if I can find someone who can tell me what the soldiers is plannin'."

The moment Ike left the room, Isobel pushed at the window casing in an effort to dislodge it. But the stout wood frame was embedded in adobe, and it refused to give. She ran to the door and tried the knob, but Ike had locked it. Frantic, she raced to the window again.

"Noah!" she shouted. Taking up a chair, she began smashing it against the window. "Let me out, Jimmie Dolan!"

"Hey, there!" Ike barged into the room. Isobel flew at him, fists pummeling as she tried to push past him. He grabbed her arms and shoved her back from the door. She stumbled and fell to the floor, sobbing.

"What's all this, ma'am?" Ike said after he'd locked the door behind them. He bent over her and laid a hand on her back. "You know I can't let you out, Mrs. Buchanan. I got my orders."

She shrugged away from his hand. "My husband is in that house! I must see him."

"You wouldn't get near McSween's place even if I did set you free."

Her heart breaking, Isobel struggled up from the floor, ran to the window and looked out.

Ike spoke softly as he joined her. "When McSween's men saw Colonel Dudley was back in town, they hightailed it out of here. He ain't got nobody left but the men in his own house. I hear they've stacked adobe bricks inside to make a barricade."

Isobel leaned her forehead against the window frame. Noah was inside Alexander McSween's house. Noah and a few others. How could they hope to hold out against an army?

"Where is the colonel?" she asked. "I must speak to him. If he fires those guns at McSween's house, he'll kill everyone inside."

"He's setting up camp down the street. Dudley may

be a hard-drinkin' man, but he's got some smarts, too. He sent messages tellin' McSween and Dolan that he's in town to protect the women and children. He said if anyone fires on his soldiers, he's gonna blow 'em to kingdom come."

Isobel moaned. "That means Dolan's men can fire on the McSween house without fear of hitting a soldier. But with troops everywhere, no one inside the house can shoot back. It's not fair."

"'Course it ain't. That's war for ya." Ike patted her arm. "Now let me bring in yer breakfast, Mrs. Buchanan. There ain't nothin' you can do. Anyhow, you won't be the first widow in Lincoln County. Believe me."

Sauntering away, he unlocked the door, slipped through and relocked it from the outside. She could hear him whistling as he banged around the stove, preparing her breakfast.

Isobel was given no opportunity for escape. Shortly after noon, Dolan's posse filled the house. The men outside the locked door were laughing about their sure victory as they loaded their rifles.

Unable to keep still despite the throbbing pain in her shoulder, Isobel drew a chair to the window. Some of Dolan's men approached the McSween house and began to pry loose bullet-torn shutters, and smash window-panes with their rifle butts.

She had no doubt that Alexander McSween must die. How many would die with him? Noah Buchanan…Billy Bonney…Sue McSween? She had barely thought of the woman when out of the house marched Mrs. McSween herself.

Head up, she strode down the street toward the *tor-*

reón. If anyone could stand up to an army colonel, it was Sue McSween with her sharp tongue and quick mind.

But the moment she was safely away from the house, Dolan's men began pouring coal oil over the windows. A flame sprang up at the back of the house near the kitchen. A pillar of smoke rose as the fire crawled from one room to the next.

Isobel sat helpless at her window. Her throat ached from choking back tears. Several times she was certain she saw Noah's silhouette, but he took cover before she could call out to him. Smoke poured from the windows as hazy figures moved around inside.

Murmuring prayers, Isobel saw images of Noah flicker through her thoughts. The evening he had lifted her onto his horse and carried her into the shadows of the pines. She could recall the smell of him…leather and dust. She remembered his clean-shaven face, the handsomest she had ever seen. She thought of the tender way he had held her, kissed her, loved her. His clear voice rang through the valley with hymns. His strong hands wrestled cattle…and wrote stories.

Oh, Noah! If only she could change the past.

"Naw, she's Buchanan's wife!" Ike's protest carried into her room. "Leave her be, fellers."

"C'mon, Ike. Let's have a look at her. Ain't she the one sent Snake Jackson hoppin' over coals?"

"Yeah, Ike! Let's take a gander at Buchanan's woman."

"Boys, if I did that, ol' Dolan would skin me alive."

Someone guffawed. "He means to string her up for murder, don't ya know?"

"Murder?" another hooted. "Hoo-wee!"

Isobel swallowed at the thick knot in her throat.

Murder? But of course. What chance would she have to prove her innocence? Dr. Ealy had treated her wounds, and the surgeon had felt no compunction over lying about the condition of John Tunstall's corpse. He could certainly make it look as though she had not acted in self-defense but had stabbed Snake Jackson to death.

Feeling ill, she studied Mac's house—enveloped in raging flames. Now Sue McSween marched back down the street to her burning home and went inside, seemingly oblivious to the conflagration.

Moments later, Sue left again and crossed to John Tunstall's store, where Susan Gates and the Ealy family had hidden. At once, the Dolan posse began to set fire to that building. Mary Ealy ran out of the store carrying the two children and set them on the road. Her husband followed with a stack of Bibles in his arms. Susan raced outside with textbooks in hand and slates under one arm.

"Susan!" Isobel cried, pounding on the window. "Susan, please look at me!"

But now soldiers drove a wagon to the front of Tunstall's mercantile. The troops quickly loaded the Ealys' few possessions into the wagon. The Ealys and Susan climbed on board, Susan clutching one of the little girls in her arms, and the wagon rolled away.

"Susan!" Isobel yelled her friend's name one last time, but the petite red-haired schoolteacher evidently had seen too much. White-faced, she stared blankly ahead, her large gray eyes fixed on nothing.

The wagon made a final trip from the Tunstall store as darkness fell over the valley. It carried Sue McSween's organ, more of Dr. Ealy's books and a large sack of flour. By this time flames had raged through the entire

McSween house. The blaze lit the mountains on both sides of town. Shooting increased until all Isobel could hear was the crack of gunfire and the roar of flames.

She hung against the window frame, not caring whether she died by a random shot. No one could still be alive inside the burning house. Noah was surely dead. She ached with hopelessness. But just then, she saw several figures suddenly run from the back of the house. Gunfire intensified. A silhouetted man crumpled to the ground.

For a moment the shooting halted.

"McSween said he'd surrender," someone shouted outside her door. "Bob Beckwith is goin' in after him."

From the window Isobel tried to make out what was happening. She heard a voice cry out from the yard of the burning house. Alexander McSween?

"I shall never surrender!" he roared.

At his words bullets flew. Bodies tumbled to the ground. Rifles blazed away. Dolan's men poured out of the Cisneros house, leaving Isobel completely alone.

She saw more men—Regulators who had tried to save their friends in McSween's house—jump from the window of the Tunstall store. Dogs barked. Flames leapt higher.

Sounds of victory erupted from the McSween courtyard as Jimmie Dolan's men began to prance about and fire their guns in jubilation. Isobel sank onto her chair, watching the devilish dance around the fire.

"McSween's dead!" someone crowed as he ran past her window, a jug of whisky in his hand. "McSween's dead! McSween's dead!"

"How many killed?" another man cried from the porch of the Tunstall store.

"Got 'em all. All the Regulators are dead!"

"Six dead in the courtyard!" someone else called out. "Naw, five. All shot dead. McSween's one of 'em!"

"Wahoo! We got 'em all. Every last one of them blasted outlaws!"

Isobel covered her face with her hands and began to cry. Noah…beloved Noah. Dear God, let him rest in peace.

Chapter Twenty-Two

Isobel slumped in her chair, her arms folded on the windowsill and her head resting on them. The acrid tang of smoke filled her nostrils. Shots continued to ring out, as they had most of the night. Someone had broken into Tunstall's store, and men were still carrying away the looted goods. Isobel could hear them laughing as they drank whisky and boasted about their victory.

Sniffing, she shut her eyes. She had not slept, and now the first purple light of dawn was beginning to streak the sky. How could she sleep? How could she ever go on? But, of course, it wouldn't be long before Jimmie Dolan remembered her. She would face her own death soon. It hardly seemed to matter.

Memories of Spain and the rich pastures of Catalonia drifted through her thoughts. Horses cantering over green hills. White cliffs. A crashing blue sea. Grapes. Grazing sheep.

And then she saw New Mexico. Blue sky arching heavenward. Fragrant piñon trees. Gurgling streams. Yuccas covered with thick white blossoms. Spiny cacti garlanded in pink blooms.

She imagined she was bending to pick one of those cactus flowers. Leaning forward, her hair fell over her shoulders. She straightened and placed the blossom in a pair of strong, sun-weathered hands.

"Noah," she whispered. "Noah."

"Isobel…" The voice came from somewhere outside herself. She tried to turn her head to see his face, but the wound in her shoulder hurt too much.

"Isobel…" She heard her name again. Or was it the wind whispering through the junipers? "Isobel…"

A warm hand stroked down her neck. She jumped. The chair tumbled backward on the floor as she struggled to her feet. And there he was…the tall hero of her dreams. Noah Buchanan.

"Didn't mean to scare you, darlin'," he said, "but we don't have much time. Got to get out of this place while Ike's keeping watch."

Isobel blinked. "Noah? Are you alive?"

"Me, Billy Bonney and a couple of others made it out of McSween's house in the dark just before the shooting got really hot. I'm not sure who made it and who didn't because I took off in this direction to find you. I didn't even know you were in Lincoln till I heard you shouting for Susan this afternoon."

He stopped and rubbed his hand over his forehead. "Mac got killed, you know. Dolan's men shot him. I saw it all."

"Noah…" It was the only word Isobel could force out of her mouth.

"C'mon, darlin'. Ike won't be able to steer those drunkards away from the house much longer. Let's head out."

Isobel moaned as Noah lifted her into his arms and

carried her from the room that had been her prison for five days. She tilted her head to see Ike Teeters standing in the doorway.

"Good luck, Mrs. Buchanan," he said, giving her a friendly wave. "You're fine company, ya know? Easy to talk to. Say, send me a letter when that first little one gets borned. Juanita can read it to me. She knows her ABCs real good."

For the first time in many days she was able to muster the trace of a smile. "Thank you, Ike. I hope Jimmie Dolan won't harm you. He'll come looking for me to hang me."

"Hang you? Naw, I just made that up. Didn't want them drunks to get their hands on ya, is all. Dolan might've forgot he even had you. I shore ain't gonna remind him." He gave her a snaggletoothed grin. "Well, so long. Guess it's time for me to go join the boys."

As Ike stepped out the front door of the Cisneros house, Noah carried Isobel out the back. His horse was waiting, and Noah settled his wife against his chest before spurring the horse away from the scene of murder, bloodshed and mayhem.

They rode through the hills, skirting the road as the morning light filtered through the trees. When they had reached a clearing safely away from danger, Noah reined the horse.

"Ike told me Snake tore into you," he said gently.

Isobel gazed into eyes the color of the New Mexico sky. "I killed him, Noah. I was wrong to do it, even though I was fighting for my life. It's not my place to take a life. I know now, revenge is not the way."

"And I won't need to make Snake pay for what he

did to you." For a long time he gazed at the gray smoke marring the sky over Lincoln Town. "The minute I figured out it was you yelling at Susan Gates through the window of that house across the street, all the bluster went out of me. I just wanted to get to you—protect you. The push to avenge Dick's death seemed downright worthless compared with the chance to build a life with you."

"Oh, Noah, I was sure you had been shot or burned alive," she murmured against his neck. "I thought I had lost you forever."

"I couldn't let that happen, darlin'. I love you too much."

A smile tilted her lips. "And I love you, Noah Buchanan."

"Good," he said, giving her a hug. "Love's about all we've got, because I don't intend to take you anywhere near Lincoln County again. I'm going to write John Chisum and cancel the purchase of the land. We'll go north somewhere and start over. I can run cattle for someone up there. We'll build us a little place—it may not be much—but it'll be ours and it'll be clean and safe. Isobel, I'd like to give you children. I'd like to provide for you and protect you—"

"And write stories for me?" With the hint of a giggle, she drew out the New York letter she had transferred to the pocket of her yellow dress. "'Sunset at Coyote Canyon' is to be published, Noah. And the magazine wants more of your stories. I'll type the second one you wrote, shall I? I'll use my Remington. Maybe we'll live on the land I won back from Snake Jackson. It's beautiful, rich pasture just north of Santa Fe. Green country with mountains covered in whispering aspens."

But Noah heard nothing. He bent and kissed Isobel's lips. His arms tightened around her, seeking solace for all those empty days...enfolding the woman with whom he would share a lifetime in this land of enchantment.

Epilogue

For my readers who are as interested in the historical portrayal of the Lincoln County War as in the love story of Noah and Isobel Buchanan, I offer this final note.

BILLY BONNEY (alias Billy the Kid)—Escaped from the burning McSween house with several other Regulators just minutes before Alexander McSween was shot. Lived for three more years, during which he engaged in more killings and daring getaways. He was shot to death on the night of July 13, 1881, by Sheriff Pat Garrett, a former friend. Billy was twenty-one years old.

JIMMIE DOLAN—Financially ruined, he brought himself back to power and wealth through an advantageous marriage and several shrewd business moves. Took over the Tunstall Mercantile in Lincoln and the Tunstall ranch on the Rio Feliz. Later served as county treasurer and territorial senator. Died a natural death on February 26, 1898, at age fifty.

SUSAN GATES—Moved to Zuni, New Mexico, with Dr. Taylor Ealy and his family. Taught school to the

Indians there. Married Jose Perea, a young Presbyterian minister. Later moved with her husband to Jemez and then to Corrales, New Mexico, where she became the mother of a son.

TAYLOR AND MARY EALY—Served as missionaries in Zuni, New Mexico, from 1878 to 1881. Returned to Pennsylvania, where Dr. Ealy began a medical practice and a profitable baby powder company. More about the Ealy family can be read in *Missionaries, Outlaws, and Indians,* edited and annotated by Norman J. Bender.

JOHN CHISUM—Returned to Lincoln County after the Seven-Day War. Built a new home, the "Long House," at South Spring River Ranch. Developed a malignant tumor on his neck. Went to Kansas City and Arkansas for treatment but died in Eureka Springs on December 20, 1884. Buried in Paris, Texas. Read more about John Chisum in *My Girlhood Among Outlaws,* by Lily Klasner.

JUAN PATRÓN—Moved his family to Puerto de Luna, New Mexico, after the Lincoln County War. There he was murdered by hired assassin Mitch Maney on April 9, 1884. Patrón was twenty-nine years old. Maney's case never went to trial.

SUSAN McSWEEN—Started her own ranching venture in Three Rivers, an area distant from Lincoln. Remarried in 1884. Obtained a divorce in 1891. Became wealthy through skilled management of her vast land and eight thousand head of cattle. Considered "a woman of genius." Died in 1931 at age eighty-six.

The following books, among others, provide a well-rounded view of the history of the Lincoln County War:

Violence in Lincoln County, 1869-1881, William A. Keleher

Pat Garrett: The Story of a Western Lawman, Leon C. Metz

Maurice G. Fulton's History of the Lincoln County War, Robert N. Mullin, ed.

John Henry Tunstall, Frederick W. Nolan

Billy the Kid: A Handbook, Jon Tuska

Billy the Kid: A Short and Violent Life, Robert M. Utley

High Noon in Lincoln: Violence on the Western Frontier, Robert M. Utley

Merchants, Guns & Money: The Story of Lincoln County and Its Wars, John P. Wilson

ACKNOWLEDGMENTS

In writing *The Outlaw's Bride,* I traced the historical events of the Lincoln County War in New Mexico. Except for the fictional participation of Isobel Matas, Noah Buchanan and Rattlesnake Jim Jackson, the characters and the sequence of events are as accurate as I was able to uncover in my research. Although any errors are my own responsibility, I owe my thanks for research assistance and inspiration to Tim Palmer, Terry Koenig, Lynn Koenig, Lowell Nosker, Bob Hart and the Lincoln County Heritage Trust, Jeremy and Cleis Jordan of Casa de Patrón, Father John Elmer, Sylvia Johnson, Nita Harrell and Sue Breisch Johnson.

Deep appreciation goes to my editor, Joan Golan, and my agent, Karen Solem, for their constant support and encouragement.

Dear Reader,

Years ago, I lived in a town near Lincoln, New Mexico. While visiting there, I listened to descendants of the figures in the Lincoln County War talk about their ancestors. It was interesting to hear that some of them viewed Billy the Kid as a murderer without a conscience, while others called him a misguided and misunderstood boy. Some said he had killed dozens of people, others claimed he had lied about those killings and had shot only one or two people.

What is truth? The Lincoln County War is well documented, but even historical documents fail to agree on certain details. As I researched this story, I became increasingly frustrated about who had recorded the truth and who was lying.

Pondering the events, I began to understand one thing in crystal clarity. Jesus expressed it when He said, "I am the way, the truth, and the life. No one can come to the Father except through Me." John 14:6 (New Living Translation)

Jesus is Truth. God the Father is Truth. The Holy Spirit is Truth. Only in Him can we rest from doubt.

When trouble creeps—or bulldozes—into my life, I use the Bible as a filter. When I lay the Word of God over worries, fears, and confusion, the lies are blocked and the truth becomes clear.

Few of us have lived through anything as violent as the Lincoln County War. But we all search for truth. He's easy to find…just open your Bible!

Blessings,

Catherine Palmer

QUESTIONS FOR DISCUSSION

1. What are Isobel Matas's primary goals at the start of the story?

2. What goals has Noah Buchanan set for his life?

3. Is revenge the same as justice? Is there any good reason to seek revenge against an enemy?

4. What did God mean when He said, "Vengeance is mine"? How should we understand that statement? How should we act?

5. In what ways did Isobel change during the course of the story? Why? How did Noah's goals change? Why? What role did their Christian faith play in their transformation?

6. The Lincoln County War, as it is now known, played out in a small town with little significance in the world. Yet it affected the lives of many people. Why did those on the McSween side feel justified in their actions? How did those on the Dolan side rationalize their behavior?

7. Dozens of people died in the conflict. Were any of those deaths justifiable?

8. How did Isobel, Sue McSween, Beatriz Patrón, Susan Gates and other women in Lincoln Town behave

during the conflict? What do you see as the role of women in the Old West? Is it different now?

9. Guillermo Pascal offers Isobel the life she has always wanted. What reasons can you give for her decision to turn him down?

10. Do you think Noah and Isobel will live happily ever after? Why? Do you think their faith in God is important to their successful future?

Love Inspired. HISTORICAL

TITLES AVAILABLE NEXT MONTH

Available October 12, 2010

PRAIRIE COURTSHIP
Dorothy Clark

WYOMING LAWMAN
Victoria Bylin

REQUEST YOUR FREE BOOKS!

2 FREE INSPIRATIONAL NOVELS
PLUS 2
FREE
MYSTERY GIFTS

Love Inspired.
HISTORICAL
INSPIRATIONAL HISTORICAL ROMANCE

YES! Please send me 2 FREE Love Inspired® Historical novels and my 2 FREE mystery gifts (gifts are worth about $10). After receiving them, if I don't wish to receive any more books, I can return the shipping statement marked "cancel". If I don't cancel, I will receive 4 brand-new novels every other month and be billed just $4.24 per book in the U.S. or $4.74 per book in Canada. That's a saving of over 20% off the cover price. It's quite a bargain! Shipping and handling is just 50¢ per book.* I understand that accepting the 2 free books and gifts places me under no obligation to buy anything. I can always return a shipment and cancel at any time. Even if I never buy another book, the two free books and gifts are mine to keep forever.

102/302 IDN E7QD

Name _____ (PLEASE PRINT)

Address _____ Apt. #

City _____ State/Prov. _____ Zip/Postal Code

Signature (if under 18, a parent or guardian must sign)

Mail to Steeple Hill Reader Service:
IN U.S.A.: P.O. Box 1867, Buffalo, NY 14240-1867
IN CANADA: P.O. Box 609, Fort Erie, Ontario L2A 5X3
Not valid for current subscribers to Love Inspired Historical books.

Want to try two free books from another series?
Call 1-800-873-8635 or visit www.morefreebooks.com.

* Terms and prices subject to change without notice. Prices do not include applicable taxes. Sales tax applicable in N.Y. Canadian residents will be charged applicable provincial taxes and GST. Offer not valid in Quebec. This offer is limited to one order per household. All orders subject to approval. Credit or debit balances in a customer's account(s) may be offset by any other outstanding balance owed by or to the customer. Please allow 4 to 6 weeks for delivery. Offer available while quantities last.

Your Privacy: Steeple Hill Books is committed to protecting your privacy. Our Privacy Policy is available online at www.SteepleHill.com or upon request from the Reader Service. From time to time we make our lists of customers available to reputable third parties who may have a product or service of interest to you. If you would prefer we not share your name and address, please check here. ☐

Help us get it right—We strive for accurate, respectful and relevant communications. To clarify or modify your communication preferences, visit us at www.ReaderService.com/consumerschoice.

LIH10R

*See below for a sneak peek at
our inspirational line, Love Inspired®.
Introducing HIS HOLIDAY BRIDE
by bestselling author Jillian Hart*

Autumn Granger gave her horse rein to slide toward the town's new sheriff.

"Hey, there." The man in a brand-new Stetson, black T-shirt, jeans and riding boots held up a hand in greeting. He stepped away from his four-wheel drive with "Sheriff" in black on the doors and waded through the grasses. "I'm new around here."

"I'm Autumn Granger."

"Nice to meet you, Miss Granger. I'm Ford Sherman, from Chicago." He knuckled back his hat, revealing the most handsome face she'd ever seen. Big blue eyes contrasted with his sun-tanned complexion.

"I'm guessing you haven't seen much open land. Out here, you've got to keep an eye on cows or they're going to tear your vehicle apart."

"What?" He whipped around. Sure enough, mammoth black-and-white creatures had started to gnaw on his four-wheel drive. They clustered like a mob, mouths and tongues and teeth bent on destruction. One cow tried to pry the wiper off the windshield, another chewed on the side mirror. Several leaned through the open window, licking the seats.

"Move along, little dogie." He didn't know the first thing about cattle.

The entire herd swiveled their heads to study him curiously. Not a single hoof shifted. The animals soon returned to chewing, licking, digging through his possessions.

Autumn laughed, a warm and wonderful sound. "Thanks,

SHLIEXP1010

I needed that." She then pulled a bag from behind her saddle and waved it at the cows. "Look what I have, guys. Cookies."

Cows swung in her direction, and dozens of liquid brown eyes brightened with cookie hopes. As she circled the car, the cattle bounded after her. The earth shook with the force of their powerful hooves.

"Next time, you're on your own, city boy." She tipped her hat. The cowgirl stayed on his mind, the sweetest thing he had ever seen.

Will Ford be able to stick it out in the country
to find out more about Autumn?
Find out in HIS HOLIDAY BRIDE
by bestselling author Jillian Hart,
available in October 2010
only from Love Inspired®.